THE DEBT

C. J. PETIT

TABLE OF CONTENTS

THE DEBT 1
PROLOGUE 4
CHAPTER 1 12
CHAPTER 2 76
CHAPTER 3 115
CHAPTER 4 156
CHAPTER 5 261
CHAPTER 6 296
CHAPTER 7 336
EPILOGUE 352

PROLOGUE

August 12, 1885

Mattie Foster stepped from the train steps onto the platform at Green River, Wyoming. Three other passengers disembarked, were greeted by family or friends and left as she stood beside her travel bag. Ten minutes later, two departing passengers boarded the train, yet she remained standing alone on the platform, filled with a mixture of fear and disappointment with an undercurrent of anger at her own foolishness.

As the train resumed its westward journey behind her, she finally accepted the fact that no one was coming, picked up her travel bag and walked to the ticket agent.

He smiled at the young lady as she neared his window and asked, "May I help you, miss?"

"I hope so, sir. Do you know where the Rocking F ranch is located?" she asked.

The man looked at Mattie, scratched his chin whiskers and replied, "I'm sorry, miss, but I don't recall ever hearing that name."

"Are you new here?" she asked.

"No, ma'am, I've been living here for more than fifteen years now. I just never heard of a ranch with that brand. Of course, I'm not a rancher, so you might want to check with the sheriff's office."

THE DEBT

Mattie was confused as she replied, "Thank you, sir," then asked, "Will they hold my travel trunk here?"

"Yes, miss. You just keep your claim ticket and you can pick it up when you're ready."

She thanked him again before taking a seat at one of the benches to think about what she would do next.

She had hoped that her father would be waiting for her or at least one of his ranch hands, but this was something she hadn't expected. Mattie had suspected by the tone in his letters that he didn't want her to come to Green River, but she had written that she was coming anyway. She wanted to at least meet her father, whom she hadn't seen since she was a little girl. If he wasn't waiting at the station, she could rent a buggy and drive to his ranch, but the ticket agent said he didn't know where it was at all which had surprised her. Her father had written that it was one of the biggest ranches in the county.

With a sinking stomach, Mattie picked up her travel bag and walked to the Railway Hotel where she checked in and went to her room. She left her bag, took a bath and then returned to her room, afraid that she had made a terrible mistake. There was a chance that the ticket agent was wrong. After all, he wasn't a rancher. She decided to take his suggestion and visit the sheriff's office.

She left the room, crossed the lobby and then left the hotel, turned onto the boardwalk, and after five minutes of searching found the office of the county sheriff and stepped inside.

The deputy at the desk saw her enter, smiled and stood as he asked, "Good morning, ma'am. How can I help you?"

Mattie smiled back and asked, "I hope so. Can you tell me where the Rocking F ranch is located?"

Again, there was the initial pause followed by, "I'm sorry, ma'am, but I've never heard of it."

"But it's supposed to be a very large ranch. My father, Russ Foster, has eight ranch hands working for him."

The deputy really wished he could help the pretty young woman but shrugged and replied, "I'm sorry, ma'am. The only Foster I know of is Tom Foster, and he's a teamster, not a rancher."

Mattie knew that the likelihood that her father had been lying to her for some reason loomed even larger, but there was one more place she could check.

"Thank you, Deputy. Where is the land office?"

"If you turn left on the boardwalk, it's four buildings down on this side of the street in the county offices."

"Thank you."

Fifteen minutes later, she exited the county offices and stood on the boardwalk, having had no better luck at the land office. There simply wasn't a ranch in the county registered as the Rocking F, nor was Russ Foster listed as any landowners in the county. *Why had her father lied to her?*

Whatever the reason, Mattie was now bordering on panic. Here she was in Green River, Wyoming, a thousand miles from anything she knew, and she was in deep trouble. She had taken an extraordinary gamble when she'd boarded the train in Columbia, Missouri and had lost. Her friends had all told her that she was being foolish, and now she agreed with them. But that didn't matter right now. What mattered now was what was in her purse, or more correctly, what was *not* in her purse – money.

THE DEBT

Her funds had been getting low since she had graduated from the Christian Women's College in Columbia, Missouri in May. Her father's letters had stopped arriving three months before she graduated and so had the money he had been sending.

She was worried about her father but had written to him telling him she would come to see him as soon as she cleared up all her affairs in Missouri. She hadn't expected it to take as long as it had, but she had accepted an offer to spend part of her last summer in Missouri with her good friend Isabel Perez and she didn't begin her journey until the beginning of the month. Now, here she was in this nice, but unknown town and her father was nowhere to be found, nor was his ranch.

What was worse was that she didn't have enough money for the fare back to Missouri, not that she had any reason to return there anyway. Wyoming, even though she barely remembered it at all, was where she was born, but she needed to find someplace to earn some money, and it had better be soon. Her college degree, while it may have marked her as rare, especially in this part of the country, did nothing to help her in finding employment. There were simply few jobs available for women that didn't involve laying on your back.

―――

She walked to the town library and asked the librarian where she could find employment listings and was directed to the town bulletin board in the back of the library. She thanked him, then walked to the large board which was covered with a wide variety of sizes and colors of postings.

After almost a minute of perusing the board, she found a scrawled card on the bottom left of the board that read:

**SCHOOLMARM NEEDED
$40 A MONTH AND FOUND
SEE JACK CAMPBELL AT
CAMPBELL DRY GOODS
BURNT FORK**

Mattie wasn't sure what Burnt Fork meant, if the position was already filled or what 'and found' meant, but she pulled the card from the bulletin board and walked up front to the desk.

"Excuse me, can you tell me about this position?" she asked as she held out the card to the librarian.

He took the card, glanced at it and replied, "Yes, ma'am. It's still open or the card wouldn't be there."

"That's good news, but what does 'Burnt Fork' mean?"

He grinned and replied, "That's the name of the town, ma'am. It's about six hours south of here."

"Oh. Can you tell me what 'and found' means?"

"It's a ranching term, ma'am. It means they'll provide room and board in addition to the pay."

Mattie looked at the card again and saw it as a lifesaver, then thanked the librarian, kept the card and left the building to return to her hotel room. She stopped at the stagecoach depot on the way and bought a ticket to Burnt Fork on tomorrow's stage that would be leaving at nine o'clock.

THE DEBT

She thought she could teach for a year or so and save enough of her salary to find what had happened to her father. She was still confused about the non-existent ranch but was concerned that something bad had happened to him, too.

The next morning, Mattie Foster boarded the stagecoach with her small travel bag as her large trunk was hoisted onto the roof. As it rolled out of Green River, she had less than ten dollars in her purse and a lot of questions in her mind.

August 25, 1885

"We found her, Frank," Bill Nelson said as he entered the old bunkhouse and found Frank playing cards with Fritz.

It was where they always met when they didn't want the boss to know what they were doing.

"Where was she?" Frank Lewis asked after tossing down his hand.

Bill Nelson grinned and replied, "She took a job as a schoolmarm down in Burnt Fork."

Frank shook his head and said, "I'm still mighty put off. If we had gotten that letter on time, we could have picked her up at the station and just run her off to the Mitchell place. This wasted too much time."

Nelson shrugged and said, "But we can get her now that we know where she is. I know the place and it's not much. It'll just cost us some more time, that's all."

Frank Lewis was still irritated but asked. "Do you think it'll be tough gettin' her outta there?"

"Nah. The law in that burg is some fat sheriff who doesn't like to get outta his office in case he might miss a meal. I'm sure he won't even bother saddlin' his horse, if he got one."

Frank nodded and said, "Alright. You and Dick go down and round her up. Take her out to the old Mitchell place and you treat her good. Do you hear? At least until I decide otherwise."

"Yeah. I hear ya. It'll take us a couple of days to get down there and probably another three to get her to the Mitchell place. We're gonna need a lot of supplies."

"Swing over to Green River and load up on what you need. Take an extra horse and a packhorse, too. Just get down there late in the day and snatch her. Head straight to the Mitchell place and just send Dick back with proof that we have her."

Bill nodded and said, "We'll leave the day after tomorrow."

"Don't screw this up, Bill," Frank snarled, "I don't want to have to do it the old-fashioned way. The boss may be gettin' old, but he's pretty damned good with that hogleg and I ain't ready to find out how good he is if I don't have to."

"It'll be easy, Frank. One quick pop on her head with my Colt barrel and we're outta there. They won't even know she's gone for a day or two, and you should be the boss just a couple of days after that."

"They all look easy until the action starts, Bill. You remember that."

"Sure enough, Frank," Bill replied, then chuckled and left the room.

THE DEBT

Frank watched him go. It may be an easy job, but nothing ever was easy when Bill Nelson and Dick Pierce were involved. He thought they were two of the biggest morons he'd ever met, but they were all he had.

CHAPTER 1

John Clark was at his desk, staring at the ranch's books, knowing he had to make a decision soon. Cattle prices were down for the second year in a row, but he had to move some animals. The question was how many. He was looking at his bank balance and was wondering if he could risk going another year or two without selling a full shipment of critters, then leaned the straight-backed chair on its back legs and blew out his breath.

"Having a difficult time, John?" asked his mother, Winnie, as she walked in with a cup of coffee and held it out to him.

John sat the chair down and accepted the cup.

"Kind of, Mama. They're only paying $15.60 a head this year. Last year, I thought it was bad at $16.10, so we didn't sell any at all. Now, it's worse. We have enough cash to hang onto the herd as it is for another year or two, but there's no guarantee that it won't be lower next year, and we have to move some anyway to keep the herds healthy. The question is how many do we want to drive to Green River."

"How many are you thinking of moving?"

"Around three hundred head or so."

"Well, your father had to do that twice as I recall."

"I remember. How he ran this place with just two hands is beyond me."

THE DEBT

"You were there too, don't forget."

"I haven't. We have ten hands now and it seems like we never get caught up."

"Are you sorry you came back?"

"No, Mama. It was time. My only real concern is who they hired to take my place."

"Frank Baker's not a bad man, John."

"I didn't say he was, Mama. He's just not cut out to be a lawman. He's been lucky so far because nothing has happened. I can't imagine what he'd do if we had another incident like that attempted bank robbery three years ago."

"He'll be all right, John. It'll be nice and quiet as it usually is. They really didn't have a lot of choices."

"I know, Mama. It still bothers me sometimes, you know?"

"I understand."

The screen door opened with a light squeal and then banged closed.

Winnie looked at John, turned and walked out of the office to see who had entered the house. The ranch hands usually didn't come into the house without knocking, and that left her grandson.

John heard his mother exclaim, "Jamey Clark! What are you doing home? Why aren't you in school?"

"They sent us home, Grandma. They said there wasn't going to be any school for a while."

"Did they say why?"

John rose from behind the desk to talk to his nine-year-old son as he answered, "No, Grandma. They just sent us home and said to come back next Monday."

"Jamey, did anything else seem odd? Was the school building still standing?" asked John as he approached his son.

"It was okay, but when we got there it was locked, and Sheriff Baker was there and told us kids to come back next Monday but didn't say why. I asked, too."

John sighed, then looked at his mother and said, "Mama, I'm going to get Bolt saddled and find out what's going on."

"Let me know. The children need to go to school."

John kissed his mother on the forehead and tapped Jamey on the head as he headed for the doorway. Jamey grinned at his father and watched him leave the room.

"I hope they don't make papa mad, Grandma," he said.

"He'll be fine, Jamey. Now that he's not sheriff anymore, he doesn't need to show his angry face. He's never shown it to you, has he?"

Jamey smiled, and replied, "No, Grandma, not when he's mad. But I've seen it when I ask him to show me, and it's scary."

"It is. If he were smaller, maybe it wouldn't be so scary."

"Maybe. Could I have a cookie, Grandma?"

"Just one. No spoiling your lunch," she admonished as Jamey shot into the kitchen.

THE DEBT

John had no idea why school would be cancelled on the first day. Miss Hall was scrupulous about following her rules and the schedule. He remembered that once he tried to get Jamey out of school to go fishing in one of the wide creeks that crossed their ranch. He'd had a bad weekend as sheriff and wanted to enjoy a day with his son.

She was appalled at the idea and refused his request, sheriff or not. Maybe he should have fibbed and told her that his grandmother was ailing and asking for him, but he couldn't do it. He never could get the knack of lying, even those innocent lies that everyone used. He didn't think any lies were innocent. So, he had gone fishing on his own and landed three nice trout for dinner, too, but still wished Jamey had been there. At least now, with his law work behind him, he'd been spending more time with his son.

It was a healthy forty-minute ride north to Burnt Fork. His ranch butted against the edge of Wyoming, and he thought it was a good half-mile into Utah too, but had never heard from them about any taxes and intended to leave it that way.

Bolt was moving at a good pace along what passed for a road. There was still grass growing in the center, but at least the ruts weren't deep enough to cause any harm to the horse.

Bolt was just about the fastest horse that John had ever seen. He was almost totally black except for a white slash down the center of his forehead. He was taller than his previous mounts as well, standing over eighteen hands. It was too bad he had been gelded as he would have made one hell of a stud. He bought Bolt two years ago when he had gone to Ralph Phillips' horse ranch to add some animals to the ranch's stock and had to pay a fancy price for him, but never regretted it. That was his first year after taking over his father's ranch.

He still thought of the Circle C as his father's ranch. His father was the one who had built it from nothing and made it the showpiece of the county. It was a massive spread, sixteen sections, and John was trying to expand it. The ranch had every conceivable type of landscape within its boundaries, even a hundred-acre patch that looked like a southwestern desert. Right now, he was running over four thousand head of cattle. There were sixty horses in the remuda in addition to their private stock. When he had first taken over the ranch, they had only sixteen horses in total which weren't nearly enough. That's how he had found Bolt.

Forty minutes later, he was riding into the town of Burnt Fork. He had grown up on the ranch outside of town and had attended the same schoolhouse that Jamey did now, but his schoolmarm was the dreaded Miss Harrington. She was old when he was a first year, at least to the eyes of a seven-year-old, and by the time he left her classroom ten years later, she was still terrifying her students. She had finally given up her position the same day she gave up breathing and Miss Alice Hall had taken her place.

That was eight years ago. Jamey wasn't overly fond of Miss Hall, and he wasn't unique in his opinion. She seemed to dislike the boys and barely tolerated the girls, but she was a good teacher, nonetheless. She was just a taskmaster and not a friendly sort. She wasn't really bad looking, but it was her domineering presence that must have frightened away any prospective callers.

John had been a widower for nine years now, his beloved Nellie having died in childbirth. He had more than a few opportunities to remarry, but none could come close to Nellie, and with his mother still at the ranch, he felt that Jamey wasn't deprived of any female guidance. He didn't think that he was deprived of any female companionship either, but did occasionally visit the ladies in Green River when he had to go to the bigger town for some supplies or move the cattle to the stockyards. It was only another forty miles to Green River, but it took a good part of the day to ride and six days to move the cattle.

He stopped Bolt at the sheriff's office and stepped down, flipped Bolt's reins over the hitching post, then took two long steps, opened the door to the office and saw his replacement, Frank Baker, sitting behind the desk. He had his Colt out of its holster and was just staring down the barrel of the loaded pistol for a reason that John couldn't fathom. John wanted to say something, but just quietly stepped inside.

Frank looked up and said, "Mornin', John. What brings you to town?"

"Jamey's unexpected return to the ranch from school. He said that there wasn't any school until next Monday? What happened?"

"We ain't got a teacher. The schoolmarm has gone missin'."

"Why would Miss Hall suddenly disappear?"

"She didn't. She married Harry Cooper in July. This was the new schoolmarm, Miss Foster. You gotta come to town more often, John."

"Maybe so. What do you mean that she just went missing?"

"Jack Campbell saw her at the school settin' things up yesterday morning and today, she wasn't in town. Nobody knows where she went."

"Did you find out what happened to her?"

"I figured she just decided she didn't wanna do it and up and left."

"Did you ask Hank if she bought a ticket to Green River?"

"Nope. It ain't my business. A growed woman can make up her own mind."

John shook his head and said, "I'll see you later, Frank," then walked out the door.

He knew Frank Baker wouldn't do anything that required work and hunting down a missing person and a newcomer at that was work.

He headed for Campbell's Dry Goods just three blocks north, walked through the doorway and saw Jack Campbell in his accustomed spot behind the counter. He was talking to Bill Hughes, the owner of the feed and grain store. Jack was the mayor and Bill was one of the three council members of Burnt Fork, which was hardly unusual for a small town.

They looked over as John entered, and the mayor said, "John! Are we glad to see you! We were just going to send someone out to see you."

"Is it something to do with the missing schoolmarm, Jack?"

"It has everything to do with the missing schoolmarm. Frank doesn't seem to think there's a problem, but we do. Miss Foster was very enthusiastic about the first day of school and then she just disappeared. No one has seen her since."

"Did anyone ask Hank over at the stagecoach depot if she left?"

"Not to my knowledge."

THE DEBT

"Who is Miss Foster, anyway? I don't recall any families with that name in the area."

"She responded to a notice we posted in the Green River library looking for a schoolmarm. She seemed like a big improvement over Alice Hall, and seemed really nice, too. She even had a college education."

"No offense, Jack, but if she was that qualified, then why would she come to Burnt Fork?"

"I asked her that very question before we hired her. She said she just liked the rural setting."

"I thought everything west of St. Louis was a rural setting."

Jack Campbell shrugged and said, "Anyway, John, we wonder if you could find out what happened to her. Aside from the town needing a schoolmarm, we really don't want anything bad happening to her."

"I'll do some preliminary investigating and then I'll let you know what I find. I'll decide how far I need to take this after that. Where was she staying, anyway?"

"At Fletcher's Boarding House."

"I'll come back and see you when I find out what's going on."

"We appreciate it, John."

John left the store, hating to admit that he liked returning to what he enjoyed doing the most. His father's sudden death from an infection after a simple cut had made it necessary for him to give up his sheriff's job and return to run the ranch. He could be gone for a couple of weeks from the ranch, if necessary, but he couldn't be a full-time sheriff. He owed it to his father, his son and mostly to his mother.

He walked to the stage office first, opened the door but couldn't find Hank Ward anywhere.

"Hank!" he shouted before he heard a muffled shuffling from the back room.

He waited while Hank put his britches on. Hank had a reputation as a lady's man and seemed to thrive on the notoriety and relished enhancing it at every opportunity. He must be taking advantage of the lull between the stage's arrival not expecting anyone to enter to purchase a ticket.

John had to wait for almost three minutes. As he waited, he wondered who Hank was spending his time with this morning and hoped she wasn't married. When he'd been caught with Mrs. Ida Dempsey, it had been quite the scandal.

Finally, a disheveled, poorly dressed Hank Ward emerged from his back room and asked, "John! What can I do for you?"

"Hank, did the new schoolmarm, Miss Foster, buy a ticket out of town or just get on the stage yesterday?"

"No, sir. I was wondering why nobody asked me. I would have been sad to see her go, too. She was a real looker, John."

John rolled his eyes and asked, "You wouldn't happen to know if she had a horse, do you?"

"She came in on the stage a couple of weeks ago, and I didn't see her on one since, and I've been looking. You might want to go and ask Paddy, though."

THE DEBT

"I will. Sorry to interrupt you, Hank," he said as he smiled then turned to leave.

"Not a problem, John," Hank said as he waved and returned to his back room, disrobing as he went.

John turned to his right and walked three buildings down to Fletcher's Boarding House, stepped up the two steps and onto the porch. He opened the door and looked around for either Fletcher, then gave up looking and walked down the hallway, entering the kitchen to find Evelyn Fletcher cleaning up after breakfast.

"Evelyn, how are you, besides perpetually busy?"

Evelyn turned to see John and broke into a big smile.

"John! It's wonderful to see you again. What brings you to my kitchen?"

"The missing schoolmarm. No one seems to know how she just disappeared."

"I didn't find out until Emily returned from school this morning."

"Is her room empty?"

"I haven't gone inside. I was waiting for the sheriff."

"He's not going to do anything, Evelyn. Can I see her room? The mayor has asked me to check into it."

"That was a smart thing to do. Let's go up there."

"What can you tell me about her? All I have so far is that Hank Ward described her as a 'looker'."

Evelyn Fletcher dried her hands on her apron as she walked from the kitchen with John following.

"Well, she was that. I'd guess she's about early to mid-twenties with light brown hair and brown eyes. She was fairly tall, about the same as Walter, five feet and eight inches or so. She had a nice figure, too. To be honest, I was rather surprised that she would become a teacher. Usually, the women who had no opportunity to find a husband went that other route."

"Sad, isn't it?" John said as he followed Evelyn up the stairs to the second floor.

"I think so. Her first name was Mattie. She was a very pleasant young woman."

"Quite a change from our last two schoolmarms," he said before he chuckled.

"Remember Miss Harrington?" Evelyn asked as they reached the upper floor.

"I never did get a chance to arrest her as a form of payback."

"That would have been fun."

She opened the second door on the left and let John inside.

"It looks like all of her clothes are still here," she said as she opened the chifforobe.

"That's not good. Either she's had an accident somewhere or someone has taken her against her will."

"That's a scary thought, John. Can you find her?"

THE DEBT

"I will if I can find the trail. That'll be hard if I don't know where she was last. Well, Evelyn, I've got to get this thing going."

"You take care, John."

"I will, Evelyn. Say hello to Walter for me."

"I will."

John trotted down the stairs and left the boarding house. Evelyn Fletcher was Evelyn Brown when they were in school, and she and her husband Walter were both in the same year with him. He and Evelyn had been paired off when they were young, but Nellie had started school the following year and there was no hope for Evelyn after that, but she didn't resent it at all. She and Nellie had become good friends. Everyone liked Nellie.

John fast walked south to the other end of the street where Paddy Sullivan had his livery. Paddy had the honor of being the only man in Burnt Fork who was bigger than John. He was the same height but carried another twenty pounds. Neither man was overly tall, at six feet even, but there just weren't any tall men in town.

He approached the open door of the livery and shouted, "Yo! Paddy!"

Seconds later, Paddy Sullivan, his bright red hair almost glowing in the morning sun, stuck his head out of the livery.

"John! Haven't seen you for two months. I thought you might've died or something."

"Not that I know of. Just staying busy. Paddy, did the new schoolmarm have a horse?"

"Nope."

"Have you seen any strangers or strange horses around?"

"Sure did. Two fellers rode in yesterday afternoon. One rode a bay gelding with two white stockings on the hind legs and the other rode a light brown gelding with a black mane and tail and no markings. They were trailing a third saddled horse and a packhorse, too. The reason I noticed is that they didn't even stop by to get them taken care of. They must've left town right away. I figured they were heading for Utah."

"Sounds like they took our new schoolmarm for a ride instead. Did you see which way they rode in?"

"I didn't see them ride in. I only noticed them when they rode past."

"It should be easy to track four horses, I think."

"Good luck. You gonna go after them?"

"I think so. It's not my job, but it just doesn't sit right with me, Paddy. Besides, we need a schoolmarm."

"Are you taking anyone with you?"

"I don't think so. I'll need to arm up and move fast. They're already a few hours ahead of me and I've got to find them first, too."

"Go get 'em, John."

John waved at Paddy and headed for the store to talk to the mayor, already mulling over the situation in his mind. Two men and a packhorse with an empty trailer, probably for the teacher. That means there were going a long way, which wasn't good news for Miss Foster. But this was a chance to save an innocent life and he wasn't about to let it pass.

He reached Campbell's and walked inside finding Jack Campbell and Bill Hughes still there.

"What did you find out, John?"

"It's pretty obvious that Miss Foster was kidnapped or at least taken away. I don't think she went willingly because her clothes were all still in her room. Paddy says he saw two men ride in yesterday afternoon and they were trailing an empty horse and a packhorse. He didn't know which way they came from, but they rode south. I'm going to start at the schoolhouse to check for tracks. It's far enough away from the other buildings, so I might pick up their trail from there. Then I'll head back to the ranch and get ready to go."

Then he added, "Jack, can someone go to see Evelyn Fletcher and ask her to pack a dress and whatever else she might think Miss Foster will need? She'll need some clean clothes. If she doesn't have a heavy jacket and gloves, get those and a scarf and put them in there as well. Oh, and a riding skirt, too. I doubt if she has one. Put them all on my account. I think it'll be at least a couple of days before I can catch up with them. I'll pick the clothes up when I come back to start trailing."

"I'll take care of it," offered Jack Campbell.

"Thanks, Jack. I'm going to get going."

"Good luck, John," said Bill Hughes.

John had already reached the door and waved as he crossed the threshold heading for the street. He walked down to where he'd left Bolt outside the sheriff's office, mounted, then turned the horse to the south, rode out of town and stopped at the schoolhouse. It was only a couple of hundred yards outside of town, but it was far enough to allow someone to sneak the teacher out of town, which also limited their escape routes to the east and west because south would take them past his ranch.

He stepped down, tied off Bolt and began walking around the schoolhouse. It didn't take long to find the hoofprints and would have been shocked not to find them. They had been tied up behind the school as indicated by the piles of horse manure. He kicked them and guessed it was less than a day since they'd been gone. He could see scuffling on the ground nearby and two grooves leading from the school's back entrance to the horses. They must have knocked her unconscious, dragged her out to the horses, then went east away from the town. This would be his starting point.

He returned to Bolt, stepped up, then set him at a fast trot back to the ranch. He was running through what he would take with him. His Winchester '76 was already in his scabbard. He didn't have his gunbelt on and hadn't worn it for other than target practice since he'd returned to the ranch. He did have a nice shooting range set up that he used and used often. He let the ranch hands practice as well.

It was a two-gun rig, but it wasn't for show. John used both hands proficiently and it had saved his life on one occasion five years earlier when he had been shot in the right forearm by a highwayman who had been plaguing the traffic between Burnt Fork and Green River. John had then hit him twice with well-placed shots with his left hand. He'd bring a shotgun as well. He'd just pack enough food in his saddlebags for three days because the kidnappers already had a packhorse. He'd bring a couple of boxes of .44 cartridges for his Colts, two boxes of the

THE DEBT

.45 center fire cartridges for the Winchester and a box of shells for the shotgun.

Thirty-five minutes later, he rode onto his access road and soon brought Bolt into the barn and let him eat and drink but left him saddled and added the second scabbard before he took his saddlebags with him to the house.

He jogged to the house, not slowing as he entered the front door.

"Mama, I need to get some food together," he shouted as he walked to his bedroom to get his gunbelt.

Winnie didn't ask questions as she had anticipated his request after watching him riding in at high speed and had already headed for the kitchen by the time that he was taking care of Bolt in the barn.

John didn't pack any extra clothing. He was going to move quickly. He needed his bedroll, his slicker, and his heavy jacket as it was already getting cooler. He didn't pack his shaving kit, but he did pack his emergency medical pouch, which he called his gunshot kit.

After fastening his gunbelt into position, he pulled his boxes of ammunition for the Winchester and Colts and set them on his bed. He returned to the main room and took the shotgun off the wall, opened the drawer in the cabinet underneath and grabbed a box of #4 buckshot shells then returned to his room and set the shotgun and shells next to the four boxes of cartridges.

John left his room and walked to the office, opened the secure desk drawer and took out three hundred dollars and three bank drafts. It was a lot of money, but it was better to have too much than not enough. He had no idea what he would need on this mission and money was flexible. He closed the door then left the office to walk to the kitchen.

"What happened, John?" his mother asked when she saw him enter.

"They hired a new schoolmarm and it looks like the new teacher was kidnapped. Two men took her just a short time ago and it wasn't an impulse thing. This was planned. I know where they grabbed her and where they left Burnt Fork and I'll trail them as fast as I can. They have a head start, but I think they would have stopped last night and made a camp, so I can make up some time. They can't move very fast with her and the packhorse, either."

His mother understood her son's need for urgency, so she didn't ask any of her many questions but said, "I've made you four sandwiches and then put some smoked beef and some ham and a loaf of bread. I added some other things as well," then handed him a cloth bag with the food.

"Thanks, Mama. I'm pretty much ready to go. Where's Jamey?"

"He's out back with his horse."

"Is he close? I can't spend too much time hunting for him."

"He was the last time I saw him."

"Alright. I'll pack my saddlebags and be gone."

"I'd tell you to be careful, but I won't bother," she said as she smiled.

She had a lot of confidence in her son.

THE DEBT

He gave his mother a hug and a kiss on the forehead before saying, "Take care of Jamey. I hope to be back in a few days."

John returned to his room, slid the cartridges into one saddlebag and the shells into the other. He'd hang the food over his saddle horn along with that bag of clothes he'd pick up in town. He put the saddlebags over his shoulder, took his shotgun in his right hand and the food in his left, then nodded to his mother as he passed.

"Bye, Mama," he said as he exited the back door.

"Good-bye, John. Do what you do and save that girl."

"I will, Mama."

John saw Jamey trotting toward him as he stepped onto the porch. He must have seen him ride Bolt to the barn.

"Papa, are you leaving?" he asked from twenty feet.

"Yes, Jamey. You have a new teacher and she's been kidnapped. I'm going to bring her back."

"You can do it, Papa."

John smiled at his son and replied, "I hope so, Jamey. I'll be back in a few days."

John walked quickly to the barn, hung the bag over his saddle horn and slid the shotgun into the second scabbard, tied down his saddlebags and mounted.

He rode Bolt out of the barn, headed down the access road, then turned north on the road toward Burnt Fork at a fast trot. He was asking a lot of his big equine friend but knew he would do anything his human friend asked of him.

Mattie Foster was confused, hungry and sore. When she'd awakened from being struck on the head yesterday, she found herself bound and bobbing on the saddle of a horse. When she asked what was happening, the men who had abducted her stopped and ordered her into the saddle, despite her inappropriate attire. But the embarrassment of showing her bare legs was nothing compared to the fear that gripped her as she saw nothing familiar in her surroundings. With her head still pounding as they continued to ride, the terror began to grow, knowing what they would be doing to her when they stopped, but they hadn't. They hadn't spoken to her much other than to order her to cook their food.

But now, on her second day of captivity, she was still bound and feeling every jolt of the horse's gait as the two men led her horse further into the wilderness. She hadn't ridden a horse in years, and this wasn't a good way to be reintroduced to it. Her legs were already cramping, and it wasn't even noon. But when she looked at the packhorse, what scared her the most was the presence of a pickaxe and a shovel. She had an idea what it was for, and they didn't look like farmers.

Through all the pain, fear and discomfort, there was the overwhelming sense of confusion. *Why had they kidnapped her? Was it intentional or was it a mistake? Was it because of her mysterious father or did they believe she was someone else?* She was so unfamiliar with this land, she wondered if they were just taking her to be their common wife. Mattie simply had no idea why they had abducted her.

She was certain of one thing, however. She knew that no one would be chasing them. She had met the sheriff twice, and he didn't seem the type to chase anything more than the next meal. They seemed to think the same thing as they didn't hurry or even look behind them after the first two hours that she had been awake. She had been kidnapped and had no chance of rescue.

They had brought a lot of supplies, but nothing in the way of clothing or anything else for a woman. She didn't have anything warm to wear, either. Last night, she had slept in a bedroll, but had a rope securing her inside, making for an uncomfortable night's sleep. When she had to get up in the morning, it was chilly, and she wasn't allowed much privacy when she needed it. They had been riding now for four hours and she had no idea where they were going. She knew they were riding northeast, but now, she was far from panicked but was seething in anger.

———

After stopping back at the dry goods store to pick up the large bag of women's things for Miss Foster and hanging on the other side of his saddle from his crowded saddle horn, John returned to the schoolhouse and didn't bother dismounting as he turned east following their clear trail.

John continued east for about three miles before they turned east northeast. It was an easy trail, and in fact, it was so easy, John began wondering about an ambush. They didn't even make any effort to hide their tracks. Either they weren't worried about being trailed or were planning on taking out any potential trackers. As a potential tracker, that would put him in their sights, but as he rode and watched the trail, he never saw any deviations or pauses as they stopped to look behind them. They weren't even looking at their backtrail, but just riding as if it was a Sunday jaunt.

John decided that they might have already done some preliminary work and found that it wasn't likely that the sheriff would make chase, but it still didn't explain why such a planned kidnapping had even happened and that bothered John a lot.

Schoolmarms usually weren't the targets for kidnappings. He figured it must have something to do with her family. *But why would anyone belonging to a family wealthy enough to warrant a kidnapping want to teach in Burnt Fork?* Maybe she was disgruntled with her wealthy way of life, was trying to rebel, and her parents had hired these two to bring her back. It was still illegal, parents or not, because she was an adult. But even that seemed far-fetched and just didn't make a lot of sense.

He gambled that they had no intention of stopping and waiting for trackers, so he kept following the trail at a fast pace, ignoring any ambush threats. It was a calculated gamble, but he just didn't want Miss Foster to be in the hands of the two men any longer than she had to be. He could save an innocent life and hopefully keep her from being molested if he could catch up soon enough, although he would be surprised if she hadn't already been raped. Men like this didn't bother with niceties, whether she was college educated or not. Especially as she had been described as a 'looker'.

He stopped briefly for lunch a little after noon when he came upon a nice stream and grazing area. He let Bolt rest, graze and drink as he had one of the sandwiches and drank directly from the stream with his tin cup. Fifteen minutes later he was moving again.

When he started the hunt, he was thirty-eight miles behind Bill Nelson, Dick Pierce and Mattie Foster. When he broke after lunch, he had already cut the difference to less than thirty miles. He knew he had a real disadvantage in that he'd have to stop when he lost light because he needed to see the tracks, but he hoped that they would stop for camp as well. So far, he noted that they kept a heading of northeast until the stream and were now shifting ever so slightly toward the east in a slow arc. In a few more hours, they'd be going due east. He wondered

THE DEBT

what was down that way. There were no towns, but there were a few ranches, just no big ones.

He found their campsite from the previous night just around six o'clock and didn't even bother dismounting to examine it for any more information, but he did swing past and didn't see any signs of a struggle, so maybe she hadn't been violated yet. He just kept riding, wanting to close the gap as much as he could today and was depending on Bolt to do it, but he was losing his light and he'd have to pull over soon. He didn't realize that he was only sixteen miles behind them when he finally had to stop, having made up eight miles in the last hour alone because his targets had stopped earlier.

―――

Bill Nelson had decided to pull over almost an hour before John had stopped because he was hungry. So, he told Dick Pierce to pull over at a likely camp site.

"Let's go, missy," Dick Pierce said to Mattie.

It was the first time either had spoken to her in hours, so she thought she could try to get some information.

"Why are you doing this?" she asked as she sat in the saddle looking down at one of her captors.

She didn't get an answer, but she wasn't surprised. She sighed and stepped down from the horse slowly. It was awkward with her wrists bound while wearing a full dress and her legs tight from cramping. She knew they were watching her as she slowly managed to dismount then, even with her bound wrists, straightened out her skirts before she gingerly walked to a rock and sat down. She was sore, felt dirty, and still wondered why they had kidnapped her. She was sure of only one thing. She was on her own, had no help anywhere, and it wouldn't be long before one or both of them took her, then killed her and made use of that pickaxe and shovel, but still with no idea why they were doing this.

They cut her leather bindings and had her cook their dinner which was difficult with her sore legs and other nether regions, but she was unable to glean any more information about the reason for her abduction as they talked to each other.

―――

John was up with the predawn, had a second sandwich and more water before saddling Bolt. It didn't take him long to get ready to move. The trail was still so easy to follow, he thought he could trail them even in the predawn light. After mounting, he kept his tracking slow until the sun rose, and as the light improved dramatically, so did Bolt's speed.

He had already gained almost five miles when Bill Nelson was waking up. It took him and Dick Pierce almost an hour to get Mattie up and ready to move.

John was only nine miles back when Nelson and Pierce bound Mattie, put her on her horse and hit the trail. They crossed a wide stream and changed their direction even more to the east, not to throw off any pursuers, but because Bill had recognized the terrain and knew they were only five or six miles from the Mitchell place.

The Mitchell place was an abandoned ranch that the boss, Russ Abernathy, had found more than twenty years ago. He hadn't fixed it up but used it for a staging area for jobs until they had moved forty miles to the northwest six years ago after it had gotten too hot to remain there. Their new location was another decrepit ranch roughly twenty miles northeast of Green River. The Mitchell place had been abandoned and very few people even knew it existed. They'd hold Mattie there until

THE DEBT

Frank's plan for taking over the gang had succeeded. Then, after Frank took over, they'd start making some real money. What happened to Mattie wasn't their concern after that. Bill Nelson was already making some plans of his own about what to do with Mattie when Dick left the Mitchell ranch to tell Frank that they had her.

———

    John was still gaining on them when he reached the stream and pulled to a stop. He let Bolt have a long drink as he apologized to him for pushing him so hard, but he knew that the horse would handle it. John then crossed the stream and had to spend almost twenty minutes picking up the trail again in the rocky surface. He was surprised by the direction shift, maybe they knew he was back there after all.

    He kept on the trail, but now began keeping an eye for potential ambush sites. It slowed him down, but he was still gaining, just not as quickly.

    An hour later, Dick Pierce spotted the entrance to the old Mitchell ranch and they soon turned down what used to be the access road.

    Mattie saw the house and wondered what awaited her there. She didn't think they'd want to harm her until they got what they wanted and still hoped that it was only ransom.

    Not doing anything to the schoolmarm may have been the orders they'd been given, but Bill Nelson didn't think Frank would mind a minor deviation from what he had been told. Besides, after Dick rode off to tell Frank of their success, what he did was his business.

———

John knew he was close after checking their horse's dropping and guessed he was less than an hour behind, probably only half that. If they were going to try to drygulch him, it would happen soon, provided they knew they were being followed, but their continued steady pace seemed to make that less likely.

———

Bill Nelson led Mattie's horse around the back of the dilapidated ranch house. Dick Pierce followed and after dismounting, they tied the two lead horses to the rear porch's support posts.

Mattie struggled to get down from the horse, her muscles protested their treatment by cramping viciously, making her drop to the dirt. Bill Nelson grabbed her by the arm and half carried, half dragged her up the single porch step and into the kitchen, then dropped her on the floor as she writhed in pain from her leg cramps.

"When you finish squirmin', you'd better start cleanin'. We're gonna be here for a few days, missy. Just you and me. My partner's gonna head back and tell your pappy that we got you," said Bill.

"*You know my father? Where is he?* I've been looking all over for him," she grunted through clenched teeth, her legs still fighting any attempt at control.

She knew from his tone that ransom wasn't the only reason for her abduction. *But where was her father and why did they know where he was when no one in Green River knew?*

Bill grabbed at her and replied, "Your pappy is back at the ranch. You're gonna be mighty useful to Frank, missy."

THE DEBT

"*Which ranch?* Nobody heard of the Rocking F. Who's Frank?" she demanded.

Bill snickered, then replied, "Rocking F? Now, ain't that a hoot. There ain't no Rocking F. The ranch we're usin' is our hideout, girlie. Frank is the man who's gonna be the new boss after your old man is outta the way."

Despite her leg cramps, Mattie was stunned. *What was he talking about?* He made it sound like her father was an outlaw, not a rancher. And not only an outlaw, but an outlaw who was now in danger.

Dick Pierce began unloading the food from the mule. He'd only take enough with him to get to the new hideout about five hours ride away, but he'd get a good fifteen miles ridden today, so he should get there tomorrow.

While Dick was unloading, John had been watching the ranch from the road. He couldn't see the movement behind the house, but he surely wasn't going to go down that access road. He turned Bolt back the way they had come and rode a quarter of a mile to a tree line, then he turned east into the trees. He wanted to get a good look at the house from the side. The tree line curved toward the house, which made things easier. By the time it was parallel to the house, it was less than a hundred yards out…Winchester range.

Dick said, "I'm ready to start out, Bill. I should be able to get fifteen miles out of the way today. I'll be talking to Frank this time tomorrow."

"Good. This was easier than I figured."

"Good plannin'. I think Frank will do right by us once he takes over."

"Get goin'. I want to get outta this place sooner rather than later," Bill said, not mentioning the real reason that he wanted his partner to leave.

He really just wanted some private time with Mattie.

"I need something from her to take to Frank," Dick said.

Bill looked down at Mattie, then grinned and said, "I could take her dress off."

Dick shook his head and said, "Just have her write a note and have her sign it. Have her say that we have her."

"Yeah, alright."

Bill walked to the supplies and pulled out a scrap of butcher paper as Dick pulled out a stub of a pencil from his shirt pocket, handed it to Bill, who gave them both to Mattie.

Bill said, "You write that Bill and Dick have you and sign it."

Mattie did as they asked then handed the note back to Bill.

Bill gave the note to Dick, then said, "Now, get riding."

"See you later," Dick said as he gave a short wave then walked out the door.

Bill waved back and took a seat in a wobbly chair and just stared at Mattie with greedy eyes.

Mattie looked at him and knew that her time of being unmolested was about to end. Her wrists may not be bound anymore, but her leg cramps made the leather bindings

THE DEBT

unnecessary. Her own tight muscles were just as effective as a pair of steel shackles.

Dick swung his saddlebags onto his horse and secured them before he mounted, then wheeled his horse and rode back down the access road. He knew what his partner was going to do, but it wasn't his call.

———

John saw him leave and debated about chasing him down or letting him go, before deciding to let him ride on. He'd just watch him go down the road to be sure he wasn't going to be back soon, then he'd take the shotgun and walk toward the house. There wasn't much cover, though. He just didn't want to risk leaving the teacher alone with one kidnapper for very long.

He watched Dick take the turn and start his horse trotting north, before he stepped down and looped Bolt's reins around a branch. He pulled the shotgun out of the scabbard and pulled back both hammers. Then he stopped, released the hammers and slid it back into the scabbard. There was too much risk with the wide scatter of the pellets. He pulled the Winchester out instead, cocked the hammer of the repeater and began to walk quickly toward the ramshackle ranch house.

———

In the kitchen, Bill Nelson thought he may as well announce his intentions.

"Well, missy, it's just you and me now. I think we should get better acquainted, don't you?" he asked as he smiled.

"My legs are cramping! Leave me alone!" Mattie snapped.

"Well, I'll come over there and give your legs a nice rubdown, after I make sure you're not going to put up a fuss."

He pulled out some pigging strings from his pocket and hooked them through his gunbelt. Then he approached Mattie and grabbed her by her hair, flipped her onto her stomach then put his knee on her back. He pulled her wrists behind her back and tied them with one of the pigging strings, then stood up and yanked her to her feet by her upper arm as her legs cramped so badly, she couldn't support her own weight.

Bill didn't care as he held onto her and said, "Now, the beds in here are probably all dusty and broken down. I think we can use the floor just fine, don't you?"

Mattie's legs were still torturing her and didn't know how she'd be able to prevent what he was planning to do to her. He dropped her to the floor and pushed her onto her back, then began pulling her dress up over her legs. Her muscles were already like rocks as Bill Nelson began running his hands up her legs and was grinning when he heard a loud creak from the back porch, startling him.

John swore silently. He had his boots off to prevent noise and now this. He set the Winchester aside quietly. This was going to be an in-close gunfight. He slipped off his right-hand hammer loop, pulled the pistol and cocked the Colt. It sounded louder than it was, and he suspected that the man inside had heard it. He was right.

Bill Nelson forgot all about Mattie. He had more urgent things to worry about as he mimicked John's actions and pulled his Colt out of his holster then tried to quietly pull the hammer back, but that wasn't possible. John heard the sound and slipped quietly to the unwindowed side of the porch. He didn't know what to do next as it seemed like a standoff with two armed men just feet away from each other but neither knowing where the other was.

Bill took one quiet step to look out the window at the back porch and saw nothing, which wasn't really a surprise. Whoever was out there was either on the windowless side of the kitchen or behind the door. He was tempted to start firing at the door and then move to the kitchen wall but knew that would be a last chance kind of thing. He only had five shots and couldn't afford to waste them.

John stood there for thirty heart-pounding seconds when he thought he'd try something to distract the man inside. He released his left-hand Colt's hammer loop and pulled the revolver out of the holster. He was going to count on the fact that very few men carried two-gun rigs as he tossed the revolver to the porch, just three feet beyond the door. When it hit, he muttered, "Damn it!"

The sound of a pistol hitting the floorboards and the uttered curse had the effect John needed.

Bill didn't need any more incentive. He unloaded his first shot through the door at the sound and then quickly ran to the door, cocking his hammer for the second round, only this time expecting to have a target in sight. He threw the door open, looking for either a downed man or a dead man.

John shouted from Bill's right, "Drop it!", but Bill had a loaded Colt in his hand with the hammer back. *Why would he even think of doing something as stupid as dropping his pistol?* He quickly turned it toward the voice, but as soon as he had begun to swing the gun, John fired. His Colt's .44 caliber bullet quickly passed through Bill Nelson, entering on the right side of his chest and exiting just two inches left of his backbone. The bullet continued and punched a hole through a dry board on the kitchen wall as Bill Nelson hit the floor, his life's blood pouring onto the old porch.

John stepped quickly to the body and made sure he was dead by the expedient method of delivering a hard kick to Bill's unmoving chest. With no reaction, John quickly entered the house, saw Mattie on the floor, her wrists bound, and her dress pulled up. He stepped to her side and pulled her dress down before she could even speak.

Everything had happened so fast Mattie had no idea what to say or do. One moment she was about to be raped and just a minute later the would-be rapist was dead and the man who'd killed him was tugging her dress back down.

John asked quickly, "Miss Foster, are you okay?"

Mattie nodded and looked at John. This wasn't the sheriff. *Who was he?* She may not have known who he was, but she was flushed with relief at her last moment reprieve from every woman's nightmare.

John then said, "I'm going to turn you on your side and cut your bonds. Don't move."

She tried to hold still, but her legs were still cramping as John rolled her onto her side, pulled out his big knife and cut the pigging strings. Mattie felt the blood flow return to her hands as she pulled her arms back to her front and began rubbing her wrists.

"Who are you?" she asked as she tried to sit.

"My name's John Clark. I own a ranch outside of Burnt Fork. Can you stand up?"

"My legs are cramping horribly."

THE DEBT

"I'll get a bedroll and you can massage them."

"My hands are almost useless right now."

"Let me get the bedroll. The feeling in your hands should come back well enough by the time I return."

"Okay."

John trotted back outside and removed a bedroll from one of the horses, assuming it had belonged to the dead man. He also took a quick look down the access road to see if the other man was returning. The gunshots could be heard from more than a couple of miles off, and it was more than likely that he'd be back and fairly soon.

―――

Dick had heard the gunshots and had a short debate with himself about whether to return or not, but curiosity ruled, so he wheeled his horse around and began to ride back to the Mitchell place. He was still a mile out when John had first looked down the road.

―――

John took a few seconds to pull his boots back on, then returned to the kitchen and spread the bedroll on the floor near Mattie.

Mattie looked at him and said, "Thank you for coming. I thought no one would come."

"You're welcome. Can you move to the bedroll?"

"I think so," she answered as she tried to slide over, but failed.

43

"I'll help you and pardon my being so familiar."

"I understand," she replied, and John lifted her easily onto the bedroll.

Mattie laid back onto the softer surface, sighed and said, "This is much better."

"Miss Foster, I'm going to go back outside. That other man probably heard the gunfire and I've got to be ready."

"Alright. I'll be okay now," she said as she began to flex her legs slightly. *He was a rancher?* He acted more like the sheriff than the sheriff did.

John hustled out the door and picked up his second Colt, returned it to its holster, then stepped around the edge of the porch and watched the access road where he spotted some dust billowing down the road a few hundred yards from the access road. The other one was returning.

He picked up his Winchester and walked around to the other side of the house, then stayed in the shadows as he watched Dick Pierce make the turn and begin trotting toward the house, his own Winchester already in his hands. He was scanning the house looking for movement, but John stayed unmoving in the shadows. Even returning toward the back porch might be seen. The man kept coming and John glanced down at his Winchester, making sure that he had left it cocked.

In the house, Mattie was massaging her legs to reduce the cramping, still wildly confused about the kidnapping, what the kidnapper had said, and her sudden, unexpected rescue. She was thoroughly grateful for what he had done but didn't understand why he had done it if he was just a rancher.

THE DEBT

John was still watching the second man approach the house. He was well within rifle range and John had every legal right to shoot him, but he never played the legal rights game. If it didn't feel right to him, he didn't do it.

Dick Pierce hadn't spotted John, but he thought something might be wrong, so he rode wide around the house before he spotted the same three horses that he had left tied to the back post, which changed his mind. There wasn't a new horse there, so he began to wonder if something else had made those sounds. The gunshots weren't that close, so it might have been from a hunter. But as he got closer to the back, he suddenly saw the upper half of Bill Nelson's body on the porch, stopped his horse and began to wildly search the area, still seeing nothing.

John had been watching when Dick rode around the north side of the house and had walked along the south side until he was near the back porch and waited. He listened to Dick's horse clopping on the other side and waited as the sound grew louder. When the sound stopped, he had to look rather than give the second man a chance to get into the house.

He popped out to challenge the rider to drop his rifle when Dick, who had his Winchester already aimed at the back porch, picked up the sudden flash of movement and fired. His .44 smashed into the back corner of the house above John's head and ripped through the aged wood, sending splinters everywhere, and the rain of wooden shards and splinters peppered John's Stetson, but not him.

John's hat was tossed aside by the barrage of flying wood and he quickly dropped to a crouch. He held the Winchester tightly his hands, then jumped forward and barrel rolled across Dick's vision. Dick had already levered in a new cartridge in case he hadn't hit him with his first shot and fired just as John began his roll and was high again as John suddenly regained his feet. Dick was levering in another round but was too late. John fired his Winchester at point blank range at a motionless target. The powerful .45 caliber round punched a hole in Dick's chest, and another was blown out in his back when the bullet exited almost immediately. He was thrown from his horse, falling to the dirt awkwardly, raising a cloud of dust before he rolled once and then laid still.

The silence returned as the large clouds of gunsmoke began to dissipate.

John quickly ran to the second man to make sure he was down, giving him another hard kick that was just precautionary. He had seen the round hit and knew the devastation it had wreaked. It was just an old habit, never leave someone you just shot behind you unless you were sure he couldn't shoot you in the back. He quickly grabbed the reins of the man's horse and tied it off to the packhorse temporarily.

Before he examined the two bodies, he walked over and picked up the first outlaw's Colt from the porch. He gave it a quick once-over, then slid it into the dead man's holster and looped it into place. He stepped back around the side of the house, picked up his injured hat, noting all the holes and wood shards still sticking out of it at odd angles. He'd probably need a new one after he pulled out all the splinters, but it had saved him from a lot of discomfort. He carried it and the Winchester as he stepped back onto the porch and entered the kitchen.

Mattie saw him enter and asked, "Are they both dead?"

"Yes, ma'am. One of them looks familiar. I may have seen his face on a wanted poster."

"He was going to rape me," she said quietly.

THE DEBT

John didn't comment on the obvious and just asked, "How are you feeling, aside from the cramps in your legs?"

"I'm all right. The cramps are finally easing."

"Miss Foster, I need to go and get my horse. I'll be back in a few minutes."

"Alright."

John stood and carried his Winchester with him but left his Stetson on the floor, not wanting to have one of those splinters stick into his head. After he had gone, Mattie picked it up and looked at all the splinters sticking like porcupine needles along its surface, and absentmindedly began plucking out the splinters and began to think.

Why had she been kidnapped? Was her father a criminal, or was the man just saying that? She was at such a loss for information, she was completely confused. She didn't know anyone or anything. It was as if she'd been dropped off in Siberia.

As Mattie was contemplating the mysteries of her return, John was slipping his Winchester into his empty scabbard, then untied his reins before mounting Bolt and set him to a walk out of the trees.

He was pretty sure that the first man he shot was Bill Nelson. He and the rest of the Abernathy gang had caused havoc among travelers, whether on trains, coaches or personal conveyance for the past four years. They hadn't murdered anyone yet, but he knew it was only a matter of time. The other one's identity wasn't quite so clear. He might be Dick Pierce, but he'd see if he could find any papers or anything else to identify them to confirm his guess.

His new question was why would Abernathy's gang swing into the kidnapping game? They had strictly been into theft before. It was a big step up in the criminal arena. As he walked Bolt toward the house, he wondered why they had decided to begin their kidnapping ventures with Miss Foster.

He reached the house and stepped down, tying Bolt to one of the empty porch support posts. He removed both the food bag and the bag of clothes that Evelyn Fletcher had packed, as well as both of his canteens, then stepped over Bill Nelson's body and entered the kitchen.

"Miss Foster, I had Mrs. Fletcher retrieve some of your things that you might need," he said as he handed her the bag.

"Thank you so much. I was concerned about that. That was very thoughtful."

"It's been known to happen," he said as he smiled.

Mattie Foster was indeed a looker, to use Hank Ward's term. But there was more to her than how she looked. She seemed to be a true innocent, which made the chase and shootout worthwhile. He had saved a truly innocent life, and maybe that counted for something.

Mattie smiled back and tried bending her knees, not experiencing nearly as much pain and thought that walking might help.

She then embarrassingly said, "Excuse me, things were so hectic that I've forgotten your name."

"John Clark."

"Would you mind if I call you John?"

THE DEBT

"Not at all, miss. Pleased to meet you, Miss Foster," he replied, offering his hand.

She smiled and shook his hand, and he found that he couldn't help looking into her eyes. They were honest eyes.

Mattie then asked, "John, can you help me up? I think I can walk a bit. It'll help."

"Certainly."

He took her hand again and easily pulled her to her feet. She was a bit wobbly but was soon walking gingerly around the room.

"Miss Foster, I've got to see to those two bodies outside. You stay in here. I've got some food in the bag here and my canteens are full, so help yourself. I'll be back in a little while."

"Thank you, John," she said as she hobbled about.

"You're welcome."

John walked past Bill Nelson's body again with a long stride, then grabbed his shirt by the shoulders and began to drag him across the porch. He decided to put him and the other man over where his Stetson had been showered with splinters for now but would have to figure out what to do with them more permanently in a little while.

He went through the pockets finding no identifying information, and just $6.45 in cash. He put the cash in his pocket and pulled Nelson's gunbelt from around his waist. When he looked inside the belt, he found 'Bill Nelson' burned into the leather.

John then stepped back onto the porch, crossed it and dropped back onto the ground to check out the second body. Again, there were no identifying papers but $7.15 in the pockets. He pulled his gunbelt, and just like his partner, Dick Pierce had burned his name into the leather.

His pistol was already secured, so he set it on the porch and dragged Dick's body around the horses and then left it beside Bill Nelson's corpse. John had noticed the relatively small amount of blood on the porch, which meant that both men must have died almost instantly. But now he knew that Abernathy was involved. Why they had kidnapped Miss Foster continued to be the dominating question.

He returned to where he had found Dick Pierce's body and picked up his Winchester '73. He just slipped it back into the horse's scabbard for now, knowing he'd have to do some gun cleaning soon.

He looked at the packhorse and was surprised to see a pickaxe and a shovel, almost as if they were miners, but suspected that they were going to be used for Miss Foster's body. If they were holding her for ransom, that was a likely outcome; get the money, kill the victim and run. At least, he'd put them to good use shortly.

John then pulled both sets of saddlebags and dumped their contents onto the ground. Each had a spare box of .44 cartridges, but little else. He carried the two boxes of ammunition and their gunbelts into the kitchen as Mattie was having a sandwich.

"Did you find anything?" she asked.

"Just their names. One was Bill Nelson and the other was named Dick Pierce. They did have something a bit different, though. Did you notice the pickaxe and shovel on the horse?"

THE DEBT

She swallowed, then nodded and said, "I think that was for me after they got what they wanted," then felt a chill even as she said it.

"I think so, too. I'll use them to get those two underground shortly. Miss Foster, do you have any idea why they would kidnap you? Schoolmarms in an out of the way place like Burnt Fork aren't exactly common targets."

"I don't know. I came here after graduating from college in Missouri to see my father. He said he was on his large ranch called the Rocking F, but no one seems to have heard of it or him."

"Well, I'm a rancher and I've never heard of it, either. What was your father's name?"

"Russ Foster."

That Christian name wasn't very common and gave John the connection that may provide the reason for the kidnapping.

He said, "The only Russ I know about is Russ Abernathy. He runs a gang of outlaws that has called the Green River area home for quite some time. His gang hasn't shot anyone yet, so there really hasn't been a big push to track him down. Both of those dead men were in his gang."

"That man," Mattie said, her voice shaking slightly, "the one you shot first, the one who was going to rape me, said that my father was at his hideout and that I would be useful to a man named Frank. He said that Frank was going to be the new boss."

It suddenly all clicked into place in John's mind. There was a power play in the Abernathy gang. Frank would be Frank Lewis, Abernathy's right-hand man for a long time now. They must have found out about Mattie's being in Burnt Fork and were going to use her as a pawn to force Abernathy out.

"I think I see it, miss. You're not Russ Foster's daughter, you're Russ Abernathy's daughter. Those two men worked for your father and it looks like Frank, his name is Frank Lewis, by the way, is trying to take over the gang. He had these two men kidnap you and were going to use you to force him out."

"Why wouldn't they just pull their guns and tell him to leave?"

"Your father's reputation was that he was very fast with his pistol. He may be getting a bit slower now that he's older, but he's a lot wiser about men, too. Men like Frank Lewis and those two outside don't like even odds. They want an advantage. Even trying to drygulch a man like your father would be hazardous. No, they needed a wedge, and you were the wedge."

"What's drygulch?" she asked before taking another bite of her sandwich.

"It means shooting someone in the back from hidden cover."

"Oh. You said you were a rancher. How come you seem to know so much?"

"I was the sheriff in Burnt Fork for six years. I read a lot about things that helped me do my job better and I kept up with what was going on."

"Why aren't you the sheriff any longer? The one they have now isn't much of a sheriff."

"Frank Baker isn't a bad man; he's just not cut out for being a lawman. He was all they could find to replace me. My father died suddenly, and I had to return to take over the ranch."

THE DEBT

"Oh."

"Well, I'm going to go out and bury those two before it gets any hotter. But before I do, let's see if we can get the pump working. It's a long shot, though."

John picked up one of the canteens and primed the pump. It was tough to get going, but after about a dozen strokes, water gushed out of the spigot.

"Well, that helps. I don't think we should be leaving today. Aside from my having to bury those two and get all the animals settled, you shouldn't be riding again so quickly."

"Thank you. I don't think I could even get on a horse again right now."

"Okay. I'll be back in a while."

John unbuckled his gunbelt, then set his rig on the old table near the sink and was surprised it didn't collapse under the weight.

He walked outside, headed for the packhorse and removed the shovel and pickaxe. He didn't want to go too far from where the bodies were stretched out near the house. Besides, the ground there would be marginally softer because the afternoon sun wouldn't be baking the ground as much as the other side.

He removed his shirt, set it on the edge of the porch and collected the tools. He picked out a spot and began punching a hole in the ground with the pickaxe. Once the dirt was loosened, he began shoveling. It was hard work, but it was good, manual labor. John enjoyed that kind of work because felt like it cleansed the soul, no matter how much it made him filthy on the outside, and this was definitely hard work.

He finally reached a depth of four feet, which was good enough for those two. He dragged one and then the other to the edge of the hole, rolled them into the pit and then began shoveling the dirt back on top of the bodies. When he finished, he was about to make some smarmy comment over their grave but didn't want to tempt Providence, so he just turned with his two tools and sat on the edge of the porch to dry off. He closed his eyes and felt the sun on his face. This was the simple part of life that he enjoyed, hard work, and when it was done, taking a break.

Five minutes later, he felt he was dry enough, so he pulled his shirt back on and leaned the tools against the porch. His next job was caring for the animals. He removed the two Winchesters, left them on the porch, then untied the four horses and led them away from the dry dirt to a grassy area. He kept walking until he found a source of water about a quarter of a mile from the house. It wasn't much, but it would do the job. He could step over the stream without even stretching, but the horses appreciated it. He let them drink and when they were satisfied, he turned them toward the house and hitched Bolt to a heavy bush and extended the trail rope to the other three animals. Then he unsaddled them all, leaving their saddles on the ground, then covering them with their blankets to keep out the morning dew. Satisfied that they had enough leeway to graze for a while, he headed back to the house.

He guessed it was after two o'clock by now, and he needed to eat something. It looked like the Abernathy boys had brought enough food for a few days and wondered if the cookstove was still functioning.

He snatched up the two Winchesters as he crossed the porch, entered the kitchen and found Mattie missing. He guessed that she was walking around the house trying to get her blood flowing into her legs again, so he set the two

THE DEBT

repeaters near the other guns before he looked into the bag of food his mother had prepared. There were no more sandwiches, so Mattie must have been hungry. He pulled out the smoked beef and cut off a piece, then ripped off a chunk with his teeth and began to chew, before he took a canteen and washed down the meat. He kept it up until the piece was gone, then cut off a piece of the ham, and as he was chewing, Mattie returned from her exercise.

"Oh! I'm sorry. I should have left you a sandwich. I was just so hungry. They didn't let me eat much, even though I had to cook their food."

"It's alright. This is fine."

"Are they gone?"

"Yes, ma'am. You seem to be walking better."

"Finally. I'm still sore, but it's getting better."

"Good. After a good night's sleep without being tied up, you should feel all right in the morning. I'll take it slower on the way back, and you tell me if you start getting uncomfortable and we'll stop. They provided enough food for the trip. Paddy told me you didn't have a horse. Did you want one of the ones outside?"

"I can just have one?"

"Sure. When I walked them out to the pasture, I noticed that the bay had a nice gait. He'd probably be the best choice."

"I've never had a horse," Mattie said.

"Where did you grow up?"

"I grew up here in Wyoming, believe it or not. After my mother died, my father sent me away to a convent school in Missouri and then college."

"Am I wrong in assuming you decided to come back and visit your father?"

"No, you're not wrong, that's why I came back. Then I was in trouble when I realized that his ranch didn't exist, and no one knew who he was. I had less than twenty dollars left when I went down to Burnt Fork."

"That took some courage, Miss Foster, but it still leaves me a bit puzzled."

"I'm more than puzzled but traveling all that way alone was more like stupidity than courage, if you ask me."

"Would you mind taking a seat, so we can help each other solve some of those puzzling questions?"

"I hope we can," she replied as they carefully sat in the two rickety chairs.

John asked, "Miss Foster, obviously you didn't know that your father was an outlaw, but what made you decide to come back here? Did he ask you to return?"

Mattie sighed and replied, "No, if anything, I had the impression that he wanted me to stay away. I never received letters of encouragement or affection from my father, but each month he'd send some money to let me continue my education. It wasn't a lot, but it was enough. I had friends in college who asked me to stay with them, but I felt an obligation to come here and thank him. I was curious about him, too. He was all I had for a family now. I rationalized that he was writing so indifferently to me because he didn't know me anymore.

THE DEBT

"When I got off the train, I was disappointed and then when I discovered that his ranch didn't exist, I was lost and quite ashamed for my silliness. The job in Burnt Fork was like a life preserver."

John said, "Okay. That's why you are here, and I can figure out why they kidnapped you, but the next question is what do you want to do next? If you'd like to return to Burnt Fork and still be a teacher, I'm sure all of the folks would be overjoyed to have you there. But if you'd prefer to return to Missouri and your friends, then I'll provide you with enough money for the trip."

Mattie was more than mildly surprised by his offer and asked, "Could I think about it for a little while? I'm still trying to sort things out in my head."

"I believe that's a good idea. While you do some thinking, I'm going to go and inspect this place and see if we can find anything useful."

Mattie then surprised John when she asked, "May I come along?"

"Yes, ma'am."

Before he rose, Mattie said, "John, could you call me Mattie? I'd feel more comfortable if you would."

"I'd be honored, Mattie," John replied as he stood, then smiled and they began his search of the derelict ranch house.

John thought he'd see if the bedrooms were useful at all as Mattie would need some privacy. The one closest to the kitchen was the worst. There were gaping holes in the wall and roof, and no furniture at all. The second appeared to be the best of the three. There were only a couple of holes in the roof and the walls were intact. There was a bed frame and a woven surface in the corner that appeared to be serviceable.

He approached the bed and said, "This might work for you. Put a bedroll on there and it should be comfortable."

Mattie walked tentatively toward the bed and pushed on the weave. It held, but a lot of dust fell to the floor when she had poked it.

"I'll clean it up after I test it," John said.

Mattie asked, "How will you test it?"

"I'll take it outside, get all the dust off and then I'll lie on it. If it can support my weight, it won't have any problem with yours. Let's check out the last room."

The one closest to the main room was only slightly better than the first one that they had examined, and as they left, John said, "It looks like the middle one is the only one that will work. I'll drag that bed frame outside and clean it off."

"Can I do anything?"

"You might want to check the clothing bag and make sure it has everything you need."

"Okay."

John returned to the middle bedroom, turned the bed onto its side, then slid it out of the room and down the hallway to the front of the house. As he dragged it along, it pushed the thick coat of dust on the floor aside, leaving a distinct path.

THE DEBT

He got it to the porch and began smacking it with his open palm. The dust cloud was impressive, and there was little wind to move it out of the way.

Mattie opened the clothing bag and was surprised to find things that weren't hers. A jacket, a riding skirt, some gloves and a scarf. She suspected that John Clark had those added because he knew she'd need them. He seemed to be an extraordinary man. He was taller than she was, which wasn't always the case. He was handsome too, with those fascinating gray eyes and thought there was one lucky woman on his ranch.

When John was reasonably satisfied that it was as clean as it was going to get, he returned it to its feet and began pushing on the woven rope lattice to test its strength. It seemed in acceptable condition, so he gently sat on the bed and it held.

He felt more confident, so he pulled his legs up and laid down, heard the rope supports stretch, but hold as he smiled. He was satisfied and began to sit to get out of the bed when he heard a loud pop followed by a horrendous series of loud snaps as the supports gave way. John dropped through the frame, crashed to the porch floor and didn't stop there. Two of the porch boards underneath him gave way as well and John found himself bent at the waist with the bed frame keeping him in that precarious position as his behind was wedged into the hole created by the departing boards.

Mattie had heard the crash, dropped her clothing bag, then hurried to the front door as best she could and saw John in his jackknifed predicament and did the only thing she could do…she started laughing.

John looked at her and despite his humiliation followed suit. Even as he laughed, he was able to work his right arm over the side rail of the bed and push himself up and then with a strong shove, throw himself over to the other side. Mattie was still laughing with her hand covering her mouth as John was able to extricate himself from the broken boards and roll onto his stomach.

"I hope I provided you with sufficient entertainment, Miss Foster," he said looking up at her as he was stretched in the prone position.

"It's the only entertainment I've had since I've been here, Mister Clark."

"Obviously, the bed failed its test. That means you'll have to make do with a bedroll again."

"At least I won't be tied inside."

"No, ma'am."

John sprang to his feet, dusted himself off and they returned to the house as John slid the useless piece of furniture into the main room. It might be useless to sleep in, but it would burn.

Mattie was still trying to come to a decision about what to do about her father and John's offer. Frank was trying to take over, maybe kill her father, which presented a moral issue for her.

Her father was a criminal. He had kept her away from his life by sending her to the boarding school and then college. Now she had returned to see him and found out the truth. She knew that the best solution for her was to return to Burnt Fork with John and assume her new teaching position, but something else was bothering her, and had been there even before she knew about her father's background.

Mattie had a deep sense of obligation to her father. She believed that if it wasn't for him, she'd probably have been left

THE DEBT

in an orphanage and not been able to receive the education that now enabled her to have some measure of control over her life. Mattie Foster felt she owed a debt to her father, nothing less.

Maybe she could convince him to stop his life of crime and began toying with the idea of taking the chance as she tried to remember him from all those years ago but found it almost impossible.

She recalled even less about her mother. She had died when she was young, and Mattie never knew why she had died. Death was a common companion out here.

Now she had a difficult choice. *Did she just return with John Clark to Burnt Fork or did she try to find her father to at least try to repay her obligation?* She still had almost no money left, but she'd have a horse tomorrow. Then there was the perpetual question of danger from being a woman alone.

If she decided to help her father, she would have to ask for help from John Clark. But he had his ranch to run, and if he wouldn't help, she'd have to return to Burnt Fork. But she had all night to make her decision and to get a better read on John Clark. He would be key to giving her the opportunity to not only meet her father but try and convince him to leave his criminal path.

Mattie Foster may have been a very intelligent young woman with a college degree, but she was incredibly ignorant and naïve when the subject was men and especially those men who viewed the rest of society as prey.

———

Forty-one miles northwest of the Mitchell place, Russ Abernathy sat with his four remaining gang members: Frank Lewis, Fritz Thompson, Big Ed Howard, and Prince King.

"Frank, where are Bill and Dick? I haven't seen them for four days now."

"Boss, I think they went to Green River. They said something about having to clean out the pipes," Frank replied as he snickered.

"I warned you guys about spending too much time in town. We can't do any jobs if we spend so much time in Green River."

Frank said, "I know, boss. But they should be back today."

Prince King knew Frank was up to something, but he wasn't about to say anything. He just wanted to be on the winning side. He was the newest member of the gang and tried to keep a low profile. Whatever Frank was up to, he knew that Fritz and Big Ed were going to back Frank's play. He looked over at Russ and almost felt sorry for him, but if it wasn't for the speed of Abernathy's right hand, he would have helped Frank. He suspected that Russ's proficiency with his weapons and his uncanny ability to read men was what had held Frank in check.

Russ said, "We're gonna hit the stage coming up from Hopkins the day after tomorrow. It's supposed to be carrying the transfer from the Hopkins Bank to The First National in Green River."

"What time do we have to leave?" Frank asked.

"It's a good day's ride to get into position. I've already staked it out."

"So, we need to leave tomorrow morning."

THE DEBT

"That's the problem, Frank. I needed those two to cut off the escape route back to Hopkins."

"They'll be back, boss."

"I hope so."

Frank hoped so, too. *Where was Dick Pierce?* He should have been here by now with proof that they'd gotten the boss's daughter.

They managed a decent dinner out of the supplies after John had the cookstove functioning almost like an iron campfire pit. Mattie had slipped into silence as she contemplated her choices.

John knew she was thinking about his offer and didn't make any useless conversation. He was impressed how normal Mattie was functioning after all that had happened since she left Missouri, but still had no idea of what she was thinking.

He assumed that she still had many friends and probably more than a few potential suitors back in Missouri and was just hesitant to accept his offer so she wouldn't feel any sense of obligation to him.

John was cleaning the kitchen mostly to give her time to come to terms with what she had just learned about her father. The last thing he would have suspected was that she might be contemplating helping the man. He suspected that she'd eventually decide to accept his offer to return to Missouri and her friends, although he wished she'd decide to stay on as a teacher and not because of the town's needs, but for his own.

For the first time since Nellie's death, he was beginning to believe that he found a woman that might be worth getting to know.

Mattie was not only leaning toward helping her father, she was thinking about asking John to assist in providing that help. The idea of asking a lawman, even an ex-lawman, to help an outlaw chief didn't even seem ludicrous to her, but she needed to know more about John before she posed the idea.

"John, when you said you had to give up being the sheriff because you had to take care of the ranch. Couldn't you do both? You know, have your foreman run the ranch?"

"I could have, but I wouldn't have done either job well. It's hard to do when you're six miles away. Besides, I owed it to my mother."

"We all owe our mothers, even if we don't remember them."

"That's true, but my mother gave me my life twice."

"How did she do that?"

John debated about how much to tell Mattie but decided to give her the full story.

"When I was in school, a new girl named Nellie Branford moved to town. I really liked her, even though I was a year older, which is enormous when you're eleven. By the time we were teenagers we were inseparable. Nellie was everything to me. When I told her that I was going to leave the ranch to become the sheriff, she supported my decision and we were married soon afterwards and couldn't be happier.

"Then she told me she was going to have a baby and we were both ecstatic. She even told me it was going to be a boy. I don't know if she really knew that or was just saying it, but she made it seem as if she did. We were both anxiously waiting for the baby and had already picked out a boy's name and didn't even bother with a girl's name, that's how sure she was. She was proven right, too. But after he was born, she began bleeding again and died less than an hour later.

"I was devastated and really thought I couldn't go on any more without Nellie. I just felt totally empty. My mother gave me some leeway at first, found a wet nurse for my son, Jamey, and I almost forgot he even existed as I slipped into almost total despair. That went on for over a month and it was my mother who yanked me back into living when she brought Jamey to me while I was in the office in town. She put him in my arms and said, 'John, this little boy is part you and part Nellie. How do you think she'd feel right now if she knew you were denying him a chance to be with his father?'

"It snapped me back into my real life, and I wanted Jamey to be proud of his father. When my father died two years ago, I felt an obligation to my mother and to my son. I owed them both for almost drifting into uselessness and needed to spend time with him. No more rides back and forth to town every day, no more late-night returns and no more dangerous escapades that could make him an orphan. That's why I stopped being a sheriff, Mattie. My family was more important."

John had no idea why he went into such detail with Mattie. He hadn't done that with anyone before. They would ask why he gave up being a lawman and he'd tell them that he needed to work the ranch and nothing more. He could have done the same with Mattie, but he hadn't. He had told her the whole story, almost. Even then, he had left out the one part of the story that still disturbed him because it created a question in his mind that he couldn't answer.

Mattie was deeply moved by his story, which made up her mind about asking him because it was so close to her own situation in a way. John had an emotional depth that surprised her, and she believed that he'd understand her need to find her father and help him.

"John, I feel as if I owe my father, too. I know he's a criminal now, but he didn't have to send me away and keep me away from his life. I want to go and warn him. Maybe I can talk him into leaving this life. Maybe I can convince him to return to Missouri with me. It's where he grew up."

John was taken aback by her decision and had to take a few seconds before responding.

"Mattie, that's a very noble thing to try to do, but it's also very naïve. Your father is a criminal with a price on his head. Even if he agreed to go with you, that would follow him. There are men out there, bounty hunters, who would sniff him out and kill him for the reward. He knows that. If he cares about you enough to send you to a boarding school and then college, he wouldn't want you to get involved in what he does."

"But they're going to try to kill him, John. Maybe they already have. Those letters he sent me showed up every month until recently when they stopped three months before I graduated, and I thought he might be dead. But I need to know. He's not, is he?"

"Those two boys didn't kidnap you three months ago. I'm sure he's alive and Frank is waiting for one of them to return with proof that they had you so he could make his play."

"Won't they kill him now that those two are both dead? I have to go and try to warn him at least. Don't you see?"

THE DEBT

"Mattie, your father is a self-protective man. It's the business he's in. He needs to be constantly looking out for the back shooter. The purpose of your kidnapping was to be able to manipulate him, maybe just disarm him. They might not kill him, but just force him out."

"Why not? They're violent men."

"For the others, it's the same thing. They've got to be sure that they can kill him if they want him out of the way. If they think there's a chance they'll die, they won't do it."

"John, I can't just let it go. I need to go and warn him."

"How? You can't shoot a gun or even ride fast or far. You surely can't intimidate these men. All that can happen to you is bad things."

"Can't you take me to him? Please?"

There it was. John suddenly had a feeling he'd been set up by this supposedly naïve girl. She had heard his story and played off of it. Now she was saying that if he didn't help, she'd go anyway and whatever happened to her would be his fault, and he didn't like it one bit.

John quickly came up with the best solution he could think of at the moment, and he wasn't very happy about it at all.

"Alright, Mattie. Here's what I'll do. I'll take you back to Burnt Fork. You start teaching and I'll go and warn your father."

"Do you know where he is?"

"I have an idea now because of Dick Pierce. I think he's northeast of Green River. Exactly where I don't know yet, but I have an idea how to find out now."

"Why do you have an idea now?"

"The Abernathy gang's domain covers a large area, so they've been hard to locate. But they range beyond Green River to the west and Baxter to the east. That's over sixty miles. If you center that, they'd be north of here somewhere. Dick Pierce, when he left to return to their hideout, had enough food for one night. So, that means he couldn't reach it in an afternoon. That puts him near the railroad. They'd want to be at least a few miles on the other side. This ranch had failed and become derelict just as many others do. I'd bet that they found another one for their hideout."

"If you can find them, then why can't I come along?"

"There are almost too many reasons to mention. You're a woman. You can't shoot a gun. You have never been in this kind of situation before. I'd spend all my time worrying about you instead of watching my back. And those are just the ones I can think of off the top of my head. Give me another few minutes and I'll be able to add another dozen."

Mattie stared at him and said firmly "I'm not going back to Burnt Fork unless I see my father."

John was getting exasperated as he said, "Mattie, you're beginning to sound like a spoiled child. This is a dangerous game you're playing. If I find out where he is and enter his hideout, I won't have better than a fifty-fifty chance of coming out of there. Yours would be almost zero and if you came along, so would mine. Just a few hours ago, you were close to being raped and probably murdered, and Bill Nelson wasn't even the hardest of the bunch. Besides, what would you do if you don't go to Burnt Fork? You already said that you don't have any money. There aren't too many jobs available for women, even college-educated women, out here. You can take my offer and go back to Missouri, but I'm not taking you with me to find your father."

Mattie's dander was up, despite the logic of John's arguments as she closed her fists and snapped, "I am not a spoiled child! I am an adult and I can do what I want to do. If I have to go, I'll saddle a horse myself and ride to Green River by myself, I swear that I will."

John exhaled then said calmly, "And you'll die, Mattie. It's that simple. You think men like Bill Nelson are rare? They're not. They're everywhere. They'd look at you as nothing more than entertainment. Now I've offered to go and warn your father. You'll stay safe and if I can do it, then maybe he'll stay safe. That's the best I'm going to do."

"Then I'll leave in the morning and go to Green River."

"Fine. You do that," John said as he threw up his hands.

Utterly flummoxed, he turned then marched from the kitchen and out to the porch. He was seething. *Talk about stubborn!* He knew he couldn't let her go by herself and that's what made it worse. She probably knew it as well. *Hell! She probably didn't even know how to saddle a horse!* He sat on the porch steps and tried to calm down. He hated being manipulated and that young woman was doing it effortlessly.

Inside the house, Mattie was doing her own steaming. *A spoiled child! Who did he think he was, anyway? She'd show him! She'd get on that horse tomorrow and ride to Green River.* All the time her conscious mind was reminding her of how rudely John had treated her, a quiet voice in the back of her mind was reminding her that she couldn't saddle a horse, didn't know how to get to Green River, and she didn't know where her father was. Oh, and she had no money. But her angry voice shouted the quiet voice down. She would leave, and he could ride back to Burnt Fork for all she cared.

John calmed down first. He knew his arguments were logical, but it didn't seem to matter against Mattie's emotionally driven argument. She was worried about her father and she wanted to see him. John knew he might be able to talk to Russ Abernathy, *but could he convince him to either leave the criminal life or that there was a palace revolution?* Maybe. But no better than maybe.

In a huge reversal, and maybe the biggest mistake of his life, he decided he'd take Mattie to her father. If she felt she had an obligation, he knew she'd have to satisfy it, just as he'd been doing for nine years and failing.

He stood, then walked across the porch, entered in the back door into the kitchen and found Mattie still fuming at the table.

He looked at her and said, "Mattie, I'm going to make the biggest mistake of my life and take you to your father."

Mattie heard it and didn't believe it. *What had just happened?*

"Why did you change your mind?"

"Just leave it that I changed my mind. I still think it's the wrong thing to do, but I'll take you there. But first, you need to learn to shoot a Winchester. A pistol might be too much of a problem, even though your hands look big enough. There's just too much going on with a Colt. A Winchester is easier to use and has more shots available. I can show you how to use it on the way. Secondly, you've got to learn to ride a horse, at least so you can escape. I had them add a heavy jacket, gloves, scarf and a riding skirt to your clothes and you'll need them all."

"Thank you, John. That was very thoughtful," she replied quietly, her eyes downcast.

"You're welcome, although I think it was the least thoughtful thing I've ever done. You'll learn to at least fire the Winchester, and you'll need to be able to handle a horse. Agreed?"

"Agreed. John, I'm sorry I acted the way I did. I'm not usually that way. But I felt like I owed my father at least a chance."

"I know. I've put two bedrolls in that middle bedroom. You can sleep in there. I'll be out on the porch if you need anything. Good night, Mattie."

"Good night, John."

He just turned and walked out to the porch. The sun was already setting, but he didn't notice the spectacular sunset. Now that he had caved in, he'd need to plan on how to approach this.

Essentially, Mattie wanted to go into the lion's den. If Frank thought he could overthrow Russ Abernathy, it made sense that there were more disenchanted members of the gang. The last time he had heard, the gang consisted of eight men. Two were now buried in the ground near the house. He needed some semblance of a plan, so as he cleaned the guns, he tried to come up with anything that had even a remote possibility of success.

Mattie wondered why she didn't feel elated about her victory. *She won, didn't she?* John was going to take her to see her father. *Then what? What happened after she finally did see him again after almost fifteen years? Would he be horrified that she knew who he was? Then what would she do after that?*

She believed John was right about him being hunted down even if he left the criminal life, but she had to ask just to be sure. At least they'd be able to warn him about Frank.

She suddenly had more doubts than she had before; a lot more doubts and a lot more questions, but none of them impacted her decision. She had a debt to pay to her father.

Russ Abernathy wasn't the man he was because he was stupid or naïve. He knew that Frank and some of the other boys wanted him gone, but he had nothing firm. A lot of the money he had made over the years had gone to pay for Mattie's schooling and to keep her away. He still had a decent stash, but there were times he regretted spending the money on that girl. He had never told her about her real mother. The woman she thought was her mother was Jean Mitchell.

Mattie's real mother was a young prostitute named Prudence Foster that Russ had grown attached to and had brought from her brothel to live with him in their first hideout. She had surprised him when she told him that she was pregnant. He thought that whores all knew ways to stop the problem from occurring. He had contemplated just taking her into town and leaving her there or giving her to one of the other men, but he hadn't. Not because he cared about her that much, but because he was concerned that she would talk. If she wasn't a woman, he would have just killed her.

Just two weeks after she had the baby, it was business as usual with Prudence. Mattie was Prudence's problem, not his. There were times when he wanted to take the baby outside and leave it in the Wyoming winter when she cried at night, but Prudence was always able to quiet her down in time.

THE DEBT

Prudence lasted another year and a half before she simply disappeared while the gang was out on a job. Russ and the boys had returned and found Mattie toddling around an empty house. Russ had been visiting the Mitchell woman off and on while Prudence was in her late stages of pregnancy and even afterwards. When Prudence ran off, Russ had simply taken Jean Mitchell away from her abusive husband to act as the kid's mother and moved their hideout to the Mitchell place. He had grown accustomed to having a woman in his bed, and Jean knew how to take care of him.

She had welcomed the change of male companionship and had grown fond of little Mattie.

Then there was that dreadful argument he had with Jean Mitchell. She had let Frank Lewis have his way with her, and she had argued that Russ had never married her, so he had no rights of possession. He had smacked her hard with his open hand, knocking her into the fireplace. She had landed among the fireplace tools, been impaled and died the next day. He had buried her in the back yard of the Mitchell place, and surprising himself, had felt horrible for what he'd done. Ironically, the man who had caused the row, Frank Lewis, didn't even care about her at all. He had just wanted Jean for the night.

He had sent little Mattie away the next week. She hadn't witnessed Jean's death or burial but was missing her 'mama'. Russ knew it was only a matter of time before she found out what had happened if she stayed and one of the gang members spilled the beans. Besides, without a woman to care for the kid, she was becoming a nuisance. There was just one other reason why Russ Abernathy hadn't just abandoned Mattie to an orphanage, and it was a unique feeling for him: guilt. He had never struck a woman before and now he had killed one. He sent her to a convent school in Columbia all the way to Missouri where he had grown up.

He would write to Mattie and send her money for living expenses, which wasn't so much when she was young, just a dollar here and there. But when she went to college, he sent more, but still not a lot. He had her mail go to the Green River post office under the name Russ Foster, a bit of a joke to him as it was the name of her whore mother. He'd either go to pick up his mail or have one of the boys pick it up.

The letters he sent were little more than notes saying in effect, 'here's your money. Don't spend it all in one place'. None of the letters expressed any feelings of affection because he felt none. He was just paying off an old debt to Jean Mitchell.

The gang all knew about Mattie and thought he was a fool for sending her money but didn't dare tell him to his face.

What he didn't know was that Frank had not posted his last three letters to Mattie and had intercepted her incoming mail. He had known about her upcoming graduation and that she was planning to come to Green River where she would be a critical part of his plan. A plan where he could take over and still be alive to remake the gang as he thought it should be. The only problem was the misdirected delay in her letter saying when she was going to arrive, and that had cost him some time.

Russ knew Mattie was planning on coming to Green River and had strongly advised her not to visit in his last few letters. In fact, he hadn't advised her at all. He had told her without any wiggle room to stay in Missouri, stopping just short of telling her that he didn't care one bit about her. He had even thought about telling her the truth about her birth mother but hadn't thought it was necessary. He had hoped she had changed her mind because he just didn't want her here. She'd be in the way and probably expect him to be her father and give her a big hug or something. The thought made him nauseous.

THE DEBT

Frank's plan was simple, but incredibly flawed in that he believed that Russ Abernathy cared about his daughter. Dick Pierce would soon bring him something belonging to Mattie and he'd show Russ the proof that he had her and tell him where she was, too. They'd ride to the Mitchell place, but Russ would be disarmed when they set out. Frank would tell him that if he showed up at the door with a gun, Bill Nelson would kill Mattie. He planned on killing both Russ and Mattie when they were in the Mitchell place anyway.

Then he could run the gang the way he wanted to run it. Some victims had been so confident that the Abernathy gang wouldn't shoot them these past few years that they had refused to cough up their valuables. That would change.

Frank simply didn't know that Russ had no emotional connection to Mattie at all. Russ rarely even read the letters she sent, not wanting to be reminded of his tiny sliver of humanity. He'd just crumple them up and toss them in the corner of the room. But when she was close to graduation, he read them because of what worried him the most, her sudden appearance in Green River.

All that Russ Abernathy knew was that something was cooking with his boys.

CHAPTER 2

John woke up early with the dawn sun blasting his eyes, then crawled out of his bedroll and decided to relieve himself on the freshly turned earth on the north side of the house. Those two had earned it. Once his yellow insult was done, he walked quietly into the kitchen, started the cookstove fire and pumped some water to wash himself. He still couldn't shave, but maybe he'd remedy that in Green River. He'd need to send a telegram to Burnt Fork and see Joe Wheeler, the county sheriff, too.

He put his shirt back on after washing and put a frypan on the stove. Bill Nelson had packed a decent quantity of food for the trip, including eggs, so he soon had the bacon popping in the frypan when Mattie made her appearance.

"That smells good," she said as she smiled.

John still wasn't in a smiling mood, no matter how pretty she was and asked, "How do you like your eggs?"

"Can I have two over easy?"

John just nodded and began cracking eggs.

"Where can I get some privacy?" she asked.

"Anywhere outside. There's nobody within ten miles at least."

"Alright," she replied and hustled outside.

THE DEBT

By the time she returned, John had the bacon cooked and set aside, and had six eggs in the frypan and was waiting to flip them.

Mattie snatched a strip of bacon and sat down as John added coffee to the pot and flipped the eggs before removing them just seconds later and giving Mattie three eggs.

"I only asked for two, John."

"You'll need them, Miss Foster. I want to get at least thirty miles done today and need to show you how to use one of those Winchesters, too."

Mattie noticed the reversion to the more formal form of address, but asked, "Why can't I use a pistol?"

"Go ahead and eat. Maybe I'm wrong and you can. We'll see."

John's real reason for not showing Mattie how to use a pistol was that it would mean close in shooting, like he had done yesterday with Bill and Dick. She'd be in a lot more danger if she found herself that close to another shooter. At least if she was using a Winchester, she'd have some distance between her and the other shooters.

He put his own plate on the table and filled two cups with coffee.

"I don't suppose there's any sugar in the supplies?"

"Sorry. We can add some when we get to Green River."

"I thought we were going to find my father?"

"We are. We need to stop in Green River first. That's how I intend on finding where he probably is. The county sheriff doesn't have the manpower to search all over his county. The last time I knew he only had two deputies and one was useless. I need to talk to him then go to the land office and send two telegrams to Burnt Fork. One to the mayor telling him you were safe and the other to my mother telling her that I'd be delayed for a few days."

"Can you be away from your ranch that long?"

"I can because I don't have anything important going on right now. Pete Harris, my foreman, can handle any problems that crop up."

"How big is your ranch?"

"Sixteen sections. Just about ten thousand acres."

"That's enormous! Why is it so big?"

"To run that as many cattle as we have, you need a lot of grass and water. Not all the ranch has grass and some of the areas are sparse. But we have about half of the property in good grass with plenty of water."

"What's your ranch's name?"

"The Circle C. If you come back to Burnt Fork, I'll show it to you. It has everything you could expect to see in this part of the country. Mountains, a small patch of desert, even a waterfall. We have stands of timber, too. We could be self-sufficient if we chose. As it is, my mother tends her vegetable garden, we have two milk cows, a flock of chickens and even some hogs. We have a big smokehouse, too. It makes for busy times, but the hands all eat really well."

THE DEBT

"It sounds like a paradise."

"Until the winter hits. Then it's something else," he said as he smiled, more because of his love of the land than anything else. It surely wasn't because he was pleased with Mattie.

It did sound like paradise to Mattie. She had liked Missouri but found the West very appealing. She may be going to try to talk her father into leaving and returning to Missouri with her, but a life in Burnt Creek was beginning to sound better.

It was a small town, but the people had seemed to like her. That man at the stagecoach office had been a bit creepy though. John, on the other hand, was everything she had ever thought she'd want in a man. He was smart, pleasant, at least when he wasn't trying to get her to change her mind, and very nice-looking. He was older than she was, but not enough to matter.

She knew she was totally ignorant of the world of men. She had grown up in a boarding school for girls and had attended a girls' college. The few boys she had met had seemed more interested in trying to get close to her for reasons other than conversation.

John was the first man she had ever had engaged in meaningful conversation and had enjoyed it. She was looking forward to spending a few more days with John before that other decision had to be made about returning to Missouri.

Mattie may have been looking at John as possible mate material, but John was deep into thoughts about how he could get Mattie to meet Russ Abernathy and keep them both alive. He knew of Abernathy's reputed prowess with his Colt, but knew he was damned good himself. He just didn't want the reputation and he could fire with either hand or both at once, and rarely missed. It wouldn't help if he was facing six armed men, though.

After a silent breakfast, John walked out to the pasture to retrieve the horses and set them up for the trip. He saddled Bolt first, then he chose the bay for Mattie. He didn't have to adjust the stirrups because she was actually taller than either of the outlaws. He had them all saddled and moving back to the house forty minutes later.

When he pulled up, he saw Mattie had changed into her riding outfit, and for some reason, it was the first time he saw her as a young woman instead of a victim. She was quite a sight in the morning sun and waved as he approached, which he returned with one of his own.

John knew that his sudden recognition of her femininity could present a problem. She might start becoming a distraction, and he not only needed no distractions, he still resented being manipulated so easily.

But even as he let the recent memory of how she had gotten her way fester, he realized that there had only been two other human beings who had ever been able to control him that way. One was his mother, and the other was Nellie.

Nellie would brag to him how she could just smile and get him to do anything she wished, and he knew she was right. Mattie may have been wrong in her decision, but she had used the same tools that Nellie had used to get him to change his mind.

In the years after Nellie's death, he had to deflect the attentions of several women who had differing reasons for setting their caps on him. Initially, he had made the mistake of comparing any potential new wife with Nellie which was futile and unfair. After he realized that he'd never replace Nellie, he

THE DEBT

expected to at least meet a woman who could meet his basic standards of honesty, humor and character. He knew that Evelyn was the closest, but she was happily married, and he was glad for her.

Mattie was just so innocent and naïve that she was hard for him to read at times. Unlike Hank Ward, he placed less emphasis on the package and more on the content. If he could find both together, then that would be the one. Mattie most assuredly had the package, but it was the all-important content that mattered. Now, discovering that she had bent him to her will suddenly became a positive rather than a negative.

John arrived at the house and stepped down, then asked with a hint of a smile, "Are you ready to go, Mattie?"

Mattie noticed the change, smiled and replied, "I'm ready. My bag is in the kitchen."

"I'll start loading the packhorse and then we'll start moving."

"When are you going to teach me how to shoot?"

"I'll explain it to you while we're riding and you can practice when we break for lunch and camp."

"Alright. Do I get to wear a pistol?" she asked.

"Might as well," he answered as he exited the porch, not understanding why he changed his mind until he guessed it was just another example of Mattie pulling another one of his strings. He'd have to watch out for that.

Mattie turned and walked just in front of John as they walked back toward the kitchen and John felt that familiar tingle he'd always felt when Nellie was close.

John picked up Dick Pierce's gunbelt once he was inside, then said, "Now, this is going to be heavier than you might expect, so I'll take the pistol out and you can just try and fit the gunbelt around your waist. Don't make it too high or too tight. Let the belt just sit on your hips. Unlike a regular belt, it's not holding anything up."

She nodded, and John removed Pierce's Colt, then handed the belt to Mattie, who tried to tighten it, but the belt just fell to the floor. She looked at John and laughed as he smiled.

"Give it back to me and I'll punch a new hole, so it'll fit. They weren't designed for anyone with your waist size."

She stepped out of the fallen gunbelt, picked it up and handed it to John who had already removed his knife from his gunbelt. He dug out a new hole for the buckle and handed it back to Mattie.

"Try this," he said offering her the gunbelt, still smiling as she accepted it.

Mattie pulled it around her waist and clipped the buckle through the new hole. She slid it down to her hips and pushed down on the belt, then held her arms out to her side.

"This is good."

"Okay, here's your Colt," he said as he slid the revolver into her holster.

She felt the three pounds of metal sag the holster side, making her feel different somehow.

"Will I get used to the weight?" she asked.

THE DEBT

"After a few days, you shouldn't even notice it. Now slip the hammer loop over the pistol to keep it from bouncing out of there accidentally."

John nodded as he watched her pull the small leather strip over the Colt's hammer.

"That's right. Now you look like a regular Western gal, except for those shoes. We'll get you some boots in Green River and maybe a Stetson as well."

"John, I umm…well, I don't have any money."

"We're fine for money. I brought enough in case I was going to be gone for a while."

"Oh. Thank you."

"You're welcome. Let's get loaded and get away from here. I don't believe that Frank or anyone else from the gang will come here, but I don't want to bet on it either."

It took them another twenty minutes to load the packhorse, then John watched as Mattie mounted the bay, and once she was in the saddle, she smiled, so he knew she was ready to ride and had recovered from her discomfort. He hoped she'd be still smiling when they reached Green River.

John stepped up on Bolt and they set their horses to a slow trot as they rode down the access road. John was trailing both the packhorse and Dick Pierce's horse, so Mattie wouldn't have any issues trying to control anything other than the horse she was riding.

"Can I name him?" asked Mattie as they turned north onto the main road.

"Sure, he's your horse."

"What's your horse's name?"

"Bolt."

"Bolt? Why?"

"As in 'bolt of lightning'. He's the fastest horse I've ever ridden and has stamina, too."

"He's certainly tall enough. Between the tall horse and your height, it seems like you're a good two feet higher than I am."

"If you want to ride Bolt, you can."

"No, I'll ride mine. I just need to get him named."

"I'm sure you'll come up with something. Just remember that he may be a gelding, but he's still a boy."

She laughed and said, "I bet he wishes he were more of a boy."

John laughed and looked over at Mattie and said, "How would you know? You've spent almost all your life with nuns and other women."

"You'd be surprised what females of all ages talk about."

"Well, don't ruin my image of feminine behavior by telling me."

John wasn't surprised that he was enjoying the conversation with Mattie. Once he'd realized that she possessed so many of the traits he valued, he disregarded her naïve decision about searching for her father and was just enjoying the time they would spend together until things got dangerous.

THE DEBT

Mattie had surprised herself with her own comments. She thought they might be a bit crude, but John had laughed and seemed to accept them as normal. She was growing more comfortable talking to John and almost wished she had decided just to return to Burnt Fork.

After they had been riding for fifteen minutes, Mattie asked if John could show her how to use the pistol.

He pulled his right-hand Colt and explained the firing process. He didn't just show her but went into detail about why things worked the way they did, even how things affected the bullet's path and why rifles were more accurate.

Mattie was fascinated. She had always thought guns were just pointed and the trigger pulled. John even explained the different types of cartridges.

"John, why do you wear two guns?" she asked.

"I decided early on when I was the sheriff, that I wanted to have a backup in case I lost my first one for one reason or another and it gave me up to twelve rounds without reloading. Then I practiced a lot to be able to use both weapons. It took me a while for the left hand to catch up with the right. But I can use both now. It saved my life a few years back."

"What happened?"

"Carl Hempstead, our barber, was waylaid on his way back from Green River, about eight miles out of town. I mounted my horse, this was before I had Bolt, and rode out there. I picked up the trail easily and it led me into a rough area with a lot of big boulders and crevices which are deal drygulching conditions. Sure enough, the man was waiting for me, and took a shot that hit me in the right forearm, making me drop my Winchester and unable to shoot with my right hand.

"I saw the smoke and pulled my hammer loop off on my left-hand Colt and pulled it, cocking it as it came out of the holster. He was getting ready for his second shot and made the mistake of standing in the open, knowing I had taken the hit, and must have been more than unpleasantly surprised to find himself under fire.

"I laid three rounds of the five I had in the pistol to keep him down. Turns out that one of the rounds hit him low, just above his left hip. He dropped his rifle and was just lying there when I pulled up and took him back to town. I had to transport him all the way to Green River, so their doctor could fix up his wounds."

"What happened to him?"

"They hanged him."

"*They hanged him? For shooting at you?*" she asked in astonishment.

"Nope. They hanged him because he shot me, robbed Carl Hempstead, and had also shot another of his victims who didn't appreciate being robbed. He was named by four other victims, too. The judge wasn't too pleased with Willie Patterson."

"Was that the only time you've been shot?"

"No. I was hit once by a man named Mex Hollister. He was a typical lowlife outlaw who just enjoyed bullying folks. He rode in one day and must have been expecting an easy time of it in a small town like Burnt Fork. He started at the Firebrand Saloon when he refused to pay for his drinks and had already pulled his Colt to dare anyone to make him pay.

"One of the other patrons told me about it, so I took the shotgun from the rack and walked over there. It's called the convincer for a reason. Nobody looks down the barrels of a shotgun and doesn't turn into jelly. Nobody, it seems, except Mex Hollister.

"Now I don't have a clue where he got the moniker 'Mex' because he had blonde hair and blue eyes. But when I walked into the saloon carrying that shotgun with both hammers back, I made the mistake of expecting Mex to drop his Colt. The odds were stacked against him. If he fired, he might miss. I was thirty feet away, and he had to know I wouldn't miss with the shotgun. He would die if he pulled the trigger on that Colt.

"I was more surprised than anyone else in the room when he decided to do just that. He pulled the trigger and the bullet caught me in the left thigh. I dropped the shotgun, and luckily, it didn't go off. When I felt the shotgun leave my hands, I automatically went to my pistols. He fired again but missed. I didn't. Both of my bullets hit him in the chest. He fell to the floor and died instantly.

"You can tell because of the amount of blood. Two .44 caliber holes will make a lot of blood unless the heart has stopped pumping. Dan Esterhaus, the barkeeper, appreciated that I didn't miss and hit his mirror. It took me almost a month to get back to normal after that hit."

"What does it feel like?"

"When you're first hit, it feels like someone smacked you with a hammer. Then there's the burn followed by the pain and the dampness."

"Do they still hurt?"

"No. Why all the questions, Mattie? You aren't planning on trying it out, are you?"

"No, no. I was just wondering."

"Because if I thought that you even were thinking of putting yourself in harm's way, I'd tie you up myself and drag you back to Burnt Fork."

She laughed and said, "No, I'd rather not. I already had that happen once."

John was glad she could laugh about the experience. It must have been terrifying for her.

"I just wanted to make sure, Mattie."

"John, why aren't you concerned about putting yourself in harm's way?"

John glanced over at Mattie and replied, "It's not that I'm not concerned, Mattie. It's just that I know I can handle things like this and protect someone like you."

"Thank you, John. It means a lot that you're willing to help me."

"You're welcome, Mattie."

They rode on until almost eleven o'clock. John could see Mattie was getting uncomfortable, so he pulled over then led them to a healthy, raucous stream and let all the horses drink, then he hitched them to a nearby branch and let them graze. He pulled out his food bag that his mother had made and cut up some ham and sliced some bread for sandwiches, then brought them over to Mattie, who was sitting on a fallen tree.

"Thank you, John," she said as she accepted a sandwich and a canteen.

THE DEBT

John sat next to her and ate his own lunch. He knew what he had to do to Mattie next and he knew it would frighten her, but he felt he had to do it.

When they had both finished, John stood in front of Mattie. She looked up at him and smiled.

"Mattie, stand up, please," he said in his voice of authority.

Mattie's smile disappeared as she stood. *What was the matter with John?*

John stood six inches in front of her and took her face in his hands. She thought he was going to kiss her and began to close her eyes to accept her first kiss, but then looked at his face and she knew romance wasn't on his mind.

John's normally smiling gray eyes turned ice cold and bore into hers. His face was stoic, almost inhuman. She felt her knees weaken and she didn't know what he was going to do to her.

"Mattie, are you afraid?" he said in a deep, rumbling monotone.

"Yes," she whispered as her heart pounded against her ribs.

"Then understand this. When you shoot another human being, you will kill that person. You will take away from him everything that he has including the gift of life that God has given him. Your pistol has that power and now, so do you. Do not use it carelessly, but do not be afraid to use it if you must. You must make that decision now. Not when you are in a gunfight. You must decide now, Mattie Foster. Do you have it in you to end the God-given life of another human being if you have to?"

Mattie had never thought of it that way. It had always been so remote. But now, John had brought the moral question home with impact and she made her decision.

"Yes," she answered firmly.

The instant she replied, John's face transformed, his eyes calmed, and he smiled at her again.

"Good," he said in his normal voice and took his hands from her face then stepped back.

Mattie was still shaken by what had just happened and knew John had intended it to be that way. It was an almost religious experience.

John had resumed his seat as Mattie slowly sat down beside him.

"John, how do you do that?" she finally asked.

"What, the face?"

"The whole effect. The face, your eyes, your voice. It sounded like Satan himself."

John laughed and said, "It's what Jamey calls my scary face, but that one wasn't the full version. It's the one that I use to make a serious point. The really bad one only shows up when I'm seriously angry. I discovered that I could call on the one you saw whenever I needed it. I've actually made grown men pee on themselves without a gun."

"I was close. Were you really angry with me?"

THE DEBT

"Not at all. I wanted to know if you were serious about using that pistol. It's not a toy. It's a killing tool. I'll do the same thing to Jamey when he's older and give him his first pistol."

"You'd do that to your own son? Why?"

"Because I love him so much. If someone doesn't appreciate the seriousness of a gun, they can put themselves into dangerous situations. I've seen it before. A young man gets to feel important because he has a Colt on his hip, and he's practiced enough to think he's pretty good.

"Now he wants to show everyone how tough he is. He has no idea of what will happen to himself if he actually did kill another man. If he has any conscience at all, it will eat at him for the rest of his life. That's why I'll do it to Jamey. I know it's not in his nature to treat a gun that way, but I want to impress on him the danger that it holds. It's a terrible thing to kill another man."

"Have you killed many?"

"Before those two yesterday, I've killed three men. Does it bother me? Not as much as it should, I suppose. Every one of them had a chance to drop their weapons but chose to shoot it out. I would never shoot a man without giving him a chance. Maybe that's why the deaths don't bother me."

"How many times have you been so angry that you had that other really bad face appear?"

"Twice. Once when a local thug named Chuck Higgins grabbed Nellie when she was walking out of Campbell's Dry Goods. It was a pretty stupid thing to do, really. He knew I was the sheriff, and Nellie was my wife, but he must have figured she wouldn't say anything. He grabbed her behind when she was walking past and laughed.

"She just kept walking and turned into my office and explained what happened. That was the first time I felt the rage boil up to a point where the face made an appearance. Nellie had never seen it either and it frightened her something awful. She thought I was going to shoot Chuck, but the odd thing is that the face and the anger don't affect how I think.

"I walked down the boardwalk with Nellie behind me telling me not to shoot Chuck. He saw me coming and was going to say something, but I walked up to him, grabbed him by his shirt and told him in that voice never to touch Nellie or any other woman like that again. He just got big-eyed, nodded, and peed on himself. I let him go and returned to my office with Nellie on my arm. When I had turned back from Chuck, I smiled at her and she knew I was back to being just me.

"The second time was when Jamey was seven and had left school for the day and come to visit me in my office. I had given him a penny for some candy, so he raced across the street without looking. What happened next was his fault. He was knocked down by some yahoo on a horse that I had never seen before. That was an accident. I was at the desk in my office and I saw him run and get knocked down. I wasn't mad in the least, I was only concerned for Jamey as I left the jail and headed to make sure he was all right.

"Well, this jerk pulls his rope from his saddle and I see him getting ready to lash at Jamey. I pulled my Colt and put a .44 through the coil in his hand. The rope was yanked out of his grasp, then he turned and glared at me. I could see he was going for his pistol, even though mine was already pointed in his direction and I had a star on my chest.

"But I was mad as hell and the face arrived. I growled at him to get off his horse. He decided against pulling his hogleg and stepped down and then I grabbed him just like I had grabbed Chuck years before. By then, Jamey was already standing and watching me. He told me later how scary I was. I told the stranger that he'd better leave town now before I really got mad, because that was my son that he was getting ready to whip. He did the same thing as Chuck had done in the urinary department then climbed on his horse and rode out of town on a wet saddle. I never did find out his name.

"I turned to Jamey and asked if he wanted to go and get his licorice drops. He smiled at me, took my hand and we walked to Campbell's to get his candy. Every once and a while, he'll ask me to show him the scary face just because he wants to see it. I got better at controlling it but can't make the really bad one. The one you saw is part of my defensive repertoire now."

"It's one hell of a weapon, if you'll pardon my language. You made your point, though."

"I'm glad I did, Mattie. Did you want to learn how to fire the Winchester first? It's a lot easier."

"Alright," she answered as she smiled.

Mattie was stunned by John's tale. *He'd only been angry twice in ten years?* And both times it was because someone had threatened a loved one. In all those confrontations, he must have been involved in over the years, he had never reached that level of anger. That was amazing control and he must have been one hell of a sheriff. She already knew he was one hell of a man.

John pulled out one of the Winchester '73s provided by the two deceased outlaws. Both were fully loaded and in good condition.

"Mattie, I'm going to empty this repeater. The Winchester has a magazine of fifteen rounds that can be loaded using the gate here on the right side. When you cycle the lever, it ejects the old round pulls a new cartridge into place and cocks the hammer. It's a lot of things that happen with that lever action, but if you know how to do it, it's easy enough."

John had positioned a bedroll to his left as he began cycling the lever rapidly, throwing new cartridges onto the bedroll until fifteen shiny brass cylinders were lying atop the dark green sleeping bag.

"Okay, it's empty now. Go ahead and try cycling the lever. Don't be hesitant or gentle. You really need to move it hard and fast."

"Alright," Mattie said as she took the Winchester.

She had watched John easily work the lever and made the mistake that he exaggerated the force necessary. She placed the butt firmly on her hip as John had and tried to cycle the lever. It moved but not well.

"Shove it hard and pull it back hard, Mattie," John told her.

She did and succeeded. It wasn't very smooth at all, she thought.

"It's easier if you're wearing gloves. Did you find the gloves in the bag?"

"I saw them and thought they were yours."

John laughed and said, "No, they're yours. They aren't dainty lady's gloves. They're working gloves. They'll keep your hands warmer and protect them from abuse."

"Oh. Should I get them now?"

"No. I just wanted you to feel how the lever action worked."

THE DEBT

He bent down and picked up the fifteen cartridges then showed her how to load them into the Winchester's gate. When they were all loaded, he handed the rifle back to Mattie.

"Now, Mattie, I'm going to let you take a shot with the Winchester. The first time you're going to shoot the rifle, you need to either cock the hammer if you know that there's a cartridge in the chamber already or cycle the lever if you're not sure. Of course, you'll waste a perfectly good cartridge if you do that and there's already one in the chamber, but I've seen men do it."

He showed her how to cock the repeater and how to take a balanced stance and hold the rifle. Finally, he explained how to aim, hold her breath and squeeze the trigger. Then he had her cycle the lever to bring in the first cartridge.

"Are you ready, Mattie?"

"I think so."

"Pick out a target and focus on the target first, then the sights. If I have time, I'll focus once more on the target as I'm squeezing the trigger."

"Alright."

Mattie picked out a branch on a tree about fifty yards away. She held her breath and squeezed the trigger. The gun bucked, and the distinctive Winchester report echoed across the field. Mattie didn't know where the shot went, but John did.

"You were a little low, Mattie, but not bad. You'll get better as you get more familiar with the gun."

"Can you show me how you can shoot?"

"Sure. Do you want me to use your Winchester or mine?"

"Are they the same?"

"No. Mine is the '76 model. It uses a more powerful cartridge and has some other changes. I like it better."

"Can it shoot further?"

"Winchester says it doesn't, but I think it does. Both are rated by Winchester at a hundred yards effective range. That means that at that range the bullet will travel and still have enough power to do its job. The '76 sounds different, too. It has more of a bark than the Winchester crack."

"Can I see you shoot yours?"

"Sure."

He walked over to Bolt and pulled out his '76 then cocked the hammer without thinking. He quickly picked out a target, a small rock atop a boulder about a hundred yards away.

"I'll aim at that rock sitting on the boulder."

Mattie shielded her eyes and looked as she said, "Okay."

John brought the Winchester level, rotated it to bear, sighted the target and was immediately squeezing the trigger when his sights stabilized. His Winchester belched flame and smoke as it expelled the .45 caliber missile and the rock exploded a fraction of a second later.

"John, that's really good. How far away was that?"

"About a hundred yards."

"Can you do that all the time?" she asked, astonished.

THE DEBT

"Pretty much. It just takes practice, Mattie."

"You must practice a lot."

"I do. At least twice a week, and I didn't want to say anything, because it's not necessary, but the Winchester you shot is a carbine while my '76 is a rifle."

"Aren't they the same?"

"The only difference is the length of the barrel and sometimes the shape, but most folks call them all rifles because of the grooves inside the barrel that spins the bullet as it leaves the gun. It makes the bullet fly straighter. It really doesn't matter what you call it, but I thought you might want to know. You seem to be a smart young lady."

"Thank you for the lesson, professor, and the compliment as well," Mattie said while wearing a grin.

"You are perfectly welcome for both, Miss Foster," John replied.

After returning the Winchesters to their scabbards, they unhitched their horses, mounted and were soon back on the road for Green River.

Mattie hadn't seen anyone fire a gun before and wondered just how good John was.

Frank knew something was amiss in his plans. Dick Pierce hadn't shown up and Russ was mad about his and Bill's absence, too. Russ planned his jobs meticulously to avoid gunfire, which was the one thing that irritated Frank. He wanted to just go in, shoot the damned people and take their money. In his eyes, all this planning was just stupid. He didn't understand that the lack of deaths meant less pressure from the politicians and the law.

After waiting most of the day, Russ finally had to give up on the two absentee gang members.

"Alright, we're going to go anyway. This is too good a target to pass up. Frank, you and I will take the lead on the road. Fritz and Big Ed will handle the sides and the grab. Prince, you'll handle the back route. We'll head out in an hour, just in case those two decide to show up. Let's get things ready to go."

They all headed out of the room, Big Ed giving Frank a look and a shrug about the missing kidnappers. Frank just shook his head. He knew that something must have happened and that meant the whole daughter as a threat plan was probably trashed. He decided he'd use a more traditional and direct method to make his play after all.

———

After riding for just four more hours, John took pity on Mattie's obvious discomfort and pulled them over to set up camp.

After he stepped down, Mattie asked if he could help her down, so he trotted over and offered her his hand.

"I don't know if I can lift my other leg," she said.

"All right. I have a solution," he replied.

"It's not painful, is it?"

"No, if it is, it'll be because I did something wrong."

He climbed back on Bolt and brought him parallel to Mattie's horse.

"Okay, Mattie, lean over and put your arms around my neck."

She did and felt a rush as she found her face just inches from John's. This was so new to her and she found it exciting. It may not have been new to John, but he felt warm as well, yet he wasn't surprised by the sensation, he'd felt it before. Once she was holding onto his neck, John put his right arm right around her waist.

"Now, hold on, Mattie," he said quietly as anything louder would be unnecessary.

"Okay."

He nudged Bolt to his left and Mattie felt herself being pulled away from her saddle. It was an odd sensation. If she thought she was close to John before, she now found herself pressed against him as her feet hung in the air.

John started to lower Mattie gently to the ground, his face buried in her hair.

Mattie knew John's face was there as she felt herself being dropped gently to the ground. She felt her feet touch and reluctantly released her arms as John did the same.

"Thank you, John," she said softly.

"You're welcome, Mattie. Stay there and I'll get a bedroll for you to lay on."

"Alright."

John stepped down and quickly hitched Bolt and Mattie's horse. pulled off a bedroll and stretched it out behind Mattie, trying not to look at her but found it difficult.

"Okay, Mattie. It's there if you want to sit down."

"Can you help again? I think my legs are ready to cramp again."

He stepped around to her front and took her hands. She leaned back, and he gently lowered her to the bedroll.

"I should have stopped earlier, Mattie."

"No, it's alright. It's nowhere near as bad as yesterday."

"Let me put a saddle and a bedroll behind you so you can relax better."

"No, that's alright. I'll be fine."

"I've got to get the saddles off anyway, Mattie."

"Okay."

John walked over to her bay and quickly removed the saddle, then took it to the bedroll and set it behind Mattie's back, leaving a gap. He pulled off a second bedroll and unfurled it, then folded it over and pushed it between Mattie and the saddle.

"There you go, Mattie."

She leaned back and sighed before she said, "That's marvelous. Thank you, John."

"You're welcome. I'll go ahead and get everything unloaded."

THE DEBT

John began stripping the animals and wondered what they could do to pass the time. It was a short day, and he estimated they'd only ridden about twenty-five miles. If they got away early in the morning, they'd reach Green River around noon tomorrow. Whatever they decided to do, it would have to wait until after Mattie could walk.

Mattie was busy kneading her legs. They were nowhere as bad as they had been the day earlier, but they were still hard. As her fingers worked her muscles, she thought about what she had felt when John was so close and that brief moment where she thought he was going to kiss her. She had never been that close to any man before, much less one with John's presence. As she continued to knead her legs, she wondered why he hadn't remarried. He must surely have been the focus of many women's attentions.

John was trying to concentrate on what he would need to do tomorrow and then when they found the gang. The makeup of the gang made everything more difficult. If it had been just her father, it wouldn't have been too bad, but six or seven seriously bad men would be a lot more of a problem, especially in light of the pending coup. He'd have to get as much information on them from Joe Wheeler, too.

It was too early to cook dinner, so he walked back to where Mattie sat still massaging her legs.

"How are you doing, Mattie?"

"Much better. I think I'm getting used to riding. I felt worse yesterday morning and we didn't ride that far."

"A few more days and you won't have the problem anymore."

"John, what are you going to do in Green River to help find my father?"

"I'll go and see the county sheriff and get as much information as possible. Then I'll go to the land office and find out if there are any tax-forfeited ranches about ten to twenty miles east or northeast. We'll pick up some more supplies and get rid of the extra horse."

"Won't the sheriff want to send some deputies with us?"

"No, as I already mentioned, he only had two the last time I knew and one of them was useless as a lawman. He'll try to talk me out of going, especially after he knows you're coming along. What we need from him is information. I'll need your gunbelt as well."

"Why?"

"To prove that Bill Nelson and Dick Pierce are both dead. I'll buy you a new one if he wants to keep them."

"Okay. I'd rather have my own anyway."

John sat down on the ground near the bedroll and asked, "So, Mattie, what else do you want to talk about?"

"Can I ask you a personal question?"

"Go ahead. I think I've told you the worst already."

"Why didn't you remarry? You've been living as a widower for nine years now."

"I asked myself that a few times. If I wanted to get married just to get married again, I would have years ago. I wasn't lonely because I had Jamey and my mother in the house. After

THE DEBT

Nellie, I spent a few years comparing other women to her and realized that was unfair, so I decided that I would look at each woman differently. It helped, but even then, I found that I couldn't reach the level of just comradery with any of them.

"It sounds odd, doesn't it? Looking for a wife and a friend at the same time? But Nellie was always a friend before she was my wife. It makes the marriage so much better. I could talk to Nellie. It seemed like the women that wanted to get serious spent more time talking than conversing. The other thing that was lacking was a true sense of humor. Nellie and I would kid each other mercilessly. It made our marriage lively, as it should be. I just never found the combination, Mattie."

"It sounds like a high standard, John."

"I suppose. Getting married with low standards is asking for trouble."

"I'm kind of new to all that anyway. You're the first man I've talked to for more than a few sentences."

"That's kind of sad, Mattie, but I can understand with your background. I would have thought that even in your school and women's college there would be dances and socials to attend, though."

"There were, but I was always uncomfortable when I did go. I felt kind of nervous when the boys looked at me. I guess most of the girls liked it, but it made me feel kind of like I was on display."

"That's what dances and socials are, really. A big store with young women and men on sale."

She laughed then said, "I guess so."

John made a mental note to refrain from looking at Mattie, at least when she could notice.

Russ had them moving fast to make up for lost time waiting for Bill and Dick. Hopkins was still off the main Union Pacific line and had to use the stagecoach or freight wagons to transfer anything to Green River. It was only eleven miles from the railroad, so there was less margin for error. They'd have to hit the stage and get out of there quickly.

The spot picked by Russ may not have seemed like an ambush site, but it was ideal. It was a rise in the road with a sharp drop off after the crest. There were no rocks or boulders on either side of the road, but Russ knew that the stage would have to slow down as it reached the crest. If it didn't, it would accelerate like a falcon dropping down for its prey as it hit the steep downslope.

His plan was relatively simple. Russ and Frank would be in the road on the decline with Winchesters drawn. Big Ed and Fritz would be off to the side. Russ and Frank would stop the stage and Big Ed and Fritz would do the actual robbery. Prince would be at the bottom of the stage's approach before the rise behind a large outcropping of rocks.

As soon as the stage neared the crest, Prince would ride up quickly behind them to prevent any sudden turn, although it was highly unlikely. Even though there was room at the top to turn the stage, it would take too much time. Prince was just the backstop and should have been with Dick Pierce and Bill Nelson. Russ knew that seven would have been overkill, but he felt better with more men. It was more intimidating to the driver and shotgun rider.

THE DEBT

Frank would concentrate on the shotgun rider and Russ would do the talking as always.

Frank had made his own modifications to the plan and he was the only one who knew how it would go down.

Russ had them moving until six o'clock when they had reached his holding point just four miles to the ambush site. It was an abandoned line shack, but big enough for the five men to spend the night.

John had dug the fire pit, had the fire going for their dinner, the grate in place and the coffee pot already heating. Mattie was up and moving normally and was picking out food for dinner.

"John, tell me about your parents. I only knew my mother a little while before she died but never really knew my father, of course."

John sat back on his heels as he stirred the fire and added more wood.

"My father's name was John, too. We didn't have the same middle name, so I'm not a junior, thank God. He came out this way a long time before there was much here. He negotiated with the Shoshone and settled on the land the ranch occupies now."

"How much did he pay them for the land?"

"He didn't give them money. They had no use for it because there wasn't any place where they could spend it. He gave them sixteen Spencer rifles and thirty boxes of ammunition. The War Between the States had just ended and they were readily available. The Shoshone weren't at war with the United States at the time, so it wasn't against the law."

"That was a pretty cheap price to pay for all that land."

"The land itself meant little to the Shoshone. Their chiefs could see that they were going to lose it soon, if not to the white man, then to the Cheyenne who had pushed them out of eastern Wyoming. To get that many rifles and ammunition was a godsend, and my father went further and instructed a cadre of warriors on how to shoot correctly. He would supply them with ammunition from time to time as well."

"How did they know it was sixteen sections?"

"They didn't. The original agreement was from a lone tree to a chimney rock to a stream to the edge of a gulch. It was finally measured out to 16.34 sections, but we really control much more. There are two parts of the ranch that cross the fronts of four large box canyons. The land in the canyons is only accessible from the Circle C. That's another six thousand acres. I recently filed with the land office to have the canyons added to the property. They'll approve it shortly, I think. It'll just mean more tax money for them at no loss to anyone else because of the inaccessibility."

"Is my math wrong or is that another nine sections?"

"A little over. It'll add some nice grazing land on three of the canyons, too."

Mattie was boggled. John was talking about another nine square miles of land like it was adding another lot to a building development.

John continued, saying, "Unlike a lot of settlers, he never had any problems with the Indians. He let them harvest cattle when they needed the meat. They understood it was his livelihood and never took too many. When the railroad came through, we were far enough away that the land grants didn't affect us at all. My father went to the land office the day it opened and showed them the agreement with the Shoshone. They really didn't care much and wrote up a deed ensuring that my father was legally entitled to the property.

"He kept building it up with the help of my mother and two hired hands. It's hard to imagine controlling sixteen square miles with just three men, but he did. He worked hard to get things done. My father was my hero growing up and I was the only living child that they had. My mother had two other children, both girls, but both died when they were infants.

"My mother, her name is Winifred, but everyone calls her Winnie, was able to put the pain behind her, and I don't know how she did it. I can't begin to imagine losing one baby, much less two in a space of three years. She never became pregnant again, so you would think that she would spoil her only child terribly, but she didn't. She was firm but fair. But she was, and is, still one of the sweetest people I know, and I admire her greatly.

"She and my father were married before they came west from Ohio right after the war. I was Jamey's age when we left. My father had spent three and a half years fighting the war and came home deeply affected by what he had experienced. It never changed his good nature, but he needed to start over again, which is why he came west. They were on the Oregon Trail and my father saw this area and left the wagon train. A few others did, too. They built what is now Burnt Fork, but no one remembers where the name came from. Everything was just about perfect ten years ago.

"I had just married Nellie, and she became pregnant right away. My parents were overjoyed, and the ranch was prospering. I was the sheriff and enjoying every minute. Then, it was like God suddenly hated us. Nellie died when Jamey was born, and that's when my mother took over. She found a wet nurse and cared for Jamey. Once he was weaned, she became his stand-in mother. I told you how she straightened me out.

"I stayed on as sheriff because I was good at it and the town appreciated what I did. Then my father cut himself on the left arm while shoeing a horse. It was no big deal. He didn't even wrap it up for an hour, but it became infected and he died two weeks later. I had to go back and take care of my mother then. I owed her so much. Not just for giving me life, but for bringing me back to the living and showing me how much I owed to Jamey. We've become a lot closer since then."

"Does she spoil Jamey now?" Mattie asked.

"You would think so, wouldn't you? But she doesn't. Except for the occasional cookie, which she did for me too, she treats Jamey as she raised me. He loves his grandma, and he's going to grow up to be a good man, as much because of my mother's influence as mine."

"It sounds like you're a proud papa," she said as she smiled.

"As proud as can be, and not ashamed to show it either," he said as he smiled back.

"Why are you risking all that to help me, John? You didn't even know me before you reached that old ranch house."

"There were a few reasons. The children needed a teacher, but that was secondary. I would have come after you if you had been anyone else because you were an innocent."

"What if I had been a prostitute? What then?"

THE DEBT

"I'd still go. Prostitutes are innocents, too."

"Really? I've never heard them called that."

"The majority of prostitutes are women who had no other options in their lives. I've met some that are very smart, witty and resourceful women. If they'd been men, they'd be successful at any venture they tried. But because they were women, their only options were to marry and have children, become a schoolmarm or a librarian, or maybe a nun.

"If a woman becomes a widow and has no means of support, guess where she'll probably wind up. A lot of young girls are there because they'd either been raped or become pregnant and were shunned by their families and their communities. They have to find someplace that will provide a roof over their head and food in their bellies. Guess where they wind up? Sure, there are a few that are there by choice, but not as many as you'd believe. It's a hard life and a dangerous life. Most don't live to see forty. So, yes, prostitutes are innocents, Mattie."

"Have you ever used their services?" she asked, shocking herself for asking the question and expecting John to be offended.

"Of course, I have. A man can go crazy without being with a woman after a while. I don't know why it is, but it just is. You can't think right if it's been too long when all your mind does is think about women. The hands make trips to Green River once a month or so usually right after payday."

"I'm sorry. I shouldn't have asked that question."

"Why not? You wanted to know, and I answered your question. It doesn't bother me. My mother knows I visit the ladies and she's not bothered by it. She wishes I'd get married, but she understands. She was married to my father for thirty-one years. She understood men, Mattie."

"I guess I'm too prudish."

"Not really, it's just how you grew up. You were brought up by nuns and in a women's college. The way you think reflects what everyone else who had influence over you thought. That's the way it always is.

"Out here in the rugged country, the niceties of what some call civilized society are sometimes an unnecessary encumbrance. We can't afford to waste a lot of time. I've seen young couples get married after knowing each other for two weeks. Life is too short around here. We don't have any doctors within fifty miles and there are dangers everywhere. Who can afford to waste the time tocourt a woman for six months?

"Civilized society treats sex like it's dirty or should be kept a secret, a secret that everyone knows about. But it's what keeps humanity alive, just like all living creatures that God put on the earth. Why would something as divinely perfect as sex be dirty? God made it enjoyable, so we would produce more babies and thrive. If it felt like the duty that society seems to preach, then there wouldn't be much begetting, would there?"

She smiled and replied, "No, I guess not."

"So, don't worry about bringing up the subject. It's just part of life. We're born, we create more life, and we die. I'd rather spend time making more life than watching people die."

"You answered why you came after me but not why you are helping me now."

THE DEBT

John sighed. He may as well tell her, so he bent forward, his hands clasped.

"Mattie, I don't know why I'm going to tell you this. I really don't. I've never told another person, except my mother, who in her way, told me. It's kind of difficult to me to explain but I feel as if I must, so bear with me."

"I will," she replied softly, wondering what was so weighty.

"It's sort of deeper continuation of the story I told you about why I felt I owed my mother so much. Nellie went into labor late on the night of April 15th of '75. My mother and Mrs. Rider, the midwife, were with her, but I was terribly afraid for her, as I imagine most expectant fathers are, but Nellie was my whole world and her cries of pain had me terrified for her.

"She had a long, difficult labor and it wasn't until almost the predawn that I heard Jamey's cries replace hers. For that short period when I first listened to his wailing, I was so very happy that we had our baby and envisioned Nellie smiling as she held him in her arms.

"I stood and walked quickly to go see her, but my father stopped me and said I had to wait for my mother or the midwife to let me into the birthing room. It seemed like hours but was really just ten minutes or so before my mother exited the room and I instantly saw the pain in her eyes. I felt empty as I asked if I could go and see Nellie, and she told me that I had a son, but Nellie had died.

"I almost collapsed but leaned against the wall and asked if I could go and see my Nellie anyway, and she nodded. I stumbled past her and entered the room where Mrs. Rider held Jamey in her arms as I just looked at my wife's face. Her eyes were closed, and she was bathed in sweat, but she seemed so happy and so peaceful, I thought for just a moment that she was still alive, so I rushed to her side and softly touched her face, but she was already cold."

John paused and blew out his breath, then took in another deep breath and continued.

"I leaned over and kissed her softly on her lips and just looked at her face for a few more minutes before I slowly left the room and walked outside into the predawn. I can't describe the chilled emptiness that engulfed me. I never blamed Jamey for her death, as he was the pinnacle of innocence, but I blamed myself for causing her death.

"That's when I went into my month-long funk of self-pity. When my mother finally brought me back, one of the things she said to me was that I now had an obligation to Nellie. It's why I use the word to describe those who need help but are unable to provide it for themselves.

"Since then, I've always felt as if I had that debt to repay to Nellie, even though she had never asked it of me. It's not as if it drives me to seek out those who need help, but when presented with an opportunity, I feel that need to satisfy my obligation to her. It's why I had to help you, even though I still think you're coming along is a bad idea."

Mattie was numbed after hearing John's confession, for that's what it was.

Mattie said quietly, "Thank you for telling me about Nellie, John. It means a lot."

John nodded, still unsure why he had the need to purge himself to Mattie but felt better for having told her. Now he needed to get back to the present.

THE DEBT

"So, Mattie," he said after clearing his throat, "what do you want to make for dinner? I did my part and got the fire going and I'll even put on the coffee."

Mattie recognized his need to get past the memories and replied, "Sure, give me all the hard work while you just make a little fire."

John smiled and stood to make the coffee, the cathartic conversation in the past. After he had the coffeepot filled and sitting on the grate, he let her take over.

A few minutes later, he pulled the hot water from the grate, poured the ground coffee into the pot and then poured himself a cup of coffee then set the pot on a corner near the fire to keep it hot. He didn't pour Mattie her coffee yet because she was busy.

Mattie was elated and deeply affected by their conversation. She felt more like an adult than she had in her life before then. She was almost twenty-three, yet still thought of herself as a youngster in many ways. She just didn't know so many things, important things, and John explained everything so well.

She had never heard anyone talk about sex so openly and not in whispers, either. Some of the girls confided what had happened when they snuck off with boys and there were differing opinions about whether it was fun or not but now, she knew a lot more. She wondered if she would enjoy it, like John said. She didn't know that men could get mixed up if they abstained for too long, either.

Mattie felt mature and she liked the feeling. But the other part of their conversation, John's revelation, was much more intimate and revealing. More importantly, she felt that John had just let her into his life. It was an awesome responsibility to be given.

John concentrated on the first half of the conversation, as he must. He didn't know what to make of Mattie's questions about sex. He had answered them honestly, if she was embarrassed, she shouldn't have asked the questions. He did wonder if she was having second thoughts about her decision to see her father by her tone.

John couldn't see any positives about the upcoming family reunion, if one dared to categorize it as such. It was like the old saw 'you can never go home again'. It was the same with most people. There were exceptions, of course. But old flames who were reunited after a long separation would find changes that they didn't like. Friends from long ago may smile and shake hands, but secretly wish they had stayed away.

When Mattie finally got to meet her father, if they were successful in finding him and avoiding being shot, *would she be disappointed? Would he break her heart, either intentionally or unintentionally? Either way, what would she do after the meeting? Would she be content to return to Burnt Fork and teach school?* He'd find out in a few days. Tomorrow, though, they'd arrive in Green River.

CHAPTER 3

Mattie was the first one to awaken the next morning. She had asked John to keep his sleeping bag close, so he had set it just four feet away. She was looking at him as he still slept. *What would she do after she met her father? What if he agreed to straighten out his life and asked her to return to his original home in Missouri with her?*

She knew that she would never meet John's like again. He talked to her, not at her and seemed to like her, but she didn't know about such things. But the thrill she felt when he was helping her down was real. She closed her eyes again and relived those few minutes. *What do you think of me, John?*

When John did open his eyes, he only had one thing on his mind as he quickly slid out of the bedroll and ran to the nearby trees. Mattie had already taken care of the issue when she left her bedroll ten minutes earlier.

When he returned, he saw Mattie already getting ready to make breakfast.

"Mattie, you woke up before I did. You must be anxious to get on your horse this morning."

"I'm ready."

"Good. I'm going to start getting the horses ready too. We should reach Green River by noon."

She smiled at him and said, "Then are you going to shave? Or are you going for the mountain man look?"

John laughed as he rubbed his scratchy chin and replied, "I hadn't thought about that. Maybe it would be a good look for me. I'll let my hair grow too. Say, Mattie, can you do braids?"

Mattie convulsed with laughter as she tried to cook.

John stood looking at her, and asked, "What's the matter? Don't you think braids would work?"

She glanced at his straight face and kept laughing.

"Mattie, I am appalled at your behavior. Here you make a perfectly valid suggestion for an improvement in my appearance, yet you mock your own recommendation. I am wounded."

"It's much more likely you'd be wounded if you paraded around town wearing braids."

"Probably, but I'd go out in style."

"Here's your breakfast, Mountain Man," she said as she handed him a plate of eggs and bacon, her face still split with a big grin.

"Thanks, Mattie."

"You're welcome, John."

He set his coffee on the ground and squatted with his plate, then quickly ate his bacon and eggs. Mattie ate hers just as quickly and recalled how the good sisters would chastise the girls if they ate either too much or too quickly. If they could see her now, they would be appalled, and if they'd hear her discussing sex with a virile man while traveling alone in the wilderness there would be fainting galore. Horrors!

THE DEBT

They finished breakfast and cleaned up their camp. John put the cooking gear into its correct location on the packhorse and they were on the road less than an hour after eating.

———

Russ had his gang in position by half past nine. The stage was scheduled to leave at ten o'clock, but it would take another half an hour to reach their ambush location.

Frank sat next to Russ on their horses on the downslope as they waited for the coach. Russ didn't like to be caught unprepared and Frank was already getting twitchy. He hated waiting. He had taken a few minutes before they left to tell Big Ed and Fritz that he would make his play during the holdup. After they got their money, he would shout "Shotgun!", and that would be the signal to start firing.

He would shoot Russ and then they'd kill everyone on the coach. They'd return to their staging location, divide the money, and then return via separate paths to the ranch house. They'd figure out what to do after that. He figured that the law would probably try and track them after the shootings, but it wouldn't be right away, no sooner than a half a day. By then, they'd be long gone. He even had a plan to lose the trail from the ranch house, but this waiting was getting to him.

———

John and Mattie were making better time than John expected as Mattie really did seem to be adapting to riding.

"Where to first, John?" Mattie asked.

"I need to talk to the sheriff. It'll be an interesting conversation and you should be there."

"You wouldn't mind?"

"No. I think it would be a good idea. You'll see how real law enforcement works. People think that the sheriff has unlimited resources and can chase down every criminal in the county. He could just leave his incompetent deputy at the desk and he and the good deputy will handle their crimes. Everyone thinks his own problem is the worst and expects the sheriff to take care of it right away. He'll try to talk us out of going, but deep down he'll hope we can take care of this little problem for him. He'll never admit it, though."

"Was it like that in Burnt Fork?"

"Not at all. It was quiet most of the time with the usual alcohol inspired violence on Fridays and Saturdays, a few fights and some thefts. Serious crime was rare, maybe once every few months or so. But anyone can tell you that a lot of crimes stay behind closed doors."

"Like what?"

"Husbands beating wives or children. Some discipline is necessary for children, but I don't think you should ever leave a mark, even for a few seconds. There's never an excuse for hitting a woman…never."

"What if she throws something at you?"

"Duck."

Mattie smiled and asked, "Have you ever spanked Jamey?"

"Nope. I never had cause. I think he's just so afraid of disappointing me or his grandma, he's never done anything to deserve it. I've seen parents that wallop their kids for dropping things, like we all do, and so do they, but no one punishes them for it.

"About a year and a half ago, Jamey took my fishing pole rather than his to go fishing. He just wanted to try it. He didn't break it or anything, but when I got home that night, he was standing in the main room waiting for me. He had tears in his eyes, and I thought something horrible had happened and asked him what was wrong. He told me he had used my fishing pole without my permission, and he was so sorry and that he'd never do it again. How can you punish a boy like that?"

"I can't wait to meet him."

"He and the entire class will greet you with cheers and applause. Alice Hall, the previous teacher, was a stern taskmaster who really didn't seem to like children at all. She wasn't a bad teacher; she was just unpleasant."

"Why did she leave?"

"She married the butcher."

"Was he desperate?"

"Not really. Alice wasn't a bad looking woman; she was just severe. He may have just fancied her and never really listened to her. He'll find out soon enough. But she wasn't nearly as bad as Miss Harrington. She was my teacher and Alice's predecessor. She made Alice look like a gentle soul."

"She must have been there a while."

"We all thought she was born there and lived under the school in a cave with the other trolls."

Mattie laughed at the image. She found it difficult to fathom that she could be having this much fun on such a serious trip. She knew it would be getting more serious very soon though, and hoped it didn't turn as deadly as John anticipated.

Russ could hear the stage driver shouting to his horses from a half mile away.

"Let's get ready, Frank."

They pulled their Winchesters and cocked the hammers as they waited for the coach to cross the summit of the rise sixty yards before them.

Big Ed and Fritz pulled their pistols and readied them for action. Down in the valley, Prince had prematurelt pulled away from his hiding place, pulled out his Winchester and was trailing the stage instead of waiting for it to reach the crest. It would be a costly mistake and wouldn't have happened if Dick and Bill had been there.

Jack Rankin was driving, and Pat Travers was on shotgun as the stage rolled along the roadway throwing up its long dust cloud as it climbed the long rise. Jack was slowing the stage for the upcoming descent and were a hundred yards from the summit when Pat glanced back.

"Jack! We got a follower! He wasn't there ten minutes ago!" he shouted as he pulled back both hammers on his shotgun.

Jack glanced behind him and saw the rider with the rifle in his hands and pulled the reins hard getting the horses slowed to a stop just two hundred feet from the crest.

THE DEBT

Jack made a quick decision and it was the right one as he suspected that there were armed men just on the other side of the rise, so he started the coach moving and pulled hard on the left reins to turn the team and coach around. The six horses responded, and the stagecoach turned quickly and began to make a wide U-turn.

Russ and Frank had heard the shout and started up their side of the slope as Big Ed and Fritz trailed quickly behind. All of them kept their weapons ready to fire.

Inside the coach, bank clerk Sid Fawcett had heard the guard's warning about a rider trailing the coach and felt the driver's decision to return. He pulled his Webley Bulldog out of his jacket pocket and held it tightly in his hand, expecting the door to be yanked open shortly. Under his seat was the deposit to the First National Bank in Green River. The money was concealed in a locked valise in a hidden compartment under the seat. At his feet was an iron-strapped, double locked box containing nothing but two bags of sand.

By the time the gang had reached the crest, Jack had the wagon turned and was picking up speed as it returned down the hill. Prince had seen the turn and simply didn't know what to do. He and his horse stood in the middle of the road a half mile from the accelerating stagecoach being trailed by his four fellow outlaws that Prince never even noticed as he was fixated on the six charging horses leading the dust-trailing stage. He finally cycled the lever on his Winchester, spitting out a fresh cartridge, brought his Winchester to bear and began firing at almost three hundred yards.

Pat Travers had no idea what the gunman was trying to hit at that range, but he was ready with his shotgun as they bore down on the unmoving lone horseman in their path.

Prince kept firing rapidly and had expended twelve rounds by the time the coach was within range. His barrel was getting hot, but he was firing automatically now in an unbelieving panic. When the rifle was empty, he continued to cycle and pull the trigger on an empty chamber, never moving his horse from the roadway.

Pat didn't even bother shooting at him while the stage rocketed toward the rider as he wanted to keep his buckshot load for the four men that he had seen trailing the coach after they had turned. Pat expected that moron on the horse to move aside in another second as the hurtling stagecoach closed to within fifty yards.

Jack had thought so too, but the kid who was dry firing his Winchester was still in the road and he hoped that his horse at least had some common sense and vacated the right of way.

At thirty yards, the horse voted for self-preservation when he reared and quickly bolted toward the side of the road, away from the charging stagecoach. When he reared, Prince was thrown, his useless Winchester still leveled at the six-horse team, hitting the ground just as the hooves from the team's lead horse reached the same spot. Prince finally did his job and got in the way of the stagecoach when the middle right-side horse stumbled over his body, veering the racing stagecoach to the right. Then the front right wheel impacted his crushed body, Jack lost control and the stage flipped onto its left side after the yoke jerked violently to the right. Jack and Pat jumped as the coach began to leave the ground.

The team had been pulled to the left when the stagecoach started to go over, and lost footing as the yoke finally cracked apart. The six-horse team crashed into the road ahead of the rolling stage, the horses sprawling into each other.

THE DEBT

Russ and the other three trailing the coach watched the accident as it happened and hauled their horses to a stop as the coach began to disintegrate, striking the many boulders alongside the road.

Sid Fawcett had been tossed around the inside of the coach like an exploding kernel of popcorn, along with the moneyless, but still very heavy strongbox. His pistol was added to the mix of flying debris, but the valise stayed in place in its secured hiding place under the seat.

Sid's neck had been broken the first time he had impacted the roof of the coach while Pat and Jack had landed badly in a field of rocks. Neither was dead, but both suffered broken bones. Pat's shotgun had flown away to some unseen location.

"Jesus!" shouted Fritz as he stared at the chaotic scene.

Russ yelled, "Hold on! Wait a minute! Let everything quiet down before we go in!"

So, the gang held back as the accident played out and the giant dust cloud slowly settled back to earth. The only movement from the coach was from the team of horses, none of whom had suffered broken bones before they regained their footing. The yoke had snapped off at the attaching point and had freed them from the stage, but they were still in harness.

After thirty seconds of no movement by the coach, Russ waved them forward. Frank saw movement off to his right as Pat Travers was pulling himself up from where he had been thrown. He was dizzy from smacking his head on the ground, had a broken tibia on the right leg and his left clavicle was fractured. He was covered in blood from his head wound, but Frank didn't wait to see if he was a threat. He fired his Winchester at the shotgun rider and Pat took the slug in his chest then collapsed in a heap and died a few seconds later.

Jack Rankin heard the Winchester and stayed where he was without moving. It wasn't as if he really had a choice to run as his left foot was pointing left at ninety degrees. He could see its odd angle but felt no pain, which scared him even more. His pain was from his four broken ribs. He had missed the heavy boulders, but he laid in an awkward position while his eyes watched the wreck that had been his stagecoach. He heard the gang trotting their horses forward and listened as Russ chewed out Frank for shooting an unarmed man. They all had seen Jack, but his open eyes and lack of movement marked him as a dead man.

"Alright, enough of what went wrong. Get that strongbox and let's get out of here," said Russ after he had calmed down from the anger he had felt for Frank's unnecessary murdering of Pat Travers. Russ had realized that it the robbery would appear to be an accident if Frank hadn't shot the shotgun rider. He probably would have died soon anyway. Now the law would be after them. Frank had ruined a perfect crime scene.

Fritz and Big Ed both stepped down to retrieve their spoils as Frank and Russ stared at each other.

Once the other two outlaws were out of hearing, Russ said, "I know what you've been doing, Frank. I'm not blind or stupid. If you want to make a play to be the boss, go ahead. Show me you've got what it takes to be the leader of this outfit."

Frank decided to go with a bluff.

"You're too late, Russ. You've already lost and don't know it. Do you know where Bill and Dick are? They're hiding out somewhere and they have a guest. Do you want to know who their guest is?"

Russ didn't have to guess. He knew. He had wondered why Mattie's letters had stopped and was aware she had graduated a couple of months ago and was planning on coming to Green River. While he didn't care if they had her or not, he did care about his precarious position, and she might be his chance to get out of it. He figured if Frank was bold enough to make his move, then he must be backed by Big Ed and Fritz, and he needed time to get away from the remnants of his gang.

"You have Mattie," he said calmly.

"Yeah, I do."

"What do you want, Frank?"

"I want to be the boss. You can stay if you want, but I call the shots and plan the jobs."

"Not if you're going to keep shooting people. I'll just head back to the ranch and clear out. You can even keep my share, just tell me where Mattie is."

"I'll tell you when we get back, and you'd better remember that she ain't goin' anywhere until I show up and tell Bill and Dick to let her go."

"You're a real bastard, Frank."

"And you're just an old woman, Russ. Go back to the ranch."

Russ knew that the massacre that was the stagecoach robbery would turn the gang into a hunted group, and it was time to make his break and maybe he'd start again in Utah or California. He wheeled his horse and left the scene at a rapid pace before Frank tried to backshoot him. As he rode, he zig-zagged slightly just in case, but needed to get back to the ranch house, get his stash and then clear out before they returned.

Frank was dancing inside. He had pulled off the biggest bluff of his life. His only problem was what had happened at the Mitchell place. Maybe the boys just stayed to have fun with Abernathy's little girl. She had sent a picture a couple of years ago and she was something worth having. Frank convinced himself that Bill and Dick were just keeping themselves occupied and that Mattie was still a captive.

As Russ rode off, Big Ed had found the strongbox and was pulling it out of the coach with a giant grin on his face. It was so heavy, he reckoned that there must be thousands inside the box. He noticed Russ leaving and knew there had been a change in leadership which made him even happier as he believed his share of the take had just gone up.

Ed dropped it on the ground and shouted, "I got it, Frank!"

Frank walked his horse close to the demolished stagecoach and said, "Call me boss. Russ is gone. I told him we had his little girl and he caved. We can't take time to try and get that box open here. Just get that thing tied down on the back of your horse, Fritz, and let's get out of here."

Fritz asked, "What'll we do with Prince's body. It's a mess. I can't even recognize him."

"Leave it with the others. Nobody will know it was us, anyway. They're all dead."

"You're the boss," said Big Ed.

Frank smiled and replied, "Yeah, I am."

Big Ed hoisted the strongbox onto Fritz's horse. They would have used Prince's, but he had run too far away, and they needed to get going.

THE DEBT

After roping it down as best they could, the remaining three members of the now Lewis gang left the shattered remnants of the stagecoach with its three dead bodies behind, along with one living witness who had seen and heard everything.

John and Mattie entered Green River shortly after noon.

"Mattie, do you want to get lunch before we do anything else?"

"I wouldn't object," she said as she smiled back.

"Then let's do that."

They rode to Murphy's Café and stepped down, tied off the horses and John held the door for Mattie as she entered.

"Have you been here before, Mattie?" John asked.

"No. I ate at the Railway Hotel restaurant until I left."

"I usually eat at Murphy's when I come to Green River. It's pretty good."

"I'm pretty hungry, so anything would taste good right now."

They found a table and a waitress arrived just a few seconds later.

"Hello, John! I haven't seen you in some time, and it looks like you're growing a beard," she said as she smiled at him.

John rubbed his three-day growth and replied, "It'll be gone in a little while, Nancy. I've been a bit busy and haven't needed to come to the big city."

"And who's the lucky lady?" she asked as she smiled at Mattie.

"Nancy, this is Mattie Foster. Mattie, this is Nancy Bannister."

"Pleased to meet you, Mattie. You must be pretty special. John's never brought any women with him before."

"No, it's nothing, John's just helping me find my father," Mattie replied.

"Oh, that's good to hear. So, you're still available, John?" Nancy asked as she grinned.

"Seems that way, doesn't it? Anyway, what's the special today?"

"Fried chicken. Will that be okay?"

"I'll have that. Mattie?"

"It sounds perfect."

"Alright. I'll be back with your coffee shortly."

Nancy left with one more parting smile for John.

"She seems to like you," Mattie asked.

"Nancy likes most of the single men that come into Murphy's. She'll latch onto one pretty soon, I think. She's only been waitressing for six months after her husband died almost a year ago. She needed a way to support herself. She was very fortunate to get this job."

Nancy brought out the coffee, set down the pot, then said, "I'll be out with your orders shortly."

THE DEBT

"Thank you, Nancy."

Nancy bounced back into the kitchen while John poured the coffee.

"You can add sugar now, Mattie."

"Trust me, I noticed the sugar bowl before we sat down."

She added a teaspoonful of sugar and stirred her coffee while John sipped his.

After Nancy brought their chicken, John watched as Mattie began to eat. He had been taken somewhat aback by her response to Nancy's suggestion that they were a couple. It was probably just an automatic reply but still, to say 'it's nothing', zinged a bit.

He had been growing fond of Mattie in the two days they'd been together. He felt close enough to her to tell her the one thing that ate at him, but maybe it was really nothing and he had read too much into their short relationship. Besides, she may be leaving soon if he does what he was asked to do. He pushed it all out of his mind and began eating his chicken.

After paying the tab and leaving Nancy a nice tip, John and Mattie returned to their horses.

"Glad to see the riding hasn't bothered you so much today, Mattie," he commented as she climbed back into the saddle.

"I'm a little sore, but not bad."

"Let's go see Sheriff Wheeler."

Three minutes later, they were stepping down at the county sheriff's office. The animals were tied off and John turned to Mattie.

"Mattie, I need your gunbelt."

"Oh. That's right," she replied as she removed it from her waist and handed it to John.

After he had hers, he took the second one from the saddlebags, holding both gunbelts in his left hand.

They walked to the door, then John swung it open and allowed Mattie to enter.

Deputy Hap McDonnell saw Mattie walk in and stood with an almost lecherous smile and asked, "Well, hello, ma'am. What can I do for you?"

John almost gave him the scary face, but instead just said, "Hap, I need to see the sheriff. Is he in?"

"Oh. Hi, John. Yeah, he's in his office."

"Well, have a seat."

John took Mattie's arm and walked back to Sheriff Joe Wheeler's office, tapped on the door jamb and let Mattie enter.

"Afternoon, Joe."

"John! Good to see you again. How are things down in Burnt Fork?" he asked as he rose when he spotted Mattie.

"Slow except for what I'm going to tell you," he replied as he closed the door behind him.

John pulled out the only chair for Mattie, who sat down.

THE DEBT

"Joe, this is Mattie Foster. She was going to be the new teacher in Burnt Fork when she was kidnapped by two men. I tracked them down and killed them both."

"Good job, John, but it's nothing new, is it?"

"Actually, Joe, that was the easy part. Here's where it gets harder."

John dropped the two gunbelts on the desk and said, "I took these off the two men that I buried."

Joe pulled the gunbelts to his side of the desk and unrolled them. After looking at the first one, he glanced up at John, then read the second and whistled.

"Bill Nelson and Dick Pierce. Two of Abernathy's boys. Are you sure it was them?"

"I was pretty sure it was Nelson before I checked his gunbelt. I wasn't as familiar with Pierce."

"Well, I'm sold. I'll send notice about their deaths to the ones that posted the reward. I'm not sure how much it is. Did you want me to send it to Burnt Fork?"

"No, Joe. Just hang onto it here. Put the name of Mattie Foster on the vouchers when they come in."

"Who?"

"This young lady is Mattie Foster, Joe. Her first name is spelled M-A-T-T-I-E. And that's why it's going to get sticky after this. You see, after she had been kidnapped, she had been told by Nelson that she was going to be used to get rid of the boss and that Frank would take over."

The sheriff's eyes grew wide as he asked, "Frank Lewis, do you think?"

"That's what I thought. That would be a first-class disaster, Joe. He's one mean bastard. The only reason he hasn't killed anyone is that Abernathy wouldn't like it."

"That's an understatement. I didn't have the time to go traipsing all over the county after the Abernathy gang, but this might make it a lot worse."

"When Mattie told me about why she was here, I figured out that she was Russ Abernathy's daughter. That's why they kidnapped her."

Joe snapped his eyes to look at Mattie and asked, *"Is that right?"*

"Yes," she replied.

"So, what are you here for, John, except to give me bad news?"

"Mattie asked me to take her to her father. She wants to talk to him and maybe get him to return with her to Missouri."

"That's crazy, John," he replied, then he quickly turned to Mattie again and added, "No offense, Miss Foster."

Then he turned back to John and said, "It's really nuts if Frank Lewis has taken over."

"Joe, how many men do you think he had with him, not including Bill Nelson and Dick Pierce?"

THE DEBT

"Well, there's Frank Lewis, Big Ed Howard, Fritz Thompson, and I hear he's got at least one new guy we don't have the information on yet."

"That's not as bad as I thought, Joe. Now, I've told Miss Foster that I'd help her, so there's no use arguing because she's as stubborn as your Hilda. I have an idea how to find them and I'm willing to go in there. Maybe I'll solve your problem for you before it becomes worse."

"John, I'd love to have you solve the problem, but even if you went alone, your chances of getting them all isn't exactly even. If you drag along a young woman, your chances drop even lower."

"I know that, Joe, but like I told you, she's stubborn. But I think I might be able to pull this off."

"Well, I'd better deputize you to make it legal. No pay, of course."

"I don't need the money, Joe."

Sheriff Joe Wheeler swore John in and handed him a deputy badge.

"Don't get the badge all full of holes, will ya?"

"I'll try to bring it back in all one piece, Joe. Oh, I'm going to leave you one of their horses. Mattie's on the other one. It'll be out front."

"Any good?"

"He seems all right. More valuable than your deputy out on the desk"

"It wouldn't take much."

They shook hands and the sheriff said, "John, take care out there. Will you?"

"I'll do the best I can."

John opened the door and escorted Mattie out of the office, then walked past Deputy McDonnell without a word and left the office.

John disconnected the spare horse, taking the extra scabbard and Winchester off and attaching it to the packhorse's saddle. That would give him a '73, a '76, his two pistols and a shotgun. Mattie had the other '73 Winchester, but he'd still need to stop and get another pistol for Mattie.

"Next up, we'll head over to the land office."

"John, why did you tell the sheriff to give me the reward money."

"You're flat broke, Mattie. How can you take your father back to Missouri if you have no money? We'll be back here in a couple of days and they should have the vouchers for you by then."

Mattie didn't reply. She had pushed aside the thought of returning to Missouri for the last day. Now it loomed large again and John seemed to think that's where she wanted to go.

They arrived at the land office quickly, dismounted and tied their horses to the hitching rail.

"One less horse makes it a little easier to get around, doesn't it?" John asked.

THE DEBT

"It does," agreed Mattie.

When they entered, the cheerful clerk stepped from behind his desk. John guessed he was more cheerful because Mattie was there.

"Howdy, John. What can I do for you?"

"Harry, can you tell me how many abandoned ranches you have around twenty to thirty miles east or northeast of Green River?"

"Off the top of my head, I'd say four or five. Why?"

"I think one's being used as a gang hideout."

"It wouldn't be the first time."

"I'm looking for one that's been abandoned for at least four years."

"That narrows it down. Let me pull the records."

He headed back to his files, put on a pair of spectacles and began humming as he looked through the folders and maps.

Three minutes later, he returned to the counter with a large map and laid his finger on one square.

"Now, this property went into default six years ago. It's the Bar H. And this one, the Rocking K, failed seven years ago. Both properties may have been vacant longer than that, of course. I only record the date when they were available for sale by the county."

"Of course. Could I see the maps? I need to look for landmarks."

"Absolutely."

He swung the large map around and let John examine the chart which included topographical features. He found both ranches and burned their locations and surrounding landmarks into his mind. He noted their relative location to the railroad mile markers as well. The railroad was good for that. If you ever lose your way, head for the tracks and find a mile marker.

"Okay. Thank you for your help, Harry."

"Anytime, John."

John opened the door and let Mattie exit first.

Once out on the boardwalk, she asked, "Now what do we do, John?"

"We head to the gun shop and buy you a new rig and then we'll go to the dry goods store and pick up some more supplies. I'd recommend staying overnight in Green River and setting out in the morning. You'll be able to sleep in a bed and take a bath. I may even shave, even if it disappoints you."

Mattie was pleased that John was joking with her again and replied, "I won't be disappointed, John. I've never seen you without whiskers."

"That's right, you haven't. Well, don't be afraid, then," he said with a smile as Mattie smiled back.

They boarded their horses and trotted to the gun shop, his favorite place whenever he came to Green River. They tied up and went inside.

"Howdy, John," said the small, bald gunsmith as he saw John enter.

THE DEBT

"Afternoon, Walt. I need a .44 for Mattie, here. She'll need a rig for it as well."

"You want a full-size pistol or something smaller, like the Webley?"

"Mattie, did you want a smaller pistol?"

"How much smaller?"

"Walt, show me the Webley."

"Sure. Got four of 'em."

He pulled out one of the Bulldogs and handed it to John.

He hefted the pistol and said, "It feels good, Walt. How accurate are these things?"

"I've gotten good results out to fifty feet."

"That's not bad. Mattie, what do you think?"

He handed the pistol to Mattie, who held it her and said, "This does feel better in my hand than the Colt. Could I get one?"

"Sure. Walt, do they make holster setups for the Bulldog?"

"Aside from shoulder holsters, I might have one that'll work. It was made for a Colt Pocket Navy, but I haven't sold it yet."

He pulled out a holster from a drawer and gave it to John who slid the Bulldog into the holster.

"It's a bit tight, but I think it'll loosen up after time. Give me a cartridge belt for it as well, Walt."

"How's that '76 working for you, John?" he asked as he began marrying the belt with the holster.

"Nice rifle, Walt. Add a six-inch sheath to that, too. I'll go and pick out the knife."

"I'll take care of it."

John went to another counter and found what he thought was an appropriate blade for Mattie and brought it back to Walt, laying it on the counter.

"That it, John?"

"Let me have two more boxes of .44 cartridges and one of the .45 center fire for the Winchester."

Walt piled the ammunition next to the completed gun rig and the knife.

"$36.50, John."

John paid the bill, then said, "Thanks, Walt."

"Anytime, John."

They left the gun shop and returned to the horses.

"Did you want me to put on the gun now?" Mattie asked.

"We'll wait until we leave town. Women wearing guns seems to spook folks."

"Why?"

"Beats me. I can walk down the street with two pistols and a Winchester, and nobody notices. You walk down that same street wearing that Bulldog, and everyone would stare at you, not just the men."

"Oh."

"Let's head over to the dry goods store and pick up some more supplies. The closer of the two ranches is twenty-two miles out and the other is twenty-eight, so it looks like tomorrow, you'll be meeting your father."

"I hope so," she said, but her conviction wasn't there. She was suddenly very nervous about seeing him again.

They picked up supplies at the dry goods store, and John had Mattie buy some western boots, a Stetson, and some other clothes. He asked if she needed anything else and she added a hairbrush, toothbrush, and tooth powder. John's only purchase was a full shaving kit. Mattie smiled at him when he added it to the pile.

After paying for the order, John added the supplies to the packhorse and hung Mattie's bag of things on Bolt's saddle horn before they just led the horses across the street to the hotel and tied them off.

He took down Mattie's bag and walked with her into the hotel, where John paid for two rooms and gave Mattie the bag.

"Mattie, I'm going to take the horses down to the livery. I'll meet you here at six and take you to dinner, alright?"

"Thank you for everything, John."

"You're welcome, Mattie. See you at six o'clock."

Mattie checked the wall clock behind the check in desk. It was 3:10 and she finally had time to take a bath.

John stepped outside and untied both horses, climbed up on Bolt and led Mattie's horse down the street. No sense in making another trail rope for a few hundred yards. He stopped for a short time at the Western Union office and sent two telegrams.

The first was to Jack Campbell

JACK CAMPBELL BURNT FORK WYOMING

MISS FOSTER SAFE
WILL RETURN IN A FEW DAYS
TWO KIDNAPPERS NO LONGER WITH US

JOHN CLARK GREEN RIVER WYOMING

The second was to his mother

WINNIE CLARK CIRCLE C RANCH
BURNT FORK WYOMING

MISS FOSTER SAFE
WILL BE DELAYED FOR ANOTHER JOB
SHOULD BE HOME IN FOUR DAYS
LOVE TO YOU AND JAMEY

JOHN CLARK GREEN RIVER WYOMING

He paid his fee and then continued on to the livery.

He was almost to the livery when he approached their corral, then stopped and looked at the horses. There was one that grabbed his attention, so he nudged Bolt closer to the rails.

THE DEBT

After looking at the horse for another minute, John turned Bolt back toward the livery door where he stepped down and led both horses into the barn with the packhorse trailing.

"John! How are you doing? Haven't seen you in a while."

"You know how it is, Fred. I need to board these three for the night. Check on their shoes as well. If they need them, go ahead as long as they'll be ready by morning."

"Not a problem."

"Say, Fred. What's the story on that buckskin mare out there?"

"She's a real eye-catcher, ain't she? Got her three days ago. Real gentle with a nice gait, too. Rides real smooth."

"How much are you asking for her?"

"I'd have to get fifty dollars for her, John."

"How about this? I'll trade you that nice bay and give you twenty-five."

Fred pretended to be doing some hardcore arithmetic but was just seeing dollar signs. He could sell the bay for thirty dollars easy, so it was a great deal, but he had to play the part.

"I don't know, John. That mare is pretty special."

"Come on, Fred. You know it's a great deal. You should throw in shoeing the two other horses and the overnight as well."

"I'll take your first offer, but I'll do the shoeing and overnight for five dollars."

"Okay. Make sure the buckskin is glowing when I stop by to pick her and the others in the morning. Can you have them ready to go at seven-thirty? The bay's saddle will go on the mare."

"They'll all be glowing at seven-thirty, John," he said as he grinned.

They shook hands after John gave him the cash for the deal.

He took his saddlebags that contained the new ammunition, Mattie's new gun rig and his shaving kit and put it on his shoulder, then waved to Fred as he walked back down the street. He was going to go to the hotel, but instead returned to the dry goods store and bought himself a new shirt, denim pants, underpants, and socks as he hadn't planned on being gone this long.

He returned to the hotel and went to his room. It was too late to take a bath or shave, so he just spent a few minutes punching a new hole in Mattie's new gunbelt. He smiled as he imagined her face when she saw the buckskin. She was really a special horse.

He walked to the washroom and cleaned up quickly. He should have bought a comb but used his fingers instead. All the joking with Mattie about his appearance had made him realize how unkempt he must appear. He left the hotel and returned once more to the dry goods store and bought a nice comb. It was two cents well spent.

When he returned to the hotel, the clock read 5:35, but Mattie was already sitting in the lobby. She was all clean and shiny. He had never seen her with her hair brushed before. She was a mighty pretty young lady.

"Mattie, you're early," he said as he approached.

THE DEBT

"I know, I took a nice, long bath and brushed my hair. I feel so much better."

"Did you want to go and have dinner now?"

"Are we going to Murphy's again?"

"Not for dinner. I sometimes bring my mother and Jamey here to do some shopping and I take them to the steakhouse for dinner. That's where we'll go."

She smiled as she stood and said, "That sounds wonderful, John."

He offered her his arm and they walked out of the hotel. The steakhouse, imaginatively named The Green River Steakhouse, was three blocks over and down one street.

"It's pretty warm right now, John. Is that different?"

"Not at this time of the year. It's not unusual to be like this the first week in September, but by the end of the month, it'll be a lot colder."

They reached the steakhouse and walked inside, John feeling a bit grubby compared to most of the clientele, but Mattie fit right in.

They were shown to a table and John held the chair for Mattie before sitting down himself.

"You look prettier than usual, Mattie, and that's saying something."

Mattie blushed and replied, "Thank you, John."

The waitress arrived, and said cheerfully, "Hello, John. Not with your mother or Jamey tonight?"

"No, Elizabeth, this is Mattie Foster."

"Hello, Mattie. I'm Elizabeth Draper."

"Hello, Elizabeth."

"What can I get for you, John?"

"Give me the prime rib, Elizabeth," he answered before turning to Mattie and asking, "Mattie?"

"I'll have the same."

Elizabeth nodded, then smiled and said, "I'll bring your coffee shortly."

"Thank you, Elizabeth."

She left, and Mattie looked over at John.

"Do you know everyone in Green River?"

"Not even close. I frequent some places, so they know me."

"She seems very nice."

"Elizabeth is very nice. She's earning as much money as she can, so she and her fiancé can get married next month."

"Does everyone tell you their life stories?"

"I talk to them like regular people. I guess a lot of people don't. They see people like Elizabeth, Nancy, and Fred over at the livery as servants. They're just folks like me. I talk to them that way, so they talk to me, too."

Elizabeth brought them a pot of coffee and two cups and saucers. She also set down a sugar bowl and creamer.

THE DEBT

John asked, "You and Arthur almost ready for the big day, Elizabeth?"

"It's so close that I'm already getting excited, John."

"I'm sure you and Arthur will be very happy, Elizabeth."

"Thank you, John" she replied and then scurried to another table.

"John, you're like her uncle or something."

He nodded, then smiled and said, "It seems that way, doesn't it?"

John poured them each some coffee, leaving Mattie enough room for sugar and cream, if she decided to add some, which she did.

After she had sipped her coffee, she asked, "John, I can't take the reward money. All I did was get kidnapped. You risked your life to save me and killed them, not me."

"Mattie, it has nothing to do with who did what. I don't need the money and you do. What would I do with it? Let it sit in the bank. What would you do with it? You'd have the freedom to do what you want. So, take the money, Mattie."

Mattie didn't say why she really didn't want the money. If she didn't have the money, she'd go back to Burnt Fork and teach school, then she'd meet Jamey, and she'd be near John.

"Alright. But I won't like it."

John smiled at her and said, "I didn't say you'd have to like it, Mattie."

Mattie looked down into her coffee and said quietly, "I sound ungrateful, John, and I'm not. You've done everything you can do for me and all I've done is cost you. I've cost you money and time with Jamey and may cost you much more. I haven't been very good for you, John."

"Mattie, that's not true at all. I've enjoyed myself immensely on the trip. It was rough at times, but I wouldn't trade it for anything."

She looked up and smiled as she said, "You're not just saying that, are you?"

"I don't waste time that way, Mattie. If I say something, I mean it."

"Even when you said you wanted to grow braids?"

"Absolutely. I was going to buy some ribbons at the dry goods store, but I needed your opinion whether red or yellow went better with my gun rig."

She held back a laugh as she said, "Please don't get me started again."

"I enjoy getting you started, Mattie. You light up when you laugh."

"Lighting up is fine outside, but in here, it might ruin the ambiance."

"Ambiance? Really, Mattie. You'd better be careful using words like that in Wyoming. You can get your nose shot off."

"Maybe, but you'd probably give them your scary face first and they'd miss."

THE DEBT

"They'd probably miss your cute little nose anyway."

Elizabeth brought them their prime rib, baked potatoes and asparagus., then set down a bowl of sour cream and a crock of butter as well.

"Thank you, Elizabeth. This looks great."

"Don't forget to save room for dessert, John."

"I won't."

Elizabeth left, and Mattie stared at the plate. The prime rib was enormous, and so was the potato.

"John, I'm hungry, but this is a lot of food."

"I know. I'll have them make us some prime rib sandwiches out of the leftovers for our ride tomorrow. How's that?"

"That would be wonderful."

With the portion issue decided, they each cut into their prime rib. Mattie hadn't tried asparagus before and was still undecided after her first bite. She covered the potato with sour cream and butter, and she loved that, but the prime rib was sensational. She was only able to eat a third and John intentionally ate only half of his. He could have finished it, but he did want to save room for dessert.

He set down his knife and fork and asked, "Do you have any room left for dessert, Mattie? I was thinking of apple pie a la mode."

"Even if I didn't have room, I'd push it aside for that."

Elizabeth stopped back to ask about dessert, and John asked that they use the remaining prime rib to make those wonderful prime rib sandwiches for them to take on the trail tomorrow, then ordered their dessert.

Elizabeth took the plates back to the kitchen and returned with the apple pie a la mode just a few minutes later. John poured more coffee for each of them and let Mattie add her sugar and cream.

Mattie took a forkful of pie and ice cream and closed her eyes. This was such a perfect evening and she wished it would never end.

But it did. Elizabeth brought back a bag with two prime rib sandwiches and the check. With the sandwiches, it totaled $1.40. John left two dollars and a ten-dollar gold piece as a secondary tip before he took Mattie's arm and they left the restaurant.

Elizabeth stopped by after they were gone and saw the gold coin and smiled. It was a very nice wedding gift from John.

John and Mattie walked slowly back to the hotel.

"I should have shaved at least before taking you there, Mattie."

"John, everything was perfect. Really."

"Well, I'll surprise you in the morning when I show up with no stubble."

"That'll hurt to shave that much off, won't it?"

"Not too bad. I have warm water here."

THE DEBT

They slowly crossed the hotel lobby and walked to their rooms, and John stopped before Mattie's room and looked into her eyes.

"I'll see you in the morning, Mattie. I'll meet you in the lobby at seven and we'll go have breakfast."

"Alright. I'll see you in the morning, John," she replied, but neither moved for another twenty seconds until Mattie finally smiled and opened her door.

Mattie entered her room and closed the door, then leaned her back against it and sighed. It was such a wonderful evening, yet she felt empty. She felt as if it was all ending. Tomorrow they'd go find her father, and one way or the other, she'd discover what her future held.

By the time she slipped under the heavy quilts, she was almost wishing that John was wrong and they didn't find him at all. Her biggest concern now wasn't satisfying her imagined debt to her father, but that John might get hurt in the attempt.

John returned to his room and set the bag of sandwiches on the dresser as he stripped and prepared for bed. Once his head was on the pillow, he made several attempts to focus on how he would approach Abernathy if they found him, but finally surrendered to let his mind wander back to Mattie. There was a lot of Nellie in the young woman, but she was special in her own right and that was extraordinary.

Russ Abernathy had arrived at the empty ranch house and quickly trotted to his room. He began throwing his things into a spare set of saddlebags he kept for an emergency run in case their location became known. He was going to get ready, but figured he had time. They'd struggle opening the strongbox and wouldn't ride as fast as he had.

As he hurriedly packed, he was a bit curious about what had happened to Mattie. He had done more than enough to satisfy his guilty conscience for murdering Jean Mitchell, but he barely knew the girl. She was just letters and money. He had sent a lot of money over the past two decades, but the letters were little more than notes. He guessed the girl had cost him almost two thousand dollars over the years, so he felt no obligation to her anymore. He'd paid that debt and should just be able to forget about it now, but it still nagged at him. The fact that it did bothered him even more.

Frank was a fool to think that she would have been enough of an incentive to get him to let him take over the gang, but it was the fact that the others had backed his play that had convinced him to leave. The girl wasn't even a small part of the equation. He was annoyed that Frank had her kidnapped, but not much beyond that.

Then there was that disastrous stage robbery. Let them have the money and the notoriety. He knew he'd have to make tracks now and separate himself from the group and maybe he'd even let the law know where they were.

He snickered as he let the idea bounce around in his head. He'd do just that. He'd send a telegram to the sheriff at Green River and tell him that the gang was at the abandoned Rocking K ranch but first, he'd need to get his money together. He still had over thirty-five hundred dollars that the gang didn't know about. It was his share of all the jobs they'd pulled, or at least his share as he figured it, but probably more than what they figured it should be.

He was still packing when he heard hooves. *How could they be back so soon?*

THE DEBT

The Hopkins sheriff was overwhelmed with the news. The attempted robbery of the stage had been discovered early that evening and they had found Jack Rankin still alive, but barely. He told them what he witnessed, and the real case with the money was retrieved as they tried to put Jack on one of the stage team horses, but he died when they lifted him.

Now, the sheriff was dealing with the mayhem that resulted from the robbery, and it was beyond his competence level. He had an unidentified body, a dead driver and shotgun rider and was so caught up in the chaos that he neglected to send out a telegram alerting other law offices. He'd do that in the morning believing it wouldn't matter now because the sun was almost down, and no one would be in the Green River or other law offices now anyway.

Russ peeked out through the window to see who was outside, not surprised to see Frank and the other boys. They had the chest on the horse's back unopened, which was why they made it back so soon. He hastily returned to his room to make sure his cache of money was still hidden, then heard them laughing as they stepped down. It had been a successful trip after all. They had the money and it would only be a three-way split.

Russ walked casually out to the main room with his pistol loop off, just in case. He wanted them to see it, so they didn't even try. He could get one without a problem, but two would be impossible. He'd be dead before he got his second shot off.

The door opened and the still laughing trio entered then stopped when they saw their old boss.

"Why, Russ. Whatever are you waiting for?" asked Frank.

"I'm leaving, Frank. You have the gang now. You're short of men, though."

"I have a couple already lined up, old man."

He wasn't sure if they'd let him go without gunplay, so he played for time.

"Where is the girl, Frank?"

"Probably enjoying the favors of Bill and Dick. I'll bet she's glad to give it to 'em, too. You sent her to a convent and then an all-girls school, Russ. She probably didn't know what she was missin'."

"Just tell me where she is Frank, and I'll be gone. I'm not gonna push it."

"You ain't got much choice, Russ. I'll take you to her in the mornin' after we all have a good night's sleep."

Russ glared at Frank and snarled, "Anyone comes through my door will be a dead man, Frank. You remember that."

"I'd be surprised if you didn't, Russ. Do you wanna see how much money you ain't gettin'?" he asked with a threatening grin.

Russ just turned and walked back to his room and closed the door, then set his chair up against the door latch knowing he couldn't stay awake all night.

Big Ed had retrieved a pickaxe from the barn to open the strongbox. The heavy tool was in bad shape, but it didn't matter as it only had one job to do.

THE DEBT

Russ listened as Big Ed crashed the point of the pickaxe into the strongbox's lock. It took three swings to break it loose.

"Damn! It has another lock!" he shouted as he pulled the outer lock off, revealing the inner lock.

"The hell with it, Ed. Just smash the damned thing!" yelled Fritz.

"It must be a lot of cash in there, boys," said Frank with a grin.

Big Ed took a massive swing and the front of the strongbox itself split open.

Frank rushed in and yanked the cover off, grabbed one of the heavy bags and for a second thought it might contain gold dust, but knew the truth just a second later and slammed the bag onto the floor. It struck the edge of the pickaxe and burst open, letting the sand flow across the floor.

"Son of a bitch!" screamed Frank.

"It's just sand!" growled Fritz.

Big Ed furiously grabbed the pickaxe and began to demonically smash the box into pieces, punching big gaps in the floor of the room at the same time.

In his room, Russ was surprised but felt like giggling. The boys screwed up. They hadn't opened the strongbox right there, so they didn't search the rest of the coach. It wasn't an unusual practice, sending a dummy strongbox along with a large hidden amount of cash, and they had fallen for it.

———

John lay on his back staring at the dark ceiling that he couldn't see. He'd finally managed to pry his mind off of Mattie to concentrate on tomorrow's possible situations and there were quite a few that he could come up with quickly. They may find nothing and no one. Her father could welcome her with open arms and take her offer and return with Mattie to Missouri. He might already be dead, and they'd get into a pitched gun battle with at least four of them. Her father may act as if she was a stranger. It would not only break her heart but put them up against the whole gang.

Honestly, he preferred the first possibility. He hoped the search turned up empty. He just didn't think that was likely. His gut told him that they were on the Rocking K. It was further from there to Green River, but that was offset by the better location in that the surrounding terrain gave it better security. The road to the ranch branched off the main road that paralleled the railroad. The map didn't show the access road, but he was pretty sure it was in what looked like a pass between two large hills. The only other approach, and the one he would use, passed the ranch's access road and after a mile, he could go around the northern hill and enter the ranch from the north. He should have bought some field glasses and decided that he'd swing by after breakfast and buy a pair. He needed to know how many were there.

And then there was Mattie. He had to keep her safe, so he'd try to talk her into staying north of the ranch with a Winchester, her new Bulldog and the field glasses so she could watch. He'd make sure she knew how to get back to Green River if everything went bad. She could go to Burnt Fork and live with his mother and Jamey on the ranch if he didn't make it.

He hoped it didn't come to that, but he had to prepare for that possibility. He reminded himself he still had to show Mattie

THE DEBT

the big differences between the Bulldog and the Colt. It might be critical to her safety.

Mattie was still awake as well. Tomorrow she'd finally meet her father. She wished those two bastards hadn't kidnapped her. If they hadn't, she'd be teaching in Burnt Fork and probably have met John in a much more cordial atmosphere. Maybe he'd notice her and ask to court her, but it hadn't happened that way. She met John in the worst of situations, and tomorrow, he may be going back to Burnt Fork without her. If her father said he wanted to go to Missouri with her, she'd have to go. *Wouldn't she?* John hadn't really said he was interested. *Do men really say they are after just a couple of days?*

But what incredible two days they had been!

She still felt a warm rush when she remembered John holding her as he lowered her to the ground, his face so close to hers. They had shared so much in those two days. He had told her things he hadn't shared with anyone else except his mother, whom he seemed to admire and love. They had talked about so many different things and laughed together. She remembered how John had said his next wife would have to have a good sense of humor but wasn't sure if hers met his standards. Mattie wasn't sure if what she felt was love or not, but she knew she didn't want to be with anyone else. It may not mean anything after tomorrow, but it did to her right now.

As she closed her eyes, she only thought of the man in the next room and wished the wall wasn't there.

CHAPTER 4

Russ hadn't slept well. He had never taken his boots or his gunbelt off, and had just laid on the bed, staring at the door until he dozed periodically. He finally decided to get out of bed while it was still dark. It was chilly too, which was no great surprise.

He rose, stepped softly onto the tired floorboards then, after removing his stash, walked on his tiptoes to the door, slowly pulled the chair away and stepped outside. He knew that no one was there with a Colt or Winchester pointed his way because there hadn't been a noise in the house for half an hour. He walked quietly to the kitchen and carefully picked up some food, then continued tiptoeing out of the back of the house and once off the porch, finally walked normally to the barn.

He saddled his horse, tossed on his saddlebags complete with his stash and slipped his Winchester into the scabbard. He took a few minutes to cut the cinches of all the other saddles to keep the others from following him for a while.

He stepped up and walked his horse as quietly as possible around the far side of the barn and swung wide to the access road. He passed through the surrounding hills and reached the road, then turned south, heading for the Mitchell place to get something to eat and set up properly for his escape from the gang and the law that would soon be on their trail.

THE DEBT

John woke up just fifteen minutes after Russ cleared the access road. He walked down to the washroom with his new clothes, toothbrush and powder and shaving kit, then took a bath and washed off a few days of trail dust. Then he finally cleared his face of what was amounting to a healthy beard. His face felt a bit raw as he combed his hair this time and dressed in his new clothes.

He exited the washroom, returned to his room and began putting his things away. He pinned his deputy sheriff's badge on his shirt as he'd be wearing his jacket today, so it would only be shown if necessary. He picked up the bag with the prime rib sandwiches, then opened the top and took a long sniff letting his mouth water with the aroma.

Mattie had heard someone walk past her room and guessed it was John returning to his room. She waited until his door closed and she took her riding skirt and blouse and trotted down to the bathroom. She took a quick bath this time and returned to her room ready to ride before she packed all her clothes into the bag from the dry goods store.

She heard John's door opening again and rushed to the door.

John caught the sound of a door opening behind him and turned to see Mattie's smiling face.

"Good morning, Mattie," he smiled back as he greeted her quietly.

She trotted up next to him and said, "Good morning, John. I'm ready to go," as John took her clothes bag.

"Anxious to see your father, are you?" he asked.

Her eyes were dancing as she smiled at him and replied, "No. I was more anxious to see you, John."

John hadn't expected that and was startled into silence for a few seconds before he replied, "Well, Mattie, you've found me."

He offered her his arm and she wrapped her arm around his as they walked to the desk. It wasn't manned yet, so they left their keys and walked across the lobby.

It was decidedly brisk outside as they exited the hotel.

"I'm glad you told me to wear my new jacket, John. It's kind of chilly," Mattie said, her breath forming clouds in front of her face.

"You need to wear your gloves today, too. It'll warm up in a little while, though."

Mattie pulled closer and not just for the heat. John noticed and was pleased with her new position, but still wondered why she had done so.

They reached the café and went inside, found a table and John held the chair for Mattie. He saw Nancy and mouthed, "Coffee".

She smiled and nodded.

"Would you like some cream with your coffee, Mattie?"

"Could I?"

"Sure."

Nancy brought over the coffee pot and set it down, then asked, "What can I get you?"

THE DEBT

"I'll have four eggs, bacon and biscuits," he replied before looking at Mattie.

She said, "I'll have two eggs. No, make it three eggs over easy and bacon."

"Nancy, bring some strawberry jam and biscuits, too," John added.

"I'll be right back with the cream," she said as she smiled.

After she'd gone, Mattie smiled at John, and not just for the biscuits and jam.

He saw her smile and said, "I thought you'd enjoy a small treat this morning."

"It was a very nice thought, John," she said as she put her hand on his.

John didn't object but returned her smile and let his fingers wrap around hers.

Nancy returned with Mattie's cream-filled small pitcher, noticed Mattie's hand on John's and thought, "Lost another one," but she took it in stride.

"Thank you, Nancy," John said but still looked at Mattie.

"You're welcome, John," she replied as she caught Mattie's eyes and winked before leaving.

Mattie took her right hand from John's and poured cream into her coffee.

"John, why did Nancy wink at me?" she asked, already knowing the answer, but wanting John to say it.

John grinned and replied, "She just admitted defeat, I believe."

"Defeat?"

"She was telling you that you won."

"Oh," she said, as she received her desired answer but still blushed.

John didn't comment further, he just kept his smile down to upturned corners of his mouth.

Nancy brought their breakfast without a wink, but Mattie still blushed as the waitress smiled at her.

Mattie finished her eggs and bacon, and then enjoyed her biscuits and strawberry jam.

John ate quickly and was just sipping coffee while Mattie polished off her biscuits.

He left a silver dollar on the table, picked up the prime rib bag and Mattie's clothes bag, then stood and offered her his arm before they returned to the cool morning.

"Mattie, I need to stop at the dry goods store. When we get there, why don't you dig out your gloves and scarf."

"Okay," she said from her very close position.

They entered the store and John set down Mattie's bag and she began rummaging.

John walked to the counter and asked, "I need a pair of field glasses. Do you have any?"

"Sure."

THE DEBT

He pulled out a box from under the counter and slid it to John.

"$5.50."

John paid for the field glasses and returned to find a gloved, scarfed Mattie.

"You look warmer, Mattie. Want to go and get our horses?"

"It's that time, I suppose," she said with a noticeably unsmiling face.

He picked up her bag and slipped the field glasses and the prime rib bag inside before picking it up, then took her arm and they stepped onto the boardwalk.

"You never did name your horse, Mattie," he said as they walked.

"I know. I just couldn't come up with one."

"I'll help. You name a horse by its characteristics. I named Bolt because he was so fast. Now, I have a suggestion for your horse."

Mattie was grinning as she said, "Alright. I almost hate to ask what it could be."

"Honey."

She laughed. "Honey? For a bay gelding?"

"What? You don't approve of my suggestion?"

"Sure, but not for the bay."

By then, they had reached the edge of the livery and John said, "You're right, Mattie. It's a terrible name for the bay."

As they crossed the doorway, he added, "But not for her," as he pointed at the buckskin.

Mattie's eyes grew wide as she saw the beautiful mare.

"John, what did you do?" she asked in a hushed voice.

"I traded in the bay for your new horse. What do you think of her?"

"She's incredible. Your name is perfect for her. Her coat is the color of honey."

"And Fred says she's as sweet as can be. What else could she possibly be named?"

"I can't wait to ride her."

"Then let's go, Mattie. We need to be moving."

John walked to the packhorse and put Maggie's bag onto a hook but took out the sandwich bag and the field glasses, then returned to Bolt, slid the food bag into his saddlebags and stepped up.

They rode out of town and headed east, taking the road parallel to the tracks.

"John, do you have my new gun?"

"It's in my saddlebag with the extra ammunition. We'll stop well short of the Rocking K, which is my best guess for the gang's location, and I'll set you up. Mattie. I'm going to ask you to do something that you may find objectionable. When we find the ranch, I'll check it out with the field glasses. If they're in

THE DEBT

there, I want you to stay put where I tell you. I'll leave you with your Winchester, the Bulldog, and the field glasses, so you can see what's going on. I'll go in and see what happens while you watch. If everything goes bad, I want you to get on your horse and return to Green River as quickly as you can. Take the stage to Burnt Fork. They'll trail Honey behind on the ride to Burnt Fork. Go and stay with my mother and Jamey."

Mattie was so surprised that she pulled the newly christened Honey to an abrupt stop and stared at him making John back Bolt up a few steps.

When they were face to face, she said, "John, it's not worth it. Let's go back to Green River right now."

"Mattie, it's too late now. I've told Joe that I'd check out the gang. Everything's changed. The old Abernathy gang was just an annoyance. Now with Frank Lewis probably in charge, it is a dangerous group. I have to do this now."

"No, John, you don't. Let someone else take care of it now."

"Who, Mattie? How many people will die if they aren't handled now? There just isn't enough law in the area. I really wish I didn't have to do this. If you want to go back, I'll escort you back to Green River. You can stay in the hotel until it's over."

She knew he was going even without her and said, "I'll come along."

They began riding into the morning sun again as John said, "Mattie, I'll admit something to you. I'd rather have you with me than in Green River."

Of all the things that John could have said to make Mattie feel warmer, that was it.

Then he said, "On a technical point, I need to explain some differences with your new pistol. The Bulldog uses the same cartridges, but only five of them, not six. The biggest difference is that it's a double action revolver. That means you don't have to cock the hammer like you do with most pistols. You can just aim it and pull the trigger. You can still cock the hammer first, but it's not necessary."

"Okay, but when we stop, can you show me?"

"Yes, ma'am," John said as he smiled at her.

Mattie smiled back, still warmed because he wanted to keep her with him.

Frank was throwing things around the main room he was so livid.

"That bastard cut our cinches! I'll bet he guessed where Bill and Dick took that bitch daughter of his, too."

"Do you think they're still there?" asked Fritz.

"How the hell do I know?"

"Boss, I can fix those cinches," said Big Ed quietly.

Frank whirled around and looked at him and asked, "You can?"

"I used to work in leather. It'll only take me a half an hour, and we'll need to get them replaced, but they'll hold up for a few days."

"Go ahead. We're gonna go and get him before he reaches Mitchell's place. You know why? Besides the fact that he

THE DEBT

pissed me off something fierce, he's probably got all his money from the other jobs, too. I always figured he was taking a bigger share. Go and get those cinches repaired, Big Ed. We're gonna run him down."

"I'm on it, boss," he replied as he trotted out the front door.

———

Sheriff Joe Wheeler looked at the telegram he just received from Hopkins. The Abernathy gang had added murder to their repertoire and sounded like Frank Lewis had taken over. He'd killed the shotgun rider who wasn't even armed. This changed everything. He wished he could warn John, but he didn't mention where he was going, so he'd have to wait until either John returned or he didn't. He simply didn't have any other choice. Besides, the best man was already on the job.

———

Frank Lewis, Big Ed Howard and Fritz Thompson were crossing the tracks heading south and Frank's mood hadn't improved much.

"What will we do if we find him, boss?" asked Big Ed.

"We can wait him out. He's only got maybe twenty rounds altogether. Even if he brought a spare box of .44s, we've got six boxes and full Winchesters."

Big Ed and Fritz nodded but were still a bit nervous about going up against Russ.

———

Russ had his horse trotting south and had about a twenty-five-mile lead on his ex-partners and had another two hours or so before he reached the Mitchell ranch. He wasn't sure what he'd find when he got there, and he really didn't care. He needed a place to hang out for a little while and get some rest before moving on. He was already drifting off after the lousy night's rest, and if Bill Nelson and Dick Pierce were there, he could handle them easily, but he didn't think he'd find anyone there. He figured that Frank was bluffing, because if Nelson and Pierce had kidnapped Mattie, they would have sent someone back to tell him of their success. It still begged the question. *What had happened to Bill Nelson and Dick Pierce?*

The two who could answer that question were about five miles west of the road leading north to the Rocking K.

Mattie was regaling John with stories about her life at the women's college. It had started when John needed to change the direction of the conversation and had asked Mattie about what life was like at the college. The behavior of one hundred and forty-three young women supposedly there for educational purposes surprised him.

Mattie's first tale was relatively benign, but they expanded into more salacious material after that. Mattie was surprised at herself for divulging the stories at first, but soon found herself thoroughly enjoying telling them. She had never had an opportunity to just tell the stories, and what made it much better was that John seemed to be genuinely appreciative. She was completely comfortable telling John anything and even more in making him laugh.

"It sounds like you ladies suffered from a lot of misconceptions about the male sex," John said.

"We used our imaginations a lot."

THE DEBT

"It sounds like it. I wouldn't have imagined some of that stuff myself."

"John, why didn't you go to college? You're certainly smart enough and it sounds like you could afford to go."

"I didn't want to. It was simple enough. People should choose what they want to do with their lives by doing something they enjoy, not forcing themselves into a life of drudgery doing something they hate just to make more money or because they think it's expected of them. I wanted to be a lawman. I loved the job; I was good at it and wanted to get better every day. I read everything I could about tracking, criminal behavior, law, and other things. When I gave that up to run the ranch, it wasn't as difficult as it could have been because I ran the ranch and had to solve problems all the time. I was still asked by the mayor to help with dangerous incidents from time to time, so I was happy doing what I was meant to do. How about you, Mattie? Will you be happy being a teacher?"

"Honestly, I don't know. I've never done it before."

"Do you like children?"

"You know, it's odd, but I've never been around that many children except when I was one myself. Obviously, I've never had nephews or nieces."

"I'll tell you, Mattie, if all the children were like Jamey, a lot more folks would want to be teachers, but too many are young hellions that think they can get away with anything. They'll try your patience. Most parents will support you, but there will be some that will take the sides of their precious darlings. You'll have a ten-year-old boy pulling up the skirt of a nine-year-old girl and if you report him to his parents, they may yell at you for making it all up. Their innocent boy would never do such a thing."

"You think I shouldn't teach?"

"Not at all. You just have to balance the negatives with the rewards you get when the good students, who will far outnumber the bad, tell you how wonderful you are or how much they're learning. You'll feel like a queen when one of your students shows improvement because of you."

"Most of the women who graduated went into teaching because it was all that was available. I know of four that hated children. It was why they didn't want to get married, too, because they didn't want any babies."

"That explains my teacher. She hated the boys and barely tolerated the girls. How about you, Mattie. Do you want to have babies?"

"Oh, yes. I've always wanted to have children of my own, especially a little girl. I want to give them everything that I was denied."

"What can you tell me about your mother?"

"My mother was kind to me, but not affectionate. You know what was odd about it? I never felt like she was my mother. She was more like an aunt to me. My father treated her like a servant more than a wife, too. Maybe that's why I felt that way."

"You were shortchanged as a child, Mattie. My mother, like I told you before, was firm but I never had a moment of doubt about how much she loved me. It was in her eyes. She could be scolding me for one of my many transgressions, but the love was always there in her eyes. It still is. When I left to go and find you, she knew it was dangerous, but all she said when I left was 'do what you do and go save that girl'."

THE DEBT

Mattie smiled and said, "And you did, John. You saved me from a lot more than just being kidnapped. You opened up my life to a whole new world, a bigger and more wonderful world."

"Well, you've helped me every bit as much, Mattie, by letting me tell you things that I'd kept bottled inside. It helped more than you'll ever know."

They had reached the turn off to the road to the Rocking K when John stopped.

"What's wrong, John?"

"Mattie, look down at all that horse traffic. It's all fresh, too. It came from north and headed south. Let's pick up the pace a bit, alright?"

"Okay. What do you think it means?"

"I have a feeling that our boys are doing something. Maybe going out on a job. It may mean the ranch is empty right now, but it'll give us an idea of what to expect. The good news is that there were only four horses heading south. The bad news is that maybe one or two are still back there, but there's no time like the present to find out."

"Let's go and find out."

John looked over at the determined Mattie and smiled before they set off north at a medium trot.

―――

Russ had ridden harder than he should have for ten miles and now his horse was as tired as he was. He only had another six or seven miles to go, but he had the horse at a walk and really needed some sleep. Maybe he was getting too old for this sort of life. He was almost forty-five now, and he'd never known anything but a life of crime since he was ten.

He'd begun by stealing things people left lying about and selling them. It wasn't so much for the money either, just stealing gave him a thrill. When he was caught, he found he could lie easily and make it look like he was sincerely repentant, but he never felt guilt for a moment.

He moved up to stealing money when he was twelve and by the time that he was sixteen, he was in a gang and had a reputation with his revolver. When other young men were going off to fight in the war, he used it as an excuse to pad his pockets. With so many men away, he found he had his choice of young women, but he never bothered getting emotionally attached to any of them. He just took from them like he took from everyone else. He started his own gang during the war and made easy pickings.

The one thing he had never done was to hurt a woman. It was the one line he refused to cross, until that night with Jean Mitchell, and he hadn't meant to kill her. That may have been an accident, but he had hit her. Her death may have been unintended, but he had caused it.

For the first and only time in his life, Russ had felt the weight of guilt on his miniscule conscience. It was the only reason he kept Mattie around and then sent her to school and college, but that debt had been paid in full. A life for a life. Now, he owed no one but himself as he absent-mindedly patted his cash-filled saddlebag. Just a few more miles to go and he could get some of that much-needed sleep.

―――

Frank and the boys were twenty-two miles behind Russ. The gap had been expanding when Russ had his horse moving at a

THE DEBT

canter, but now that his horse was plodding along at a walk, they were gaining, but their horses were tiring now as well, and they'd have to stop soon.

"What'll we do if he's got the Winchester ready and waiting on us, boss?" asked Fritz.

"The same thing we were gonna do. We expect him to fire at us, so we keep up the fire and keep him penned in until he runs out of ammo. We'll get him, boys, and we'll get his money. I'll bet he's got over five thousand on him."

"That much?" asked an incredulous Fritz.

"Sure. He's been taking more than his share for years and thought we were all too dumb to notice."

"That back-stabbing bastard!" cried Big Ed.

"You remember that when we get there."

"When will we get there, boss?" asked Fritz.

"That'll be tricky. He'll get there in mid-afternoon, but we won't get there until almost sunset. I don't want to go into a darkened house wondering where he is, so if it's too late, we'll sleep outside tonight and go in early in the morning."

"We don't have any food, boss," Big Ed complained.

"We can go without for food for a single night, Big Ed."

"We're gonna miss lunch, too," he mumbled loudly enough for Frank to hear.

Frank mumbled back, "You can afford it, Ed."

John and Mattie arrived at the entrance to the Rocking K, and John pulled his new field glasses from around his neck to his eyes to examine the property.

As he scanned the abandoned ranch, he said, "There's no smoke from the chimney or cookstove, Mattie, so it's not likely that anyone's in there. I don't think we'll bother going around the hill as I originally planned, but I want you to take the packhorse and ride a hundred yards behind me. Alright?"

"Okay."

"I'll give you the field glasses, too. When I get within a hundred yards of the house, you stop and can watch with the glasses. I just don't believe anyone's there."

"Alright, John."

John pulled the field glasses from around his neck and handed them to Mattie, then unhitched the trail rope to the packhorse from Bolt and tied it to Honey's saddle.

He pulled his Winchester and cocked the hammer, then set Bolt off to a slow trot as they rode down the access road. Mattie waited until John was about a hundred yards ahead, probably just eighty or so, then started Honey and the packhorse after him, matching his speed.

John's eyes were trained on the ranch house, expecting a shot at any moment as he looked for any sign of movement at all. There was a barn, but he discounted its importance right away. They wouldn't have expected his arrival and he had seen no movement in the barn while they were watching. If someone was here, it would be in the house.

It was warmer now, but there would still have been at least a wisp of smoke if anyone had been inside.

THE DEBT

John approached the deathly quiet house, and when he was close, stepped down from Bolt, his eyes still locked onto the house. He looped Bolt's reins around the hitch rail without looking and walked slowly up the porch steps, made it to the front door and opened the screen door. It squealed loudly, but John had expected it, so he stood off to the side of the doorway to see if anyone fired through the inside door. He waited thirty seconds and after hearing no sound from inside, he opened the inner door to more screeching.

He stepped inside and shouted, "Deputy Sheriff John Clark! Come out with your hands in the air!"

His voice echoed through the empty house.

He then rapidly side-stepped to avoid any sudden gunfire, but none came. He was more confident that he was the house's lone occupant now and quickly went from room to room to verify that fact. Then he released his Winchester's hammer and walked back onto the porch and waved Mattie in.

She set Honey off to a trot and soon reached the house, dismounted and tied off her new horse.

"You were right. It's empty," she said.

"There is something interesting inside, though," he said as he walked to Bolt and slid his Winchester back into the scabbard, opened his saddlebag and pulled out the prime rib sandwich bag and then removed his canteen.

Mattie smiled and said, "I had forgotten about the sandwiches. They sound really good right about now."

"They still smell good, too. Let's go inside and I'll show you what I found."

He took her gloved hand and led her up the stairs. Glove on glove wasn't the same, but Mattie was pleased, nonetheless.

They entered the messy room and John released her hand and pointed at the destroyed strongbox.

"Look at that, Mattie."

"What is it?"

"It's a strongbox, or what's left of it. They opened it with that pickaxe right there. The damaged box is fairly new, too. Look at the damage they did to the floor when they tried to open it with the pickaxe. They must have just hit a stage somewhere, but there's something else, too. Do you notice anything odd about the strongbox?"

"Other than it's a total disaster, nothing at all."

"That's it, Mattie. It's been almost destroyed. If they just needed to open it, one side would be a mess, but the rest would be okay. Whoever opened it was really mad. I'd guess it was because it didn't contain any money. See the split bags of sand? Sometimes they have a decoy strongbox for the robbers to steal and a hidden strongbox with the money. It looks like they got the wrong one."

John pulled off his gloves and tucked them under his gunbelt. Mattie watched and did the same.

"Let's eat these sandwiches while we check out the rest of the house. They may be back in a few hours."

John opened the bag and pulled out a soggy prime rib sandwich.

THE DEBT

"I think we'll need a towel or something," John said as he smiled and held up one sandwich.

"Maybe, but it sure looks good," Mattie replied as she grinned and took the prime rib-filled bread.

The juice ran down the sides of her mouth as she bit into the juice-soaked bread.

"Oh, my! This is the tastiest mess I've ever created," she said then followed it with an appropriate giggle.

John laughed at the sight and walked toward the kitchen. He found a towel hanging on a peg and returned to Mattie, gave it to her and watched as she wiped the juice from her still smiling mouth and chin.

John took out the second sandwich and was able to avoid too much drippage because of his bigger mouth, but he still found himself grinning like Mattie. It was very tasty.

They finished their lunch and had cleaned their faces before they began their inspection of the house.

As they scanned the rooms, John said, "It looks like four different men were here, judging by the boot prints. One was a big man who I'm guessing was Big Ed Howard. I can't tell whose belong to whom after that, but the boots were different."

Then he smiled at her and said, "I hope you appreciate my grammar. I didn't want you to give me a D."

Mattie laughed, then left to walk down the hall and entered a different bedroom.

It didn't take long for her to realize that she was standing was in what used to be her father's room. She knew it was because in the corner she found some crumpled sheets of paper that she quickly recognized as her letters. She could tell by the stationery as she pulled the light blue wads out of the corner of the room from amidst the other trash, then straightened them out enough to read the envelopes and found most were still sealed.

Her father had just crushed her letters and tossed them away like any other trash. They meant nothing to him. She knew his letters to her were almost sterile in their presentation but thought it was because he didn't want to show his true feelings. Looking at the letters, she knew he didn't care about her at all.

John had been watching from the open door as Mattie had picked up and flattened out the letters and didn't have to ask whose they were. She didn't cry, but he could tell that when her father had crushed those letters, he had crushed Mattie's heart.

He stepped behind her and put his hand on her shoulder.

"Are you all right, Mattie?"

She answered quietly, "He didn't care, John. He just threw my letters away like trash."

"Mattie, maybe those letters were intercepted by Frank, so he could find out when you were coming. Maybe your father never saw them."

"No, these are older letters. I hadn't even graduated yet."

John didn't understand why he was standing up for Russ Abernathy. He knew he wanted to lessen Mattie's hurt, but still, it was a stretch for him. Abernathy was a criminal. *Besides, what kind of slob throws trash into the corner of the room and leaves it there for six months?*

THE DEBT

Mattie tossed her letters back toward the corner. As they floated to the floor, she turned to John.

"I'll be all right now, John."

John had no choice, really. He pulled Mattie close and hugged her. They were both still wearing heavy jackets, so it was just a comforting hug, but Mattie wrapped her arms around John, and they stood there in the dusty, dirty room and said nothing.

Finally, John said, "Mattie, let's go out the back entrance. I want to check the trails of the horses."

She sighed as they let each other go, but he took her hand and they walked out to the kitchen, then left the house through the back door and walked to the barn.

As they walked, John was examining the ground and said, "There are no tracks back here, so the horses must have all been kept in the barn. We'll see the tracks before we get there, so that's where we'll start. I want to see something."

"What?"

"I want to see if they all rode out together or if Frank took over the gang."

"You can tell?"

"Not for sure, but I can get a good indication. Those tracks this morning were different. One set was older than the others. They were made when the ground was still dry. The others were made after the frost had melted. It looked like three were trailing the one. But it's a subtle difference and I could be wrong."

Mattie looked up at John with admiring eyes and said, "You haven't been wrong yet, John."

"I've been lucky so far, Mattie."

"Me, too," she answered quietly.

John then saw the tracks coming out of the barn and said, "Let's follow those and see what happens."

"Okay."

Mattie was getting excited by the chase and had forgotten her melancholy over finding the letters. They walked, and John had to let her hand go to examine the hoofprints more closely.

After about a hundred feet, one set turned to the south, away from the front yard and the others went straight toward the access road.

"See the set that moved away from the house? That's the early set. He didn't want to wake anyone in the house, so he swung wide and he was walking his horse to keep the noise down. The others set off at a faster pace. I'd guess your father took off and the others are after him."

"Why would they chase him if they wanted him gone?"

"Beats me. It might have something to do with that empty strongbox. I have no idea. I may not know the reason why, but it's obvious that one of them left and the others chased. Maybe it wasn't your father. Maybe Frank Lewis is the one who snuck off. Maybe he stole money from your father, and they were after him for that. I just don't know, but we'll follow and find out."

"I'm ready, John."

THE DEBT

"Let's get that Webley set up for you. I've already punched a new hole in the gunbelt, and I'll want you to take a shot or two as well, so you can get used to it a bit."

"Alright."

They swung around the front of the house and John stopped by Bolt to remove the Webley and a box of .44 cartridges from his saddlebags.

"Okay, Mattie, open your jacket and try this gunbelt on while I load the Webley."

She unbuttoned her jacket, took the empty gunbelt and tightened it around her waist and snugged it down over her hips. It was a good fit. John slipped four cartridges into the pistol.

"I left one chamber empty, so it can't go off accidentally, even if it's dropped."

He paused and then stepped off to her right side.

"Alright, Mattie. I'll fire the first round to show you how it fires. It's smaller but expect a good kick. Don't try to fight it, though. Hold the grip firmly, but when the gun fires, let it pull your hand and wrist back. Okay?"

"Okay."

John pointed the gun toward the barn, but not at any specific target.

"I'll show you how a double-action pistol works."

John held the pistol level, then squeezed the trigger. The hammer snapped back, dropped back to the firing chamber, the firing pin smacked the rimfire cartridge and the gun fired the .44 into the barn with the same amount of flame and smoke as his Colt.

"Now don't get fancy. Just point the gun at your target like you do your index finger and squeeze the trigger. Are you ready to try it?"

"I think so."

John handed her the Bulldog. Mattie's hands were large for a woman's, so she had no problem with the grip. She brought the pistol to bear, mimicked John's action and squeezed the trigger. Again, the small pistol discharged, and Mattie did a good job of maintaining control of the gun after it had jumped upward.

"Can I fire it again?"

"Fire both of the remaining shots, if you'd like. I want you to be comfortable with it."

She grinned at him, then turned back to face the barn. She was enjoying this.

She leveled and fired. Then immediately fired a second shot. Both of her shots were within a foot of each other.

"Excellent, Mattie. You did a wonderful job. Give me the pistol and I'll reload it for you. I'll also give you ten extra cartridges to reload the pistol if you need to. Watch as I do a reload, so you'll know how. Normally, I'd want to clean it right away, but I want to get moving. I can clean it later."

Mattie focused on John's hands as he emptied the spent brass and reloaded each chamber with a new cartridge.

THE DEBT

"Got it?"

"Got it."

He handed her the pistol, and she slammed it home into the still tight holster. John was pleased to see her flip the hammer loop over the pistol.

"No one except us will know you have that pistol, Mattie, because it will be under your jacket. Keep it that way until we get this problem resolved."

"Okay. It's not as heavy as the Colt."

"That and the absence of the extra cartridge should make it noticeably lighter. I think we're ready to go, Mattie. I believe they're heading for the place where you were held, and I'll bet it was one of their old hideouts."

"Are you going to track them, John?"

"Sort of. I'll track them until I'm certain that's where they're going. It's about forty miles, so we won't get there today, but we can get close. Judging by the state of their horse manure, they left a few hours ago, so they won't get there today either. The first rider probably will, but I don't believe the others will risk going in at night. I wonder if they packed anything to eat before they left?"

It was almost sundown when an exhausted Russ and his weary mount approached the entrance to the Mitchell ranch. He slowed down even more and pulled his Winchester, cocked it and began moving forward a little faster. He reached the house and stepped down but didn't hitch the horse. He wasn't going anywhere. Russ took a route around the north side of the house, walking quietly and almost reached the corner when he spotted the large mound of earth a few feet from the house. He also noticed the large bullet hole and smashed wood on the corner of the house. There had been a gunfight here and he guessed that Bill Nelson and Dick Pierce were under the mound, which was fine with him, but the real question was: *who had done it?*

He turned the corner with his Winchester covering him, but there was no need. He stepped up onto the porch and saw traces of blood but not a lot. That meant either it wasn't a bad wound, or it was an instant death shot. Whoever had taken out the two outlaws was good with his pistol, and he stored that away for future reference. Bill and Dick weren't as good as he was, of course, but they weren't slouches either. To get them both took some amount of skill and guts. After the question of the shooter's identity, came the second. *Why had they been killed?* They hadn't pulled a job in almost a month, so maybe it was a bounty hunter. Some of them were pretty good.

Right now, they were just questions and he needed some sleep. He walked back out front and led his horse to the back, unsaddled him and let him drink from the trough. He then led the horse to the nearest patch of grass and hitched him to a bush, pulled off his saddlebags and Winchester and went into the house. He checked for beds but found none. He spread out his bedroll, took off his Stetson and stretched out. He was asleep in minutes.

———

John and Mattie were making good, but not spectacular time. John didn't want to get the horses tired, nor did he want to unexpectedly surprise the three men who were trailing the first.

"So, how is Honey?"

'She's marvelous, John. She's so smooth and comfortable. Why did you buy her for me?"

"When I was dropping the horses off at the livery in Green River, I saw her in the corral. She was too pretty to leave there, and I thought that you should have her."

"Thank you, John. She is a wonderful horse."

"You're welcome, Mattie."

"Where are we going to camp for the night, John?"

"Between five and ten miles from that ranch. I intend on having a nice campsite where we can have a fire to keep away the cold. I wish I had brought a tent, though. I can make a sort of tent that might help."

"Out of what?"

"Our two slickers. They'll keep the dew from settling and frosting up and it'll keep some of the heat in as well."

"I think that would be a good thing."

"Wait until winter sets in, Mattie. But, honestly, I don't mind winter at all. We get the work done, and then we get to sit in front of that big fire. Jamey and I will make some popcorn and my mother will make some hot cocoa."

Mattie smiled and said, "That sounds like a scene out of a book."

"It does, doesn't it?" he replied as he smiled at her.

"Do your hands get to come into the house?"

"They can, but generally they prefer to stay in the bunkhouse. It has a good heat stove and is well built, too. I think they like the privacy, to be honest. You know, so they can tell their nasty stories and bad jokes. It's tough to do that with a lady around like my mother or a young boy like Jamey."

"How big is the ranch house?"

"There are two, really. The original house my father built and the house we use now. The new one is pretty big. We have five bedrooms, two bathrooms, a library and office, and a large sitting room and kitchen. It's really my mother's house. My father had it built for her. Once the ranch became prosperous, he promised her he'd build her a proper house, even though she insisted that she loved the old house. He had it built eleven years ago. She may have loved the old house, but even she admitted that the new house was pretty special."

"I'd love to see it."

"I'd love to show it to you, Mattie, but it's the land that makes the ranch so special. I'll show you the mountains, the large lake, the trout streams, and the waterfall. The canyons will be added soon, and they're beautiful as well. Taken altogether, it's a perfect example of God's handiwork."

Mattie smiled and said, "John, that's poetic."

"When you see it, Mattie, then you'll understand."

They pulled over when John estimated they were around eight miles out. Besides, he had found an ideal location. After the horses were stripped and brought to a creek to drink, they were hitched to some tree branches in a grassy area to graze.

John pointed and said, "See those two boulders over there? If we camp right in between, we can build a fire that can only be

THE DEBT

seen from the west. The rocks will reflect the heat as well and keep out any wind."

"How can I help?"

"Pick out what you want for dinner and breakfast. I'm going to go and get some wood and some branches for our little tent."

"Okay."

Mattie went to the packs to get the food while John took out his big knife and walked into a stand of pines. Mattie could hear branches snapping as John broke off ones that met his requirements. He used his knife to trim off the branches into useful staffs and spent another five minutes hunting for dry wood for the fire before he headed back with his knife in its sheath and his arms full of wood.

He dumped the load near the boulders and quickly built a fire pit. There were more than enough large rocks lying around to make it a sturdy one, and after he had placed the kindling into the pit and had the fire going, he added some bigger sticks and put the cooking grate in place.

"You're up, Mattie. I'm going to get the tent built."

"I'll handle the food, sir."

Making the tent wasn't difficult. He just made a basic frame with the branches and laid one stretched out slicker on one side and the second on the other and anchored them with rocks on the edges. It took less time to set up than a regular tent. Of course, there were those two holes in the roof. John remedied that with some pine boughs that were left over after trimming the tent supports.

While Mattie was cooking, John finished the job by putting the two bedrolls inside. It would be a cozy arrangement.

———

Frank, Big Ed and Fritz were in their bedrolls and Frank could hear Big Ed's stomach growling from eight feet away. He was going to tell him to shut it up but knew he wouldn't be able to. *Why hadn't they at least grabbed a few cans of beans?*

———

John and Mattie had eaten and cleaned their plates and pans and were already in the hodge-podge tent and were facing each other in their bedrolls eighteen inches apart.

Even in the limited light available, John could see she was troubled about something and was trying to formulate a question.

After a couple of minutes of silence, he asked, "What would you like to talk about, Mattie?"

She took another few seconds to find the right words and then said, "When I found those letters that I had written to my father, I was heartbroken when I realized that he really didn't care for me at all, and I was angry, too. I thought that I'd be over my feelings of obligation to him once I discovered that I meant nothing to him, but they're still there. I know you said you felt you owed a debt to Nellie when she died having Jamey, and it still bothers you. Do you think mine will ever go away?"

"That's a question I can't answer, Mattie. What each of us feels belongs to us alone. But I probably didn't clearly explain what I felt when my mother told me I had an obligation to Nellie. It wasn't as if she said I must do something; it was more like a guide. But to me, the obligation, or debt, if you wish to call it that, is like a journey without a destination. It's always there, and I don't know if it will ever be satisfied. The best way to describe it is when you've forgotten someone's name and it nags at you until you remember it. That's a horrible analogy, but it might give you a sense of what it feels like to me. I don't think about it, but it's there.

"What you're feeling is different. You feel genuinely indebted to your father, and frankly, I don't believe he deserves it. Men like him have no compassion or love in them or they wouldn't do the things that they do. That being said, it's up to you to decide when you feel that obligation is fulfilled."

Mattie sighed and said, "I hope it's soon, John. And maybe your annoying feeling will go away, too."

"I hope so, Mattie. I hope so."

After another few seconds of individual contemplation, Mattie said, "There's something else that I've been meaning to ask since I'd been kidnapped, and I honestly wouldn't have dared to ask it of anyone before we started our ride together. It's about what everyone would think of me once I was taken from the schoolhouse. I've known girls and young women who'd been assaulted, and they were all treated as if it was their fault, especially if they became pregnant. How can I return to Burnt Fork if they all think that happened?"

John correctly suspected that she was weighing staying where everyone knew what had happened to her or returning to Missouri where she had friends who didn't know.

"I know every person in that town, Mattie, and almost all of them are honest, good people. We have our share of gossips and troublemakers, of course, but not as many as big towns have. Those nattering whisperers find the bad in everyone and can't see it in themselves. Mattie, if you decide to return to

Burnt Fork, you'll be respected and appreciated by the folks that matter."

"And what about my staying with you without a chaperone for days and nights. Won't that generate gossip as well?"

John smiled and replied, "Yes, ma'am. I'd be surprised if it didn't. Have you met the stagecoach manager, Hank Ward?"

"Oh, yes. He practically undressed me with his eyes as I was climbing out of the coach and made several suggestive remarks before I had a chance to ask where I could find Mister Campbell. He's a very creepy man."

"That's Hank. He considers himself a lady's man, and I don't believe that there's a woman under seventy…wait, let me change that to eighty, that hasn't been a subject of his advances. Hank is harmless in that he comments and suggests, but as far as I know, he's never even touched a woman without her permission. Trust me, I would have known otherwise. Yet it seems as if he always has a female visiting him, whether she's a local lady or a temporary resident. Hank is the biggest source of gossip in Burnt Fork, but despite that, he's well-regarded and looked on as a harmless character.

"Someone like you, with your background will be above reproach, and, if I may add without any false modesty, you're riding with me and my reputation is as good as it gets. Everyone knows that I would never take advantage of a woman, and even if we were out of touch for a month, there wouldn't be a hint of a scandal in town when we returned."

She smiled at him and asked, "So, if I went back to Burnt Fork, they'd all think I was not only still a virgin, but a saint to boot?"

John laughed lightly then replied, "If I said so."

THE DEBT

"Then I guess I'd better not curse or even belch between now and when we return to keep my hopes for sainthood alive."

"I'll grant you some leeway on the cursing, ma'am, but I haven't heard any belching yet."

"Give me time, sir. It was close after that prime rib and pie ala mode."

John just smiled at Mattie, happy that he'd been able to swing the conversation away from its serious beginnings.

Not surprisingly, both were already thinking of that other possible answer to Mattie's question, that if she returned as his wife, things would be even better…much better.

———

Russ awakened with a start. It was still dark outside. and it was cold in the house. He slid out of his bedroll, then quickly ran out to the backyard and after unbuttoning his britches, remembered the gravesite just to the left of the porch. He thought it would be funny, so he walked over to the mound and relieved himself there, not realizing that he was the second to desecrate the gravesite.

"Traitorous bastards!" he said aloud, "You got what you deserved. Whoever plugged you both deserves the rewards on your heads."

He began snickering at his own abusive comments, then returned quickly to the house.

Russ was sure that his old gang had fixed the cinches by now and had probably trailed him, so he initially thought it would be foolish to start a fire because they'd know he was in the house. But then he figured that if they had trailed him, and he wasn't sure that they had, they already knew he was there anyway, and started a fire in the cookstove.

He searched through the limited food he had brought with him, opened a can of beans and poured them into the frypan. After he set the pan on the hot plate, he cursed himself for not grabbing some coffee. Mornings just weren't right without a few cups of hot, black coffee.

A few minutes later, he was eating his bean breakfast, still annoyed for his lack of coffee. It was warmer in the kitchen now, but still chilly enough to keep his jacket on.

Once he finished, and the sun was up, he'd do a scan of the outside for his ex-partners, and if they didn't arrive by mid-morning, he'd continue his run south heading for Utah. If they arrived and insisted on making trouble, he'd rather have it out now than once he got on the road. He liked his odds better than having to worry about them coming up from behind and drygulching him when he was in the open.

―――

His three ex-gang members struggled out of their bedrolls an hour later, and no breakfast meant no time wasted in getting ready to ride to the ranch and get Russ Abernathy.

Big Ed was particularly anxious to get to the ranch in the hope that Dick and Bill might have left some food. What had happened to the two men had been a long topic of conversation last night, and no one had a clue about their disappearance.

Each man saddled his horse, mounted and were moving just an hour after sunrise, just three miles away from the ranch and their waiting ex-boss.

―――

THE DEBT

John's eyes opened first and found Mattie still facing him.

After their conversations last night, he had danced around the topics involving where she would go after she'd met her father because he knew that, without question, he didn't want her to leave. He would have told her straight away, but felt it was her decision to make. As notorious a man as Russ Abernathy was, he was still her father and the only family she had. It had to be her decision, but he prayed that she would decide to stay, and if she did, his next question to her might deprive the town of its new schoolmarm.

John was still thinking about it when Mattie's eyes slowly opened, and she smiled.

"Good morning, John."

"Hello, Mattie. We need to get going, and I have to go before we go."

Mattie laughed and said, "Make it fast, because so do I."

John smiled at Mattie before he quickly scrambled out of the bedroll and then their makeshift tent.

After they each took care of nature's needs, John quickly started a new fire and began saddling the horses while Mattie made a very quick breakfast. John had the trail rope attached to Honey this time as he needed the freedom of movement. He then took down the slicker-tent and packed them away as Mattie finished the cooking.

As they wolfed down their breakfast, Mattie asked, "Why do I get the packhorse?"

"I may need to move quickly, depending on what we find. I know that you're armed and are reasonably accurate with your weapons, but this is entirely different, Mattie. This could come down to a gunfight and I'm used to it. I don't want you to be involved in a hailstorm of flying lead if it can be avoided."

Mattie nodded and said, "Alright. I understand."

They finished breakfast and ten minutes later were heading south again.

———

Russ had decided to watch from outside the house, near the shell of a bunkhouse. He tossed his saddlebags over his shoulder, picked up his Winchester in his right hand and headed out the front door. He had two boxes of .44 cartridges and with the fifteen shots he had in his rifle, the ones in his pistol and on his gunbelt, so he had over seventy rounds of fire, which should be plenty.

At least that was his plan, but he was too late in putting it into operation when he stepped out of the front door and spotted the three riders passing the access road. He guessed they were headed for the tree line to the south, then quickly reversed direction and trotted back into the house, angry for his missed opportunity. He could have drygulched two of them before they knew he was even there. He'd have taken out Frank first, then Big Ed. Fritz would just run or try to join him again, as if he'd let that happen.

But now, that whole plan was wasted. They must have spent the night just a mile or two down the road. *Damn!*

He quickly searched for a new plan of defense. There were three of them, and they rode into the tree line, so he went to the southern wall where he found some loose boards and kicked one out in the kitchen wall, then trotted down to the main room and did the same in two different spots. Finally, he went to what

THE DEBT

used to be the washroom and kicked out a board there. This was his best location because the old, rusty cast iron tub was still there. No .44 round is going to penetrate that iron beauty.

He was as ready as he'd ever be, so he started in the westernmost opening that he had kicked loose in the main room. The second was eight feet to his left. He'd take his first shot from this one and immediately move to the second. Then the kitchen, the washroom and back to the kitchen, making no pattern for them to pinpoint where his next shot would come from. The smoke would hang over the house if he fired too often, so he'd have to space his shots, but the multiple locations would confuse them. When they first started firing, he'd watch. If they stayed in the tree line, he'd head for the tub and wait until the sound changed as they moved closer. Then, it would be time for payback.

"He has a fire going, boss. He's probably making breakfast," said Big Ed, his stomach still growling as he pointed at the smoke from the cookstove chimney.

"He must have figured that cuttin' those cinches would leave us stranded, but we're gonna show him he was wrong. Now we know he's in there," said Frank, "so we'll turn into that tree line and ride right in next to the house until we're about eighty yards out. Then we open fire. We'll each pick a tree for cover. Pepper the place with bullets, but don't go crazy. Let's not waste our ammo. We need to know where he is, so once he starts returning fire, we aim at his muzzle flash."

Fritz and Big Ed nodded. This was going to be easy.

They walked their horses into the tree line and after ten minutes, were at the closest point to the house, which was closer to a hundred yards than eighty.

Frank called them to a halt and said loudly, "Okay, boys. Let's split up. Twenty yards apart and find a tree. Ed, you take the kitchen end. Fritz, you take the front of the house. Aim high at first in case he's in a bedroom, then aim for his muzzle flash or smoke."

They split apart, then each dismounted, found a covering tree and readied their barrage.

Russ had seen movement in the tree line, but nothing more than shadows. He knew he'd see smoke before too long and then the hail of bullets would begin slamming into the ranch house.

Frank was the one who initiated the fusillade when he fired at the center of the dilapidated structure. The .44 caliber missile spun across two-hundred and eight-one feet, then struck just below the eaves above the bathroom and smashed into the floor of the middle bedroom.

Russ marked the spot of Frank's smoke and waited with a slight smile on his face.

Fritz and Ed fired simultaneously after hearing Frank's Winchester. Fritz almost reached the fabled *'couldn't hit the side of a barn'* level when he missed the entire house, his shot clearing the roof. No one noticed, but Russ marked both locations of the gunsmoke and now knew where all three of them were. He quickly trotted to the tub and climbed inside to let their frustration bring them into closer range and into the open ground between the house and the trees.

Big Ed's second shot broke the southern kitchen window and clanged off the cookstove. He snickered at his shot before they began to increase their rate of fire. Frank was beginning to wonder if Russ was even inside because he hadn't returned fire. He decided he'd wait until he'd at least emptied his Winchester, then he'd let it cool, reload and decide what to do if there was still no lead flying out of the house.

―――

John and Mattie were less than four miles away and heard the distant sound of gunfire.

"Do we go faster, John?" she asked after turning in her saddle.

"No, ma'am. There's no point. Whoever is shooting isn't really aiming. If they were, it wouldn't continue this long. It's such a steady rate of fire, it sounds as if they're probably shooting at the house itself. I don't know if there's any return fire yet, but I'll know when I get close enough to see. What's important now is that we need to keep our horses fresh in case we need everything they can give us."

"Alright."

"Mattie, when we get close, I want you to stay about a half mile north of the ranch. Get the packhorse and Honey into some cover. I want you to keep an eye on the road. They might try to make a break. If they do, they'll more than likely head south, but it's possible they'll head toward the railroad."

Mattie wanted to protest but knew better. This was going to be his show now.

"I'll do that, John."

John smiled at her, and said, "Thank you for not arguing."

Mattie smiled back and said, "I wouldn't have won this one anyway."

"No, ma'am. Not this one."

They continued to ride toward the gunfire at a trot, the shots growing louder with each passing yard. After twenty minutes, John knew they were close, then he heard the gunfire slowing down, and could see gunpowder clouds rising in the distance. That was a lot of firepower still being expended. He wondered just how many rounds had been fired and how many cartridges they had left.

He spotted an ideal location for Mattie and the horses and pointed, saying, "Okay, Mattie. See that nice set of boulders over there. Get the horses in there and tied down."

"I can do it, John."

"Good. Now, keep your Winchester ready. You don't have to cock the hammer but get ready to fire if you need it. If it's not me, it'll be a bad guy. Only shoot if he sees you and starts coming after you. More than likely, he won't because I'll probably be close behind him. If you see me following him, mount up and come after me. I'll only follow if none of the others are left."

"Okay, John. I'll be ready."

They sat on their horses looking at each other for a few seconds, and again, Mattie expected John to kiss her, but was disappointed a second time when he just smiled, tipped his hat, and wheeled Bolt back down the road.

Mattie sighed, turned Honey and the packhorse to the right and off the road into her shielding boulders. Once inside, she

THE DEBT

turned the horses around and rather than hitch them, stayed in the saddle and pulled her Winchester.

John had Bolt moving at a slow trot as he neared the ranch, noting that the firing had slowed down even more, then suddenly stopped altogether. He wondered if they had finally hit their target, or Abernathy had somehow picked off all three of his ex-gang members.

―――

Frank had reloaded his Winchester and emptied it at the house again because he simply couldn't come up with a plan. Planning wasn't his strong suit. But now, his own diminishing supply of ammunition was making a change in plans necessary.

He'd finally spotted Russ's horse, so he knew that Abernathy was inside, but *why hadn't he fired back yet?* He suspected that somehow, his ex-boss was waiting for them in a hidden location outside the house.

He left his tree and jogged over to Fritz.

"Frank, I'm runnin' low of ammo," said Fritz when he spotted his new boss.

"I know. Hold off for a few minutes."

"Alright."

Frank then shouted, "Big Ed, come over here."

Big Ed let one more Winchester round go and then trotted over to Frank and Fritz.

"What's up, boss?"

"We're runnin' low on cartridges and that bastard is still nowhere to be seen. I ain't even sure he's in there anymore. His horse is out back, though."

Russ waited for fifteen seconds of silence before he slipped out of the tub and snatched his Winchester as he trotted into the main room, where he hit the floor and assumed a prone firing position. He didn't let the barrel jut out from the house. He'd let it be a surprise when he fired.

But when he looked at the tree line, the three men weren't out in the open. They weren't coming closer and he wondered if they ever would, so he picked out Fritz standing near a tree talking to someone with Big Ed behind him and thought it was the best shot he'd get. He steadied his sights, then squeezed the trigger.

Frank was just about to suggest that they spread out and approach the house from three different directions when the report of the Winchester reached them and the bullet whizzed past them at the same time, making them all drop to the ground shouting assorted expletives before they turned their eyes to the house.

"He's firing back, Frank!" shouted Fritz.

"I can see that, you idiot! Hold your fire. Let's get his location pinpointed."

"Okay!" exclaimed Big Ed as each of them brought their Winchesters to bear on the smoke near the front of the house.

After firing his surprise round, Russ had quickly trotted to the kitchen and again dropped to the floor. The three shooters were all on the ground and had fired six rounds at his first firing location as Russ snickered.

THE DEBT

He finally acquired a decent target. It was a large mound wearing a plaid coat, and he knew it was Big Ed. He fired his second shot through his kitchen firing slot, and the muzzle flash and blooming smoke told his targets where he was.

"There he is!" shouted Fritz as the bullet smashed into the tree close to Big Ed's neck.

It scared the daylights out of him but did no physical damage, as each fired once, then held off firing another as Russ's changed location had them flummoxed.

After a few more minutes with no shots from the house, Frank quickly hid behind the closest tree and said, "The first game is back on, boys. This time, aim and fire at his smoke."

Big Ed and Fritz both mimicked Frank's move by scrambling to their feet and selecting protective tree trunks just as Russ fired his third round from the washroom. Frank fired almost immediately, but was high, and by the time Fritz and Big Ed fired, Russ had quickly crawled out of the washroom to return to the other main room hole.

———

John saw the smoke from the tree line as he passed by the access road, hoping that no one was glancing his way. It was a bold move, but he expected that as they were shooting, they would be concentrating on the target or not being hit and not looking toward the road. He didn't realize just how focused the three outlaws were on the house because of Russ's multiple firing location tactic. He could have ridden past waving his hat and singing a bawdy saloon tune and none of them would have noticed.

John was sure that Russ Abernathy was in the house, but it wasn't the fact that there were three shooters that needed to be dealt with first that made his decision to enter the trees. It was that Abernathy was Mattie's father and she needed to at least talk to him to see what a bastard he really was, so she wouldn't care about what happened to him.

He reached the tree line and walked Bolt into the trees, then stopped after a hundred yards and stepped down. He tied Bolt to a branch and took off his jacket. He needed the flexibility but didn't remove his badge. He hung his jacket on the saddle horn and pulled out the shotgun, but there was no point in taking extra shells. He unhooked his hammer loops on both Colts, because he knew that he'd need them both. He planned on taking out two of them with the shotgun, then dropping the scattergun and then going for his pistols. The time frame in between would be critical, as he would have to almost instantly determine who had survived the shotgun blast and how much time he would have to draw and fire at any survivors. Russ Abernathy would take a few minutes to figure out that there was no more incoming fire, so John should have time to get down there and see if he could talk to him, although he knew it would still be an enormous risk.

He took off his holed Stetson, laid it on the pine needle blanket covering the ground, then he cocked both shotgun hammers and began to walk forward, scanning the trees for his adversaries.

They were still firing at the house, hoping that Russ would fire more and use up his ammunition, but Russ wasn't playing their game. The last shot he'd taken from the washroom had resulted in a close call and he figured they'd be more prepared this time, so he now waited for them to make the sudden rush that he had expected in the first place.

THE DEBT

John had walked for two and a half minutes and knew he was close. The Winchester fire told him he was less than fifty yards out, so he kept walking, ready to fire.

Frank was thinking about changing tactics. Maybe a rush by all three spread a few yards apart and zigzagging in would flush that bastard out of the house. They could keep up the fire on the way in and then burst inside. It was more dangerous by far, but they'd win and those who survived would be richer. It was the thought of all of Russ' money that drove him now.

He turned to tell Fritz of his new plan when he thought he saw motion among the trees to the west. Then something flashed when a morning sunbeam filtered through the trees and reflected off of something shiny, which sent a chill up his spine. But he knew that saying anything would draw attention to himself, so he remained silent and continued to watch the area for further evidence of an unknown intruder. He tried to think who it could be and the only answer that made any sense was that Russ had found Dick and Bill and had talked them into joining him again. If that was true, then the odds were against them.

John had spotted Fritz and had shifted slightly to get a second outlaw in line when Frank had seen him.

John spotted him at the same time but quickly stepped behind a thick pine trunk. The enormous advantage that John had, besides the two barrels of #4 buckshot, was that he expected to see them, but they didn't expect to see John. But now, one had seen him, and he needed to act fast before the one who'd spotted him let the others know.

John quickly stepped out from behind the tree, had Fritz and Frank in line, and shouted, "Deputy Sheriff John Clark! Drop your weapons!"

Fritz jerked at the sound, and began to swing his Winchester around, but Frank already had his aimed in John's direction.

But neither Winchester ever had a chance to fire when John pulled the shotgun's trigger. Both barrels spewed their large quantities of lead pellets along with a massive cloud of gunpowder smoke among the pines, as John immediately dropped the shotgun and pulled both Colts, cocking them as they were being withdrawn from their holsters.

Fritz got the worst of the shotgun spray. His chest and face were smashed by over a dozen pellets, and he was thrown against the tree before he just slid down to the ground. Frank only caught four, but he'd been hurt badly. One hit his open mouth, smashed through his left incisor, then through the upper pallet of his mouth and lodged near the base of his brain. Two others hit his chest on the right side, but neither collapsed the lung as his blood quickly soaked his shirt. The last hit on the right side of his abdomen and caused little real damage, but it hurt like hell. It was the accumulation of his injuries that dropped him to the ground, his arms and legs suddenly useless. He watched as the mysterious lawman jogged past him with two Colts in his hands.

All Frank could think was, *"Who the hell are you?"*

John paid little attention to either man as he walked past. As soon as John had shouted, Big Ed had been as surprised as the other two and had turned his Winchester in that direction but couldn't see him and rushed for cover.

When John's shotgun had gone off, he had ducked behind the tree, but his Winchester's barrel snagged on a low branch,

THE DEBT

yanking it out of his hands. He spent a few precious seconds regaining his Winchester and bringing it level. By then, John was in sight and his two Colts were pointed at him.

Big Ed had nothing to lose. He didn't want to hang, so he pulled his Winchester to a firing position, but before he even fired, John fired both Colts. Their twin reports echoed among the trees and Big Ed, large man that he was, took both .44 slugs in the chest. His Winchester discharged but the shot went wild. Ed went to his knees, looked at John and fell face forward. John checked to make sure he was dead with a quick kick, then he turned toward Frank Lewis, who was still breathing.

In the house, Russ Abernathy had heard the shotgun but didn't see any smoke, so he knew it wasn't aimed in his direction. He knew he had no support anywhere, so it had to be the law, and it was his chance to make a break. He grabbed his Winchester, snatched his saddlebags and ran to the kitchen. He didn't bother looking for incoming fire as he raced to his saddled horse. Any survivors of the shotgun blast would be firing at the lawman. When he heard the two Colts being fired then a Winchester, he knew he had a small window for escape. He reached the back porch, threw his saddlebags over his horse, tied them down and quickly mounted. He raced his horse around the other side of the house and shot down the access road, glancing at the tree line to make sure no one was firing.

John approached Frank Lewis as he writhed on the pine needle covered ground, blood leaking from his wounds.

"You're dying, Frank," he said quietly as he holstered his pistols.

Frank gurgled, "Who the hell are you?"

"My name's John Clark. I'm a rancher down by Burnt Fork."

"What's with the badge?"

"Just a temporary badge to hunt you guys down."

"This because of that stage holdup?"

"The one that came up empty? No. I'm after you for kidnapping Mattie Foster."

"Was that you who screwed that up?"

"I did."

"Where's the girl, anyway?"

"About a half a mile north of here."

Frank then almost snickered, as blood bubbled from his mouth as he said, "You diddled her yet? You should 'cause her mother was a whore."

"I didn't, but I'll tell you what, Frank. You tell me about her mother and I'll bury you proper, so the critters don't chew your face off."

The one thing that gave Frank a case of the willies was just that, so he said, "Her mother was a whore name Prudence Foster. She had the kid a year and a half later, took off when we were off on a job. The one who raised her was Jean Mitchell who lived on this ranch. Frank killed her after I had a poke at her. Stupid bastard."

"Who, you or him?"

"Him. I ain't stupid."

"Maybe not, but you're dead. I'm going to get him now. Is he in the house?"

THE DEBT

"He was. Promise me you'll bury me, mister. I don't want no critters eating at my face."

"Yeah, I'll bury you and the other two. I already buried your partners."

"See you in hell, temporary deputy," he said as he grinned.

"Not likely, Frank."

John stood and began to walk back to Bolt, not caring if Frank lived or died. He scooped up his shotgun and returned to Bolt to go and see if he could talk to Abernathy.

―――

Russ Abernathy was almost giggling as he hit the road and headed north. He was home free. He'd catch the train and head west. He had a lot of cash and no one knew him in California.

He set his horse to a medium trot after the mad dash and checked his back trail and found no one coming. He was in a great mood.

Mattie heard the horse approaching and almost ran out to greet John, but she remembered what he had said and held the Winchester close as the horse grew nearer. As it passed, she got a good look at the rider and was stunned. Without a doubt in her mind, she knew he was her father. He was a lot older, but she knew.

She spent two minutes thinking about what she would do now that she'd found him. Then she let her emotions overrule her instructions and common sense, untied the packhorse and rode Honey from her hiding place. She needed to catch up to her father and look him in the eyes when she asked if he cared for her at all and to at least thank him for sending her away and paying for her education. She needed to satisfy that debt.

She was just almost a mile behind him when she pulled onto the road.

John slipped the shotgun into the scabbard and stepped up on Bolt. It was time to go and see her father. Maybe he wouldn't have to shoot him, but according to Frank, who had no reason to lie, Russ Abernathy had killed the woman that Mattie considered her mother. He wondered if that would finally break the sense of obligation that she held for him.

He rode out of the tree line directly toward the house, his Winchester cocked and ready. The house was quiet. He was going to ride to the front, but he decided instead to save time and ride in an arc around to the back and see if Abernathy's horse was there. Abernathy may have bolted after he heard the shotgun and it didn't take long for him to spot the absence of a horse and the fresh tracks leading out of the ranch.

He turned Bolt toward the access road and set him at a fast trot, hoping that Abernathy had gone south, and not back toward Mattie. If she had followed his instructions, she would be safe, but if he'd learned one thing about her these past few days, was that she was a determined young woman and if she recognized her father, she might try to talk to him on her own. When he reached the end of the access road, he saw the tracks turn north, cursed, then quickly turned Bolt northward and set him off at a canter.

THE DEBT

On the northbound road, Mattie had Honey moving at a fast trot. She was about two miles north of John and around a thousand yards behind her father and gaining.

Mattie saw him ahead and kicked Honey up to a canter, closing the gap more quickly as her heart raced in anticipation of the long-awaited reunion.

When she was within a hundred yards, Russ Abernathy heard the hooves and turned to see what looked like a woman chasing him. He didn't care, man or woman, it was a threat. This wasn't like Jean Mitchell. Maybe she's the one who used that shotgun, so he pulled his Colt and fired a warning shot to tell her to back off.

Mattie was shocked. *Her father had shot at her!* She was so surprised, she didn't slow down or turn, which would have prevented what happened next.

Russ Abernathy was angry that she hadn't stopped, then took a more accurate second shot with more of a killing intent.

Mattie saw his muzzle flash, then almost immediately, felt the bullet slam into her right side just the way John had described it, the punch, the heat, and now the pain. She slumped over Honey's neck as blood began to leak from the wound and Honey slowed down immediately.

Russ was elated with long-range pistol shot and kept riding, he didn't spot John because of the turn in the road that blocked his view after a mile and didn't bother speeding up or taking out his Winchester. He simply slid his used pistol into its holster, pulled the hammer loop in place and kept riding.

―――――

John had passed by where Mattie should have been, saw the packhorse and was filled with a mixture of anger and deep concern as he nudged Bolt into a faster speed. He didn't know if Abernathy had taken her or she had voluntarily gone with him, but either way, he had to find her. Then he heard the distant report from a pistol followed by another shot just a few seconds later.

His heart leapt as he finally asked Bolt to do what he was capable of doing and kicked the big gelding forward with a jab of his knees and Bolt shot down the road. He was leaving a huge column of dust behind him as he kept accelerating, the horse's hooves pounding the ground in a thunderous roar.

———

Mattie was already woozy as she held onto Honey's neck. Her father had killed her. *Why had he done this to her? She just wanted to talk to him and to look at his eyes when she thanked him,*

She was in pain, but even more than the physical pain was the harsh realization that her sudden short romance and dreams were going to die with her. She began to cry softly because it was all she could manage. She already missed John.

Bolt was flying. John's vision was trying to stay stable with the jarring ride as he scanned for Honey.

After he rounded a slight curve, John caught sight of the buckskin ahead and saw that Mattie was hunkered over Honey's neck. His heart was pounding as loudly as Bolt's hooves as they shot towards her. Honey then slowed more and finally stopped.

THE DEBT

John began slowing Bolt when he was a hundred yards out because he was going that fast. He saw blood on Mattie's right side and almost panicked, but he knew Mattie needed him and this wasn't time to do anything but do all he could do to help her stay alive.

He reached Honey and leapt from Bolt's saddle as he slowed to a stop, then pulled Mattie from her saddle carefully into his arms.

Mattie had her eyes closed and was drifting into a deep, welcoming sleep when she felt hands taking her from Honey. She thought it might be her father coming back to finish the job when she heard the soothing sound of John's voice.

"Mattie! I've got you. Stay with me," John said excitedly as he carried her off the road.

She smiled. John had her. If she was going to die, it would be in John's arms.

John laid her in the grass by the side of the road, opened her jacket and saw the wound on the right side, just below the ribs. She had lost a lot of blood, but it didn't look fatal if he could stop the blood loss. John would have to work fast to clean it up, but Mattie was a strong young woman, and it was her best defense.

John ripped open her blouse around the wound and examined it closely. The bullet had passed through her right side but hadn't even entered the abdominal cavity. He just needed to take care of the wound and get her to safety.

He left her in the grass for a moment, ran to Bolt, pulled his saddlebags and ran back to her. John dropped the saddlebags and hunted for his emergency gunshot kit and flask. He pulled them out and hoped that Mattie was unconscious while he did this.

He quickly threaded a needle with heavy thread, then opened the flask and poured some whiskey on her wound. She moaned with the pain from the alcohol striking the raw flesh, which was a good sign. He then started suturing her wound. He kept a steady hand as he repaired the damage to the woman he loved and regretted not letting her know at least that.

After he had closed the front, he cleaned the needle off with whiskey and threaded it again for the back wound. He rolled Mattie on her left side and began sewing. Every few seconds, Mattie would moan or make a short yelp as she still felt the pain, which gave John hope that she would survive. He finished sewing and rinsed it all with whiskey again before rolling her onto her back.

"Mattie! Can you hear me?" he asked loudly.

Mattie could hear John but couldn't say anything as much as she wanted to. He sounded so far away.

"Mattie, I'm going to go and get the packhorse. I need to get you to Green River!"

When she still didn't respond, John grew worried, but before he left, he leaned closer to her ear and said in a quieter voice, "Mattie, you have to stay with me. Not just now, but always."

Mattie was almost unconscious, but his words filtered through enough to make her smile at the wonderful thought.

John hated to leave her, but he had to get the packhorse.

He tied Honey's reins to a low bush, then quickly stepped back onto Bolt, wheeled him back south and set off at a canter.

THE DEBT

Fifteen minutes later, he was back with the packhorse. He quickly stripped the horse of its supplies and took his canteen to Mattie. He sat her up and gave her water, and she swallowed, which is all he could ask.

He laid her back down and grabbed the pickaxe, then ran to a nearby pine tree and used the blade end of the pickaxe to cut down two three-inch thick young trees. He quickly stripped them and cut the other ends to make two stout poles, then carried them to Honey and the packhorse. He had them six feet apart while he removed his jacket, buttoned it back up, and slipped a pole through each sleeve. Then he laid it across Honey's saddle and the pack saddle. He used packing cord to secure the poles to the saddles. He also looped regular rope around the saddle horn and the pack saddle. He finally secured the two slickers to the poles with the last of the packing cord, then tested his makeshift litter. It was the best he could do. He returned to Mattie, picked her up gently, then carried her to the horses, lifted her onto the litter and secured her with the rope.

He attached the packhorse's trail rope to secure the two horses to Bolt then mounted and started very slowly to see if the horses would act in unison. They both stepped off at the same time, and as he watched, he began to increase the speed.

Soon, he had them all moving at a slow trot. He would glance back at Mattie often to make sure she was secure. It was still early in the day, a little after nine o'clock, and at this speed, they would arrive in Green River by five or six. He just couldn't stop for a decent break. The horses would have to wait for a rest.

Russ Abernathy was riding about the same speed as John just a dozen or so miles ahead. He planned on heading to

Green River and taking the train west. He knew that his description on the wanted posters was so vague as to be worthless and there was no need to rush now.

A little after noon, John slowed to a stop. He ran back to Mattie with his canteen. She was still breathing normally and drank some of the offered water giving John more hope. John returned to Bolt and got them all moving again. Twenty minutes later the road crossed a stream and he let the horses drink. They still had five more hours to go, and as he rode, he was following a single set of hoofprints. That would be Russ Abernathy and John hoped that Abernathy didn't get away. He wanted him, and he wanted him badly. *That bastard shot his own daughter!*

Russ took a short break for lunch and to let the horse graze and drink. John was ten miles back when Abernathy finally got back on his horse.

Russ turned west on the road after crossing the tracks. He knew he was only another three hours ride out and would be in Green River soon. He wondered when the next train west would be.

An hour and twenty minutes later, John made the same turn with Mattie. He had stopped and given her water just a few minutes earlier, and was grateful that the temperature was staying moderate, just under sixty degrees. That wouldn't be true in a few more hours. When the sun began to drop, so would the thermometer.

The sun was low in the sky when Russ Abernathy rode into Green River. The first thing he did was to check the train schedule. The next westbound train would be leaving at 7:40, and when he looked at the station clock, he saw he had more than two and a half hours, which brought a smile to his face. This was perfect. He dismounted, crossed the platform, bought

THE DEBT

a ticket to San Francisco and returned to his horse. He mounted, walked it down the street and stepped down at Murphy's Café for some much-needed food.

When John saw Green River in the distance, he had to fight an overwhelming desire to speed up these last two miles. He knew it would be dangerous to Mattie. When he did arrive, he turned his precious cargo down the main street and onto Parade Street. He stopped at #16 and quickly dismounted, then quickly ran around the horse's back end to the stretcher. He untied the rope holding Mattie in place and lifted her into his arms.

Mattie felt his arms, smiled, and almost drunkenly whispered, "Hello, John."

John felt like crying he was so exhilarated when he heard her voice.

"Hello, Mattie. I'm taking you to the doctor now."

"Okay."

He pulled her close and stepped down the walkway then up the steps to Doctor David Spangler's office/house and kicked at the door a few times.

The doctor's wife opened the door, prepared to say something about using the bell, then saw John holding Mattie and waved him in.

"David! You'd better come in here!" she shouted as she led John to the examination room.

Doctor Spangler dropped his fork and trotted down the hallway.

"What happened?" he asked John.

"She was shot about eight hours ago. A .44 caliber bullet went through her right side."

"Did you do anything?"

"I sewed it closed as best I could."

"Alright. Bring her into the examination room and set her on the table."

John carried her inside, laid her softly on the table and helped the doctor remove her jacket.

The doctor quickly examined her wound and said, "You did a good job sewing that closed, John."

He took out his stethoscope and listened to her chest, nodded and turned to John.

"Her breathing is normal, and there's nothing in her lungs. Her heart is strong, so unless there's an infection, I believe she'll be alright with some rest and some food."

"I used whiskey to clean the wounds first, doc."

"That'll help a lot."

"Doc, can I leave her with you for a few minutes? I need to go and talk to Joe Wheeler. This was the Abernathy gang's doings. Russ Abernathy is the one who shot her."

"Go ahead. She's not in any danger."

"I'll be back."

THE DEBT

John trotted back outside and thought he owed it to the horses to release them from their encumbrance first. He pulled his knife and cut away all the cords and ropes, then pulled it off and then led the three horses to the livery.

Once there, he found Fred cleaning out a stall.

"Fred, I have three animals here that need medals, but I'll be satisfied getting them unsaddled, fed, watered and brushed down. They just carried a young woman who had been shot over forty miles almost non-stop."

"Do you have time to tell me the story, John?"

"No, I've got to go and see Joe. Suffice it to say that all the Abernathy gang is dead except for Abernathy himself. He shot her and he's here in Green River."

Fred's eyes grew wide, but he nodded and said, "You can fill me in later. Go."

John handed him the reins and took off at a trot to the sheriff's office and hoped that Joe was still in. When he arrived, he swung open the door and found the useless deputy at the desk.

"Where's Joe?" John asked quickly.

The deputy almost sneered and asked, "Do you mean Sheriff Wheeler?"

Without doing it intentionally, John's scary face descended, as he glared at the deputy and snarled, "Where the hell is Joe, you little bastard?"

"He's on rounds," he croaked. .

John turned and left the office looking for Joe.

He stopped and scanned the boardwalks, finding no sign of the sheriff. Maybe he stopped for coffee at Murphy's, so he stepped down to the street and started walking toward the café.

Russ Abernathy had finished his meal twenty minutes earlier and had luxuriated in having his coffee and relaxing before his train arrived. He finally put down his cup and left the waitress a nice tip. He could afford it, he thought as he smiled to himself.

He walked across the diner's floor and stepped outside. The sun was setting as he saw a man walking toward him wearing a two-gun rig and Russ snorted at the sight. The young pup thinks he's tough because he's wearing two guns. In the dying light, he didn't know how old John was, nor could he see the star on John's chest.

John had seen him exit, but while he didn't know what Russ Abernathy looked like, he did notice that the horse standing by the diner looked as if it had been ridden hard. It was covered in sweat and dust, just as Bolt was.

Russ started to turn to his horse, but as soon as he reached for the saddle horn, he heard a booming voice.

"Abernathy! You are a spineless coward! You shot your own daughter!"

He whipped to the sound of the voice and asked himself the same question Frank had: *Who is this guy?*

Russ turned to face John and said calmly, "Mister, I don't know who you are, but you're making the biggest mistake of your life."

THE DEBT

"No, Abernathy, it's your mistake. You've really pissed me off. I'm the one who killed every other member of your gang. First it was Bill Nelson and Dick Pierce because they kidnapped Mattie. Then I killed Fat Ed, Fritz and Frank for shooting at you. I should have let you all just have at each other. Now, I'm either going to bring you in to be hanged or you can die out here in the streets of Green River. It's your choice."

John's voice carried across the streets and into the café where Joe Wheeler was having coffee after his evening rounds but hadn't recognized Russ Abernathy. When he heard John's initial challenge, he dropped his cup and ran to the door, then stopped at the exit and watched.

He pulled his Colt's hammer loop off as he held the other diners from exiting the establishment. He knew that Abernathy was wanted dead or alive, but he couldn't shoot the man. He'd let John handle it. He knew how good John was and doubted if even the infamous Russ Abernathy was better. Besides, John seemed mighty angry and that made Abernathy's chances even slimmer.

It was that anger that caused part of Russ Abernathy's problem. He also remembered when he'd found such little blood at the Mitchell place. Maybe this bastard really was that good. He'd never even worried about it before.

John kept walking toward Abernathy as their eyes were locked together and stopped when he was thirty feet away.

Abernathy could see him now as he stood near a gas lamp. His face looked like a demon from hell had sprung loose from his soul. His eyes were almost glowing. For the first time in the three decades of his criminal life, Russ Abernathy felt fear. *That man was insane!*

Joe looked at John's face from the café and felt a chill. He almost couldn't recognize him. When he spoke, it got worse.

John's deep, satanic voice almost filled the street as he said, "Abernathy, I'm giving you one chance to drop that gun and I hope you don't. I'd rather just put two bullets into your chest. Right between the sixth and seventh ribs. Would you like to know how that feels, Abernathy? Go ahead and go for that hogleg. I want you bad, Abernathy. You shot your own daughter. You shot my Mattie. I want you to feel my bullets burn into your flesh. Do it, Abernathy! Pull that pistol!"

Abernathy ran his tongue across his lips. His right hand was shaking, which not only shocked him, but made pulling his pistol useless. He had no chance and he knew it, so he threw his hands into the air and peed on himself.

Joe couldn't believe what he had just witnessed. He quickly jumped the three steps to the ground, jogged behind the outlaw, pulled Abernathy's gun and handcuffed him before looking at John.

John instantly returned to the normal John and slipped his hammer loops into place and walked over to Sheriff Wheeler.

"Joe, among his many charges, add attempted murder. He shot Mattie. She's over at the Doc Spangler's office. He said she'll be fine. The rest of his gang are all dead at the same ranch as the first two, so the Abernathy gang does not exist anymore."

"John, when can you come and make a statement?"

"As soon as I get over to the doc's and check on Mattie. Tomorrow, I suppose we need to clean up that mess I made back at that ranch."

THE DEBT

"We'll go down there with a wagon. I'll need you to show me where it is."

"I can. I need to get something to eat today, and I left my jacket on the ground in front of the doc's."

"You go and check on Mattie. I'll be in the office."

"Thanks, Joe. I appreciate the help."

"No, John, we all thank you. Just never make that face again."

"I'll try not to, but I'm not making any promises."

He smacked Joe on the shoulder before he turned and headed for Doctor Spangler's. When he reached the office, he walked to the door and knocked politely.

Mrs. Spangler opened the door just fifteen seconds later and said, "Come in, John."

"How's Mattie?" John asked as he took off his hat and walked into the parlor.

She closed the door and said, "Ask her yourself. She's awake now. I gave her some broth, but she's weak and tired. All she keeps doing is asking about you."

"She's pretty special, ma'am."

"So are you, from what she tells me."

John smiled and headed for the examination room, then stopped, exhaled before he entered and saw Mattie's smiling eyes looking at him.

"Mattie, you're awake. How are you feeling?" he asked as he approached her.

She was smiling as she said, "I'm tired, but happy to be here. The doctor says you did a great job sewing me up."

"I'm just happy to see that you're doing better. You scared me to death, Mattie."

Her smile faded as she said, "John, I did such a stupid thing. You told me to stay behind the boulders and if I had, none of this would have happened. I saw my father ride past, and I had to go and talk to him. I needed at least to watch his eyes when I thanked him for what he did for me. But he shot me, John! He tried to kill me! My own father!"

John pulled up a chair and sat as Mattie closed her eyes and began to cry.

He touched her wet cheek gently and said, "Mattie, I wish I could be mad at you for disobeying my orders, but I should have known that you would have. In the past few days, I've gotten to know you well enough to understand that. It was as much my fault as it was yours."

Mattie then opened her eyes, rubbed away her tears and said, "The doctor said that you were going to find him. Did you?"

"Yes, I did. We stood face to face, ready to let the lead fly, but neither of us fired a shot when my scary face took over and he gave up."

"He really did? He just threw up his hands?"

"Yes, ma'am. I'll admit that I was disappointed because I really did want to shoot him for what he did to you, but he just gave up and the sheriff handcuffed him."

"So, he's over at the jail right now?"

"Yes, ma'am. He'll need to change his britches though."

Mattie's eyebrows arched as she asked, "You're kidding! He peed on himself?"

John smiled and replied, "Yes, ma'am. That tough, murdering outlaw was scared that much."

Mattie laughed lightly, then asked, "John, when I was by the side of the road, did you tell me that you wanted me to stay with you always, or was that just a wonderful dream?"

John read her eyes before replying, "Yes, Mattie. I was afraid I might lose you and wanted you to know that I never wanted you to go to Missouri or anywhere else."

"I wish you had told me sooner, John, but it was worth getting shot to hear you tell me. Why did it take a bullet for you to tell me?"

"For the same reason that you chased after your father. You had to be the one to decide that you owed him nothing and that he didn't love you at all. You do understand that now, I hope."

"I was a fool, John."

"No, Mattie, you were just a sweet, naïve, and innocent woman who only expected the best of people and who desperately hoped to find a family."

"Have I found one now, John?" she asked softly.

"Yes, Mattie, you've found one," he replied with a smile as he gently touched her cheek with his fingertips.

"When you're better, you'll be coming with me to the ranch, and just as I told you, I'm not going to spend months courting you and hoping you'll honor me with a kiss before springtime. I love you, Mattie Foster, and I want to marry you, so we can spend those soon to be arriving cold nights before a blazing fire and share some popcorn with Jamey and my mother, your new family."

Mattie took his fingers in her hand and closed her eyes as she whispered, "And hot cocoa."

He leaned forward, and whispered in return, "And hot cocoa."

Her eyelids slowly opened as she whispered back, "I love you, John."

John kissed her softly before sitting back and smiling at her.

Before either of them could say anything more, Doctor Spangler cleared his throat and entered the examining room.

"My patient needs her rest, John. You may have done a good job, but she still lost a lot of blood and she's not a big oaf like you."

John nodded, then slowly stood as Mattie clung to his fingers.

He kissed her fingers then said, "I'll be back as soon as I can, Mattie."

Mattie nodded and smiled, then released his fingers as he turned to Doctor Spangler and asked, "What's the plan, Doc?"

THE DEBT

Doctor Spangler looked at his patient as he said, "We'll keep her here for a couple of days. We have a bedroom across from the examining room for that purpose. She can borrow some of my wife's clothes, but you'll need to bring some more for her when you can."

"Thanks, Doc. I've got to get something to eat and tomorrow, Joe Wheeler and I are heading down to the ranch where this happened to pack up the bodies of the Abernathy gang."

"They're all dead?"

"Except for their leader. Russ Abernathy is in the jail right now."

"Well, that's good news."

Then, in what he considered an off-hand remark, he said, "Now if someone can find me a schoolteacher it would make my day."

"You need a schoolteacher?" the doctor asked with raised eyebrows.

John quickly replied, "Desperately."

"For Burnt Fork?"

"Yes, sir. Mattie was supposed to do it, but I'm going to steal her away for my own selfish purposes."

"My wife's sister just arrived three days ago, and used to teach school in Cheyenne, but wanted to be closer to my wife. Do you think they'd hire her?"

"Absolutely. If she'd like, she can come with us when we leave Green River. I'll probably buy a buggy to get Mattie down there anyway."

"That would be marvelous. Close enough to visit, but not too close."

"Trust me, I understand. Where is she now?"

"She's upstairs. Do you want to meet her?"

"I'm really kind of hungry, Doc. I can come back in an hour."

"That's fine."

"I need to get my jacket out of the road, too. I used it and some slickers as a makeshift stretcher for Mattie."

"I'll follow you outside. I want to see this contraption."

John then turned to Mattie who'd been happily following the conversation and said, "Ta-da!"

Mattie was grinning as John turned and left the examining room with a curious Doctor Spangler walking beside him.

John and Doctor Spangler stepped outside, and John picked up his emergency stretcher. He slid the poles out of the sleeves and pulled his jacket free, then undid the buttons and pulled the jacket on before picking up the remaining debris. The slickers hadn't fared well.

"Very inventive way of transporting your patient, John."

"I was scared to death, Doc. I've been looking for nine years to find her, and I couldn't lose her."

THE DEBT

"Well, you did an incredible job. She probably owes you her life."

"No, Doc. I owe her mine."

They shook hands and John waved as he headed toward the diner.

He walked inside and as he looked for a table, he was spotted by Nancy and the other diners and the room broke into applause. John was embarrassed and felt his ears flush red as he made a slight wave gesture and took a seat.

Nancy whooshed over to his table and said, "John, we all heard you out there. That was incredible. Did you really want him to draw his pistol?"

John looked at Nancy and replied, "Yes, Nancy. I wanted him to go for his gun badly. He'll hang for all the things he did, but I wanted to be the one to finish him. I was almost embarrassed for him at the end."

"No one could believe you scared him into surrendering."

"He was a bully, Nancy. He was really fast with that Colt and he used that to bully people, even his own gang. When he finally met someone who he wasn't sure he could beat, he took the coward's way out. Now, can I get something to eat? I'm really hungry."

"I'll bring you the special…and a lot of coffee," she replied with a grin.

John grinned back and said, "Thank you, Nancy," before she bounced away to get his order.

Everyone had stopped staring at him by the time Nancy brought him his coffee. A minute later she brought him the special: pork roast with roasted potatoes. She or the cook really laid on the food for some reason, and even John wasn't sure he could finish it. But he did and left a silver dollar on the table as he left the diner, which made Nancy smile a bit more when she saw the size of the tip.

As he left, a few people waved, and John waved back, but thankfully, there was no more applause.

He stopped at the jail first because there was time and when he entered, the other, non-idiot deputy at the front desk just waved him back to the sheriff's office. Russ Abernathy just glared at him as he passed, and John could tell by the smell that he hadn't been cleaned up.

He walked down the short hallway, tapped on the sheriff's door jamb and when the sheriff waved him in, sat down across from Joe Wheeler.

"So, John, tell me what happened before you write up your report."

"If you'll give me some paper and a pencil, I'll write and talk at the same time."

The sheriff replied, "That'll work out fine," before he removed some paper from his drawer and slid the four sheets and a pencil across the desk.

John began talking and writing. He didn't go into too much detail beyond the shootings and Mattie's injury, but included it in his written report. It took twenty minutes to complete both the oral and written reports, and when he slid the completed report back to the sheriff, he told Joe that he'd be in at eight, so they could go out to the ranch and recover the bodies.

THE DEBT

"Well, Joe," he said as he stood, "I've got to go and see a teacher."

"The same one you took out there to find her bastard father?"

John smiled and replied, "No, sir. I'm going to meet a new teacher. I'm planning on marrying the other one."

Joe grinned as John tipped his hat and left his office.

After leaving the jail, he crossed the street, then turned down Parade Street at a jog, knowing he was close to being late. He climbed the four steps to the doctor's house again and knocked on the door.

Thirty seconds later, the door swung wide and he found himself looking at a pleasant-looking woman close to his age with dark brown hair and eyes.

She smiled and said, "You must be John Clark. Come in. I'm Ruth White, Doctor Spangler's sister-in-law."

"Pleased to meet you, ma'am. Please call me John," he said as he removed his hat and followed her inside, closing the door behind them.

"Thank you, John. Please call me Ruth."

"Thank you, Ruth. Do you mind if I check in on Mattie before we talk?"

"I'd be ashamed of you if you didn't. Please go ahead. I'll be in the sitting room."

"I'll be out shortly, Ruth."

John stepped into the bedroom across the hall from the examining room, and soon glimpsed Mattie's smiling face.

"Did you get enough to eat, John?" she asked in a surprisingly strong voice.

"They gave me too much, Mattie. Are you still hungry?"

"Oh, no. I've been well fed."

"You look good, Mattie, especially with all you've been through today."

"Can you sit down for a few minutes?" she asked.

John sat on the edge of her bed and said, "I just came back from the sheriff's office and filed my report. We'll be leaving early in the morning for the ranch house."

"I heard."

"We won't be back until late tomorrow night, but when we go back the next day, I'm going to buy a buggy and horse to take us back to Burnt Fork. I don't want you riding that distance."

"I can ride, John. Honey is such a sweetheart of a horse."

"I know, but this way, I get to have you close, and besides, we can bring Ruth back with us and you two can get acquainted."

"Oh. That is a good idea."

"Mattie, we may need to spend another day in Green River. Is that alright?"

"As long as you don't change your mind, mister. I carry a gun, you know."

THE DEBT

John smiled at her and said, "I'm going to enjoy being your husband, Mattie."

Mattie then said quietly, "I hope I don't disappoint you, John. I'm new to all this."

He leaned over and kissed her again before he said softly, "You haven't disappointed me yet, Mattie, and you never will."

For the first time, Mattie initiated a kiss and surprised John when it wasn't one of the soft kisses that he'd given her, but a deep, passionate kiss as she wrapped her arms around his neck.

When she finally sat back slightly, she said, "I had to know if it was all that I had hoped it would be."

He tilted his head slightly, smiled and asked, "And?"

She closed her eyes, sighed and hugged herself as she answered, "Oh, no. It was so much more. I didn't want to stop."

"It will only get better, my love."

She opened her eyes and asked, "Oh, please tell me you're joking. Better?"

"Much better," he answered as he stood and said, "I have to go and meet our new teacher now."

Mattie was still almost euphoric, despite the fresh bullet wound as she said, "You go and talk to Miss White."

"I'll see you right afterward."

"You'd better."

John stood, snuck another quick kiss and left the room.

Ruth was smiling at him when he appeared as she asked, "Is Mattie alright?"

"She's doing much better."

"That must have been a very frightening experience," she said as John took a seat across from Ruth.

"I wasn't afraid in the least when going into that fight with those outlaws, but I was terrified when I saw Mattie slumped over her horse with blood all over her side. It had soaked right through her jacket. I can't tell you how relieved I am that she's doing so well."

"All because of your quick actions, according to my brother-in-law."

John shifted back to the question of employment and asked, "So, Ruth, are you willing to come down to Burnt Fork and educate our rowdy youngsters?"

Ruth smiled and said, "Tell me about the town."

"It's a small town with about two hundred residents, but I like the folks. I know all of them and all of the children, too. My son, Jamey, is nine and he fills me in on who the good ones are and who the bullies are. There are twenty-one students in the school."

"It sounds like a normal-sized classroom. Where would I live?"

John asked, "Where would you like to live?"

Ruth's eyebrows rose as she asked, "I have an option?"

"Yes, ma'am. Did you want to live in town?"

THE DEBT

Ruth was surprised that there was an option, but replied, "That would probably be better, don't you think?"

John nodded and answered, "Probably, but would you prefer your own house, or would you rather stay at a boarding house?"

"There's a house for the teacher?" she asked in surprise. She'd never heard of such a thing.

"Not yet. I'd just like to know which you'd rather have as a residence. The advantage of the boarding house is, of course, that you don't have to do your own cooking."

Ruth sat back a bit, smiled and said, "Usually, they just say, 'there's the school. Good luck'."

John laughed before saying, "Well, Ruth, I'll be honest with you. I don't want to let you get away. You're a very pleasant person and seem to have a good sense of humor. The last two teachers were a bit on the terse side, and I believe the children would be ecstatic to have you there. I know Jamey would. I'm just trying to sweeten the pot."

"That's quite a sweetener, John."

"Ruth, will you come to Burnt Fork with me and Mattie? If you don't want to stay, I'll drive you back."

"I'd be surprised if I didn't stay. When do you want to leave?"

"Two days after tomorrow. We'll meet you at Murphy's Café at seven-thirty for breakfast."

"Alright. I'll be there. You haven't asked the obvious question."

"It must be obvious to everyone but me."

"Why aren't I married and having my own children?"

"It's not a question that I would ever ask."

"Then, I'll answer it anyway. I love teaching and I wouldn't want to give it up to get married."

"Let me ask you a question then. Would you get married if you didn't have to give it up?"

"You are kidding, aren't you?" she asked as the surprises kept coming.

"Not at all. Would you?"

"I would."

"Then keep that in mind when we ride down to Burnt Fork."

"You're a very different kind of man, John."

"Sometimes there's an advantage to being different, Ruth," he replied as he stood, then added, "I'm going to visit my fiancée and then head to the hotel. It's been a long day."

Ruth rose and said, "I'll see you in three days then."

"I'll probably bump into you a few times in between, but it's been a pleasure meeting you, Ruth."

She nodded, then smiled and left the room, walking up the stairs to her room.

John was pleased as he could be with Ruth White almost from the first as he left the parlor and stuck his head into Mattie's room.

THE DEBT

She looked at him and asked, "I heard all that. How come I wasn't offered a house?"

John smiled, walked into the room and took a seat on the bed, then replied, "I offered you much more than a house, Mattie."

"I know. I'm just trying to be annoying."

"I could have made the same offer to you, but I didn't. Do you know why?"

"I have an idea."

"I want to share my life with you, Mattie. All of it. I want to wake up every morning and see your face. I want it to be the last thing I see before I fall asleep. When we have one of our spectacular sunsets, I want to have you near me, so we can share it. And, yes, I want to curl up with you with three feet of snow outside in front of the fire with popcorn and hot cocoa."

Mattie touched John's face with her fingertips and said, "I'll take that over teaching anytime."

"I'm going to head over to the hotel and get a room. I won't see you tomorrow, Mattie, but I'll make a regular nuisance of myself the next day."

"I'll be looking forward to it," she said as she smiled.

John gave her a goodnight kiss that was more passionate than the one she had given him to let her know that he wasn't exaggerating when he'd said that it would be getting better. After one last smile, he stood, left the room and then the doctor's house.

He stepped out to the street and took in a deep breath of the cool Wyoming air and looked up at the blanket of stars that stretched overhead before smiling, then heading down to the hotel, where he got a room then stepped down the hallway. He opened the door, took off his gunbelt, laid the rig on the chair near the bed, took off his still holey Stetson, set his saddlebags on the floor and kicked off his boots. He laid on the bed and looked up at the ceiling and began to talk in a low voice that bordered on a prayer.

"Nellie, I haven't talked to you in a while, and I'm sorry about that. What do you think of Mattie? I think she's very special, just as you were, only different. She's given me a new life, and one that I thought that I'd never have again. How I explained to Mattie about how I felt when you died wasn't exactly true, was it? I did feel as if I owed you something for causing your death even though it doesn't make a lot of sense.

"I know it wasn't intentional and Jamey was created by the love we shared, but I felt so guilty that all I had to do was love you and you had to suffer the annoyance of carrying Jamey for nine months, the morning sickness, and then that long labor of horrendous pain. It wasn't fair, Nellie, and I know that.

"Then, you died, and I acted like a selfish, thoughtless coward, just wallowing in my self-pity until my wonderful, caring mother told me that I owed it to you and our son to be a man. I did that, and I know that you're happy with our son, but I never was able to put aside my feelings of guilt for what I did to you. Now I found Mattie and I'll be happy again. I'll make love to her and she'll carry our baby. I can't lose her, Nellie. I can't."

John then closed his eyes and continued, saying, "Mattie almost died because she believed she owed a debt to her father for sending her away and giving her some money to live, only to find that she owed him nothing. But for nine years now, I've just had a feeling that I hadn't done enough to repay what I did to you. Is that what this has been? A debt like Mattie thought she had? If it is, how can I possibly fulfill this obligation to you? Tell me, Nellie. Please."

He waited, but after ten minutes without any change in that nagging feeling of guilt, he finally shifted his mind back to Mattie, and let thoughts of her let him sleep.

As John was lying on his bed thinking about Nellie and Mattie, Deputy Hap McDonnell took over watching the prisoner from Deputy Lee Garrison. He'd heard the story of the non-gunfight near the café and was still snickering.

He glanced at Russ Abernathy and said loudly, "Whew! It stinks in here. Did somebody pee all over himself?"

Russ snarled, "Shut up, you moron."

Hap stood, then turned and stepped closer to the cell and glared at the outlaw.

"Who are you calling a moron? I'm not the coward who peed himself rather than face a damned rancher!"

Russ snapped, "You watch your mouth, or I'll kill you."

"With what? You gonna pee me to death?" Hap shouted back as he laughed.

Russ just glared at him and said in cold, threatening voice, "You're a dead man, deputy."

Hap should have realized how dangerous his prisoner was, but he was under the illusion that he was in control because he had a pistol and the cell keys and Russ Abernathy was behind bars.

He took one more step, putting him closer to the iron bars, and whispered, "You're gonna hang, pee-boy."

Russ saw his chance, so he stood and took two measured steps closer to the deputy, not even looking at his eyes, as he kept his focus on the deputy's chest.

Hap still didn't recognize the danger, and leaned forward to toss another snide, urine-related insult when the outlaw's hands flew out between the bars, quickly grabbed his head and slammed it back into the bars before Deputy Hap McDonnell could even blink. He buckled at the knees and slid to the floor.

"Damned idiot," Russ Abernathy said as he dropped down to the cell's floor and stretched his arm through the bars for the keys that were still in Hap's right hand.

He couldn't quite reach them, so he grabbed Hap's sleeve and pulled his arm closer, dragging the keys with it. He reached again, felt the cold metal in his fingers, then smiled as he pulled the keys into the cell. He stood, then snatched his Stetson from the bunk, quickly walked to the lock and unlocked it from the outside, swung the door wide and quickly stepped next to Hap, pulled Hap's gunbelt off and strapped it on. He looked down at Hap and kicked him once and then smashed his heel into the back of Hap's neck making a nasty, loud crack as Hap's cervical vertebrae broke into pieces, severing his spinal cord. He went through Hap's pockets and found $2.17 as Hap stopped breathing.

"Cheap bastard," he growled under his breath.

It was dark as Russ Abernathy calmly walked out of the jail. He had his freedom, a gun, and all of $2.17. He needed more

THE DEBT

cash, but the thirty-five-hundred dollars in his saddlebags was probably somewhere in the county courthouse, but that didn't do him any good. He needed a horse, too. So, he headed down for the only establishment he could find both, The River's Edge Saloon.

He just stepped along the boardwalk as if out for a late-night stroll and when he arrived at the saloon, walked down the row of horses and selected the best of the bunch. Once he had made his choice, he turned and passed through the batwing doors. The large room already smelled of all sorts of human odors, so his pungent aroma wasn't noticed when he entered.

He looked around the room and found what he was looking for, a poker game. He hoped it was a high-stakes game as he sauntered that way. As he drew near, he began quickly adding up the amount on the table, and found it wasn't a lot of cash in the pot, around twenty bucks, but it was better than what he had.

He glanced over at the bartender first. He was the real danger and probably had a scattergun under the bar, so he drifted over to the wall opposite the bar, with the poker game still in front of him, and loosened the Colt's hammer loop.

Russ smoothly and quickly drew Hap's Colt from the holster, cocking the hammer as he did.

"Alright, boys! Nobody moves. I don't want to kill anybody else tonight, but it won't cause me any lost sleep if I do. Now, you boys playing poker, put all of the cash, including what you're holding in your pockets on the table and make me a nice clean stack."

They began to comply when Abernathy saw the bartender moving slightly to his left, whipped the Colt's muzzle in his direction and said loudly, "Barkeep! You stay where you are. My name is Russ Abernathy, and I don't miss."

That stopped any heroics by the bartender who put up his hands and stepped away.

Russ glanced down at the stack of bills on the table. It wasn't huge, but it should be enough.

"You!" he said as he pointed his pistol at the player to his right, "Hand me the cash and don't try to be a hero. It's only money."

The man picked up the greenbacks and held them out to Abernathy, who snatched them from his hand.

"Now, I'll be leaving. The next man who comes through that door to follow me will be a dead man."

He then backed toward the doors, watching the entire room, which wasn't an easy thing to do. As he neared the door, he heard bootsteps outside and some laughter, then waited as two new customers swung the doors wide and walked inside. They were still laughing until they saw a saloon full of hands in the air and wide-eyed faces staring at them.

"What's goin' on?" one asked as the answer came from behind him, off to his right.

Russ said calmly, "Just go inside and sit down. I won't shoot you unless you try to get all stupid and brave."

The man who asked took two steps toward the nearest table with his hands in the air as all of the others were doing. His companion's curiosity made him turn quickly to see who it was that was threatening to shoot him. It was a fatal mistake.

THE DEBT

The sudden movement kicked in Abernathy's survival mode and he expected to see a pistol in the man's hand. There wasn't, but by the time Russ realized that it was empty, his Colt's hammer had fallen, and the cartridge had fired. The bullet passed cleanly through the shocked man's left lung and struck a second man sitting eight feet behind, his hands still in the air.

Russ instinctively cocked the hammer and backed out of the saloon as everyone remained frozen. No one moved to help either wounded man as Russ Abernathy backed out onto the boardwalk, unhitched his selected mount, then stepped up and then took the other horse from the hitchrail along as well. He stopped looking at the batwing doors, expecting that his threat to shoot anyone who left the saloon was sufficient, and quickly headed south out of Green River at a fast trot.

After three minutes, the bartender finally moved and grabbed his shotgun. Once he did, chaos reigned, but nobody wanted to be the first out those batwing doors, so there was a rush to go out the back door. The first victim of Russ's Colt was dead, but the second had only suffered a weakened .44 caliber slug which stuck in his left thigh. It was another two minutes before someone exited through the front entrance and ran down to the sheriff's office to find Joe Wheeler, but when he blasted into the jail, he found Hap McDonnell's body instead.

Joe Wheeler was at home sitting with his wife telling the story of the Abernathy gang's demise when he had heard the gunshot. He stood to leave and check it out, but his wife reminded him that Hap was on duty and he'd find out what it was. It was probably just some drunken ranch hand anyway. He knew better than to argue with his wife, so he sat back down and continued with the lengthy story with frequent interruptions for wifely questions. The story was abruptly ended a few minutes later by frantic pounding on the door.

Joe stood and walked quickly to the door and pulled it open, but never got a chance to ask what Jasper wanted.

"Sheriff! Russ Abernathy killed Hap and escaped! Then he came down to the saloon and killed Ben Chambers. He stole a couple of horses and run off!"

"Damn!" he cursed and turned to his wife and said, "I gotta go!"

"Go! Go!" she shouted as Joe quickly stepped out into the cool night air and closed the door behind him.

He turned to the man who had given him the news and said, "Jasper, go over to the hotel. Tell the clerk to have John Clark meet me as soon as possible at the saloon. Tell him to come armed."

"Yes, sir!" Jasper exclaimed and rushed off to the hotel.

Joe was initially going to have Jasper get Deputy Lee Garrison, but Lee would have to stay in town now that Hap was dead. He'd send someone else to find Lee after he found out exactly what had happened. The other reason was that he knew that John really wanted to kill Russ Abernathy.

John had just drifted off when there was a loud knock on the door and his eyes snapped awake, causing a rush that set his heart pounding.

"Just a minute!" he shouted as he pulled his boots on and stumbled to the door.

He opened the door a bit and asked, "Yes?"

THE DEBT

"Mister Clark, the sheriff wants to see you as soon as possible in the saloon. Russ Abernathy just escaped and killed the deputy and another man."

"Son of a bitch!" John snapped and then said, "I'm on my way. I've got to get my guns."

Jasper left quickly, and John began getting ready even faster. He yanked on his gun rig and hat, threw on his jacket, then grabbed his saddlebags and ran out the door, leaving it wide open. There was nothing left inside anyway.

He rushed across the lobby and out of the hotel in seconds, then saw the crowd meandering toward the saloon to find out what had happened. He had to push his way through to get to the doors and pull two men out of the way. One snarled at him until he realized who was pulling him, then stepped aside.

Joe saw him enter as he was kneeling over Ben Chamber's body.

"John!" he shouted, as he waved John over.

"How did this happen?" John asked.

"I don't know. I haven't been down to the jail yet. I was told that Hap McDonnell's body is right up against the bars without a gunshot wound. He was probably riding Abernathy and got too close. Abernathy came in and robbed a poker table and was backing out when Ben here entered and from what I'm told just turned around when Abernathy shot him. Abernathy backed out and stole two horses. Can we get him at night?"

"Not usually, but there's enough light from the gas lamps to pick up which direction he's going. I'll go after him based on that. You can stay and clean up the mess here. I owe that bastard."

"So, do I. You go ahead. You're better at this than I am."

"I'm gone," John replied as he turned toward the door.

As he trotted down the road, he knew that this was an iffy proposition at best. He guessed that Abernathy was headed either east or south. If he was going east, he'd be heading for the Mitchell ranch again, but he didn't think that was likely, although he thought it would have been his best option because John knew he had dropped a lot of supplies just off the road when he had made Mattie's stretcher and there were those three dead men with horses, Winchesters, ammunition and probably some cash. But Abernathy didn't know that, so he might be headed for Utah, and Utah was south, right past his ranch. He knew that road very well as he trotted toward the livery and hoped Abernathy headed south.

Russ was heading south and kept a moderate speed. He had two horses, two Winchesters and two sets of saddlebags, hopefully with more ammunition and maybe some food. He'd need food, and that made him make an unwise decision. As he rode, he began looking for access roads, thinking that a quick stop to add to his money and supplies was necessary, not believing that anyone would be trailing him so soon or at night.

John could see the two recent sets of horse prints in the gaslight as he walked quickly along the dirt road and followed them down to the livery then went inside. He saddled Bolt quickly, then led him to the street and turned south, following the two sets of hoofprints as he walked. Five minutes later he entered the crossroads and could barely make out anything in the darkness. He lit a match and followed a few more feet

THE DEBT

before he had to light a second. When he saw the prints cross the tracks, he knew that Russ Abernathy was going south.

He stepped up on Bolt and set him at a medium trot. He'd have to trust his instincts now. He knew Abernathy would put some distance between himself and the town and had about half an hour head start, so that would put him four or five miles ahead. *Where would he go?* It was around eight o'clock, and John figured that Abernathy had a bedroll, but little else, and probably no food. He may not even have matches for a fire, not that he'd be making one tonight. He'd know that he'd be followed, but he probably thought that any posse would wait until daylight. Russ Abernathy would play the odds, and John wanted those odds to be in his favor, not the outlaw's.

———

Russ Abernathy didn't need food for tonight. He'd already eaten and wasn't hungry, but he did need to be better supplied than he was. He didn't want to break into a ranch or farmhouse at night and have to stumble around. He'd rather do it with some light, so he could find what he wanted. What became of the occupants was of no consequence.

Twenty minutes later, he found an access road and turned right. He wasn't sure if it was a ranch or a farm, but most likely it was a ranch. Farms were in a minority in this part of Wyoming. He trotted his two horses down the road and saw lights in the distance and he smiled. It was a ranch house. His first concern was the presence of ranch hands, so he reduced speed to a slow trot and looked for the bunkhouse and found it situated two hundred yards opposite the ranch house and north of the barn. He didn't know that it was empty, and all of the ranch hands were all in town. Two were even in The River's Edge Saloon and had witnessed the murder.

He slowed the horses to a walk to reduce the sound, then dismounted about fifty feet from the house and led the two horses to the hitch rail. He tied them off and pulled his pistol, cocking the hammer as he brought it level. Russ quietly stepped onto the porch and very slowly opened the door. Once it was open, he quickly walked inside and closed the door behind him before he was greeted by two sets of startled eyes.

Hal Crenshaw and his wife, Tess, had called the Lazy C home for over fourteen years and had never had a problem with outlaws or Indians until now.

"What do you want?" Hal shouted.

"I need food and your money, old man," declared Russ, who was three years older than Hal.

"I'll give you food and what we have, then you can go," replied Tess.

"Now, you're a right smart lady. Let's head into the kitchen and you can pack me up some supplies. I've already killed two men tonight and I don't have any scruples about shooting women, either. I even shot my own daughter today, so just mind yourselves and you'll live to see another day."

The couple walked down the hallway with Russ behind them, not believing him for a moment that they'd see another day.

―――

John was guessing as he trotted Bolt south along the same road that he'd be following to bring Mattie and Ruth home to Burnt Fork in a few days. He was going to gamble some lost time to check on the ranches that were just off the southern road. Abernathy would try to stock up with food and other supplies if he wanted to make good his escape, but he couldn't

THE DEBT

stay on the road. He'd know that telegrams would be going out all over the region about his murderous escape with an accurate description. John knew he'd have to avoid towns as he went as far south as he could. The more distance he put between him and Green River the better. Of course, he'd probably come to the notice of the United States Marshals now that he'd killed a law officer, even one as useless as Hap McDonnell.

Assuming he did find out where he is, *how could he take him?* He may have to wait until moonrise. There was a half moon, and it would be up in another hour or so, and that would help, but for now, he just rode, looking for the access roads. He knew that the Crenshaw's Lazy C was the first one on the road and should be coming up on the right soon.

In the Lazy C ranch house, Tess Crenshaw was putting tins of beans and beef into a bag that already contained some smoked beef and a small ham.

"I need some matches, too," Russ said.

Hal pulled a box of matches from a shelf near the cookstove and handed them to Tess, who put them in the bag.

"Now, where's your money?"

Hal replied, "We don't keep much here. We use the bank."

"Give me whatever you've got."

Tess walked to the cookie jar, opened it, reached inside and took out all the bills.

"Silver, too," growled Russ. "Put it all on the table."

She sighed, scooped out all the change and dropped it all on the table.

"Now step back," Russ snarled as he gestured with his Colt.

Hal slid in front of Tess as they both backstepped to the kitchen's far wall.

Russ noticed and snickered. "How quaint. Hubby thinks standing in front of his little wife will protect her. It won't, old man, at this range a .44 will go clean through you and kill her, too."

Hal knew he was right, but he thought he might slow a bullet down enough to let her live. He and Tess just watched as Russ began stuffing the money into his pocket.

John had reached the access road to the Lazy C and risked being shot by stepping down and lighting another match to examine the ground. As the match flared, he saw the hoof prints heading into the ranch, but none coming back out. Either he was still there, or he'd gone cross country which would make tracking impossible in the dark.

Russ Abernathy knew it wasn't much, but with the poker money and the food, it would get him another hundred miles anyway. He was going to back out when he stared at Tess Crenshaw. She wasn't young, but she wasn't bad looking, and he seriously thought of having his way with her, but time was more important. Besides, he'd have to kill her husband and he didn't really want to make the noise. It was the only thing that saved their lives.

THE DEBT

Tess knew what he was thinking as he looked at her and felt a sickening chill.

He said, "My name is Russ Abernathy. If you try and be stupid and brave and stick your head out of the door to try and backshoot me, you'll die fast."

Then he abruptly turned and left the kitchen, moving quickly toward the front door.

Hal hugged his suddenly sobbing wife, realizing that they were going to live, after all.

———

John decided he'd wait until Russ Abernathy left the house. He was gambling again. He might already be riding cross country, but John figured he'd want to get another twenty miles further away tonight and the safest way to do that was to use the road. Abernathy hopefully wouldn't risk breaking a horse's ankle in the dark.

So, John pulled down off the access road, halted Bolt and sat in the darkness as he pulled the shotgun, cocked both hammers and waited. He knew he could be seen if Abernathy looked for him but was expecting him to want to move as quickly as he could and not pay that much attention to his surroundings.

Russ Abernathy quickly left the ranch house, then hung the bag of food on the spare horse's saddle horn. He was fashioning a trail rope for the horse when Hal Crenshaw, his manhood affronted by Russ Abernathy, left Tess in the kitchen and trotted down the hall.

Tess shouted, "Hal! No!"

Her shout was all the warning that Russ Abernathy needed. He dropped the trail rope and pulled his pistol again.

John had heard the shout as well and quickly set Bolt toward the ranch house two hundred yards away. It was another few seconds before he was close enough to see the horses then picked up the shadow of a man that he assumed was Russ Abernathy.

Hal reached the main room and reached above the door for the shotgun.

Russ Abernathy wasn't sure what that rancher was planning, but he saw Hal Crenshaw reaching for something, and quickly brought his Colt level and cocked. He took that extra half second to make sure that he wouldn't miss, when there was a thunderous roar behind him.

John had fired the shotgun into the air to distract him from shooting, and it did the job as Russ whirled to see the shooter and kill him if he could.

Hal heard the shotgun blast himself and dropped to the floor, thinking it might be another outlaw fighting off a posse.

Hal Crenshaw was quickly forgotten as Russ Abernathy rapidly thought of ways to handle the newer, more serious threat. He hadn't seen the flash of the shotgun, nor could he spot the gunsmoke in the moonless night, but the sound had come from the northeast. He had to get away from the light that silhouetted him, so he quickly hopped to the ground as he strained to pick up the shadows but cursed his reduced night vision.

After firing the shotgun, John had quickly slammed it into its scabbard and pulled the Winchester, cocking its hammer as he pulled it out, then set Bolt moving forward.

THE DEBT

Russ Abernathy could hear hoofbeats in the distance and was getting nervous. *Who would hunt him at night?* Then, he knew. It was that same damned rancher who had stood him down in front of the café. He had been so humiliated by what had happened that he wanted payback more than he wanted to run.

"That you, rancher?" he shouted.

John shouted back, "It's me, Abernathy. I've come to take you back or kill you. I'd rather kill you."

Despite his desire for payback, the words chilled him. He remembered the eyes, the face, and decided to keep him talking and fire at the voice.

John knew he was putting himself at risk by announcing his position and he decided that he'd have to take an even bigger gamble. He'd let Russ Abernathy have the first shot and he'd fire at the muzzle flare.

He pointed his Winchester where he had heard Abernathy's voice and waited.

Russ kept moving, expecting the rancher to be aiming at his voice, "You aren't gonna kill me, rancher. I'll get you."

John got a better read and was tempted to fire but didn't…not yet.

He replied loudly, "Abernathy, you don't get it do you? I want you dead."

As soon as John had finished, Russ Abernathy thought he had him and could just about make out his form in the shadows, so without any more hesitation, he fired.

John didn't bother wondering where Abernathy's shot went, as he fired his Winchester at the Colt's flame and levered in another round to fire a second shot, but it wasn't necessary.

John's .45 caliber round had left his Winchester's muzzle and a little over a tenth of a second later, had traveled the length of Russ Abernathy's right forearm before ripping his elbow joint out of its socket and shattering the bones in the joint as it left. He screeched loudly and fell to the ground, trying to grab his elbow, but it wasn't there anymore.

John released the hammer of his Winchester and trotted Bolt over to the wailing outlaw chief. He slid his Winchester back into its scabbard and stepped down. He wasn't worried about Russ Abernathy playing possum. Humans didn't make those kinds of sounds voluntarily.

Tess Crenshaw had raced from the kitchen immediately after she had shouted to her husband and seen her husband on the floor. She thought he might be shot, so she quickly ran to him and bent over him. She realized he was healthy when he grabbed her and pulled her to the floor with him, but just to protect her. They had been flat on the floor, listening to the verbal exchange, then the two shots. Russ Abernathy's nearby scream told them that their unwanted guest had been shot, so they were both standing as John reached Russ Abernathy.

John kicked his pistol away from him. In the light from the house, he saw the damage his shot had caused, and it was impressive. He was bleeding heavily, so John jogged back to Bolt and pulled out some pigging strings, then returned to Russ Abernathy and tied one tightly around his upper arm and the bleeding stopped almost immediately.

John stood and pulled Russ Abernathy to his feet and sat him on the porch steps.

THE DEBT

"Hal? Tess?" he shouted.

Hal Crenshaw opened the door, having recognized the voice.

"Did you get him, John?" he asked.

"I didn't kill him. I just made him a one-armed man that'll hang. I'm going to bring him back to Green River. Is Tess all right?"

"He just took our money and some food."

John looked at the horse with the bag.

"I'm sure the food is all there. Let's get your money back."

John stood the shaking Russ Abernathy and began going through his pockets. He pulled out all the money and handed it to the Crenshaws.

"This is a lot more money than he stole from us, John."

"The rest was taken from some poker players at the saloon. They were expecting to lose it anyway. Keep it. Call it the wages of sin."

"Are you the sheriff down at Burnt Fork again, John?"

"No, sir. I'm a temporary deputy though, and just helping Joe Wheeler."

Tess wanted to go and deliver a good, hard kick to cause Abernathy more pain, but just said, "I'm glad you got him, John."

John nodded and said, "Go ahead and grab your food. I've got to get him back to town. Doc Spangler's probably going to have to fix him up a bit."

"Thank you so much, John," said Hal.

"Not a problem."

John yanked Russ over to his stolen horses and he managed to wrangle him into the saddle. He was a bit woozy, but still able to maintain his balance, not that John cared if he didn't take a nosedive into the hard soil.

John extended the trail rope that Russ had made to include both horses, then he used another pigging string to tie Abernathy's left wrist to the saddle horn to keep him in the saddle. He made the binding tighter than necessary, remembering having to cut the bonds from Mattie's wrists when he'd first seen her.

He climbed on Bolt, waved to the Crenshaws and turned back down the access road, then north toward Green River. He never said a word to Abernathy as they rode at a medium trot.

John felt denied by not killing the man. He deserved it for what he had done to Mattie, even if he didn't know she was his daughter. The bastard had shot a woman. It wasn't like Mattie had a gun out or anything. But he knew he couldn't kill him once he was wounded. Hell, he couldn't even let him bleed to death.

They arrived back at Green River just a few minutes later. There was still some activity in the streets, but it had quieted down considerably. He stopped at the sheriff's office first, and left Abernathy on the horse. John stepped down, made sure Abernathy was still alive and then walked into the office.

THE DEBT

Hap McDonnell's body had been removed and Joe Wheeler was at his desk writing reports.

When he saw John enter, he asked, "Did he get away, John?"

"No. He's outside on his horse. He needs to see the doc, though. He doesn't have a right elbow anymore."

Joe jumped out of his chair and exclaimed, "*You got him?*"

"He had just robbed the Lazy C. Hal and Tess are okay. They got their stuff back and I gave them all the money that Abernathy had on him. It was the poker players' money too, but I didn't think you'd care."

Joe snickered as he passed John and said, "I don't. Let's go see him."

They walked outside, and Joe looked at Abernathy's arm.

"Jesus, John! What did you shoot him with, a howitzer?"

"I hit him with Winchester '76 at thirty feet, Joe. That .45 will do some nasty work."

"I suppose we've got to get him over to Doc Spangler's, but I almost hate to bother him."

"You and me both, Joe."

John untied the trail rope and separated the three horses. He tied off the second horse from the saloon to the trail hitch and the sheriff led the horse with a barely conscious Russ Abernathy down the road. They reached Doctor Spangler's house and John cut his pigging string that was securing Abernathy to the saddle, and as soon as the binding was severed, he fell over toward Joe Wheeler who caught him and lowered him to the ground. Both men then lifted him up the steps and set him down on the porch.

Joe knocked on the door and Mrs. Spangler opened it more quickly than he'd expected.

The sheriff said, "Ida, we've got Russ Abernathy. His right elbow is pretty much gone."

"Can you bring that piece of trash into the examination room?"

"We'll do that."

John took Abernathy's shoulders and Joe Wheeler took his legs as they carried him into the examination room and put him up on the table. Doc Spangler had been in the kitchen drinking coffee when they brought him in, but quickly walked into the examination room and had almost the same reaction as Joe Wheeler did when he saw the wound.

"Lordy! What a mess! Shotgun?"

The sheriff answered, "John got him with his Winchester '76 at close range."

"At night?"

Joe turned to John and asked, "How did you get him at night. The moon only came up a little while ago."

"We were intentionally exchanging insults to get a read on each other's position. I let him have the first shot and fired at his muzzle flare."

"Gutsy, John," Joe said as he shook his head.

THE DEBT

Dr. Spangler said, "I'm going to have to amputate that arm, Joe. It won't take long. John's already done most of the work with that Winchester. That tourniquet kept him from bleeding out. I'll be able to get him back to the jail in the morning."

Then he looked at John and asked, "I have to know, John. Why didn't you just let him bleed to death? He's going to hang in a couple of days anyway."

"I couldn't, Doc. If I had killed him outright, it wouldn't have bothered me a bit. But to let a man bleed to death when I could stop it, well, that's different."

Doctor Spangler nodded.

John then asked, "Is Mattie awake, Doc?"

"She was when all the commotion was going on. She knows that you went after him, so I think she still is. She's probably waiting for you."

John turned and left the examination room, crossed the hallway, tapped on the door and heard, "Come in, John."

John opened the door and stepped inside. The lamp was out so the only light was coming in from the hallway.

"John, are you all right?" she asked.

"I'm fine, Mattie. Did you want me to light the lamp?"

"Could you? I want to see you better to make sure you're not lying to make me not worry so much."

John smiled, struck a match and lifted the lamp's chimney. After the wick was set aflame, he lowered the chimney and sat next to Mattie.

"How are you feeling, Mattie?"

She examined him for blood, then replied, "Much better. I'm still sore, of course, but I'm feeling good."

He leaned over and kissed Mattie softly. She seemed content with just a soft message this time.

"I heard what everyone said out there. John, did you stop his bleeding because he was my father?"

"No, Mattie. It's much simpler than that. There's a difference between shooting a man who's trying to kill you and letting an unarmed man die. I know that in the practical sense giving Russ Abernathy two more days of life means very little. But that would have bothered me for the rest of my life if I had let him die. Now, earlier today, in that gunfight with the rest of the gang, Frank Lewis was dying, but there was nothing I could do about it. This was different."

"I understand. Are you still going out there tomorrow?"

"I have to, Mattie."

John paused and then said, "Mattie, I've been debating with myself all day about something. I have valid arguments on both sides, but the best argument was that I wanted always to be honest and never have any secrets between us."

"It's a good way to start a marriage, John."

"It's the only way. Mattie, when I had finished the gunfight down at the outlaw ranch. Frank Lewis was alive, and he told me some things. If he had told them to me just in normal conversation, I'd have put them down as just more lies. But he was dying, Mattie, and I made a deal with him. I told him I'd bury him if he told me the truth. He was afraid of having animals eat at him after he was dead. A lot of men do, so when I told him I'd bury him, he told me things and I could read his eyes. He was telling the truth."

"What did he say, John?" she asked, her pulse rising just from John's tone.

"He said that the woman you knew as your mother wasn't your mother. She was Russ Abernathy's woman after your mother had gone. Russ killed her just before he sent you away."

Mattie looked down at her hands as she asked quietly, "What happened to my real mother?"

"Her name was Prudence Foster. She was a prostitute. Frank said she just left to go back into the business."

"She left me there with that gang?"

John said, "She might have had a good reason, Mattie."

"So, if she were alive, she'd be around forty years old."

"Probably."

Mattie looked at him with her big brown eyes and asked, "John, could we find her?"

"Maybe. They assumed that she just ran off to be a prostitute again. What if she ran off with some cowhand or even one of Abernathy's old gang? She could have gotten married and changed her name. But she wouldn't have changed her Christian name. I don't believe she would have gone that far away either. Are you sure you want to find her, Mattie?"

"I have to know, John. I had that monster for a father, and I'll have my new family, but I would be ever so grateful if you could find her."

"Then I'll find her, Mattie. I promise."

She smiled at him, sighed and said, "I know. Thank you, John."

"Now, you need your rest and I have to do eighty miles tomorrow."

"Alright."

He took her hands in his, looked into her eyes and said, "I love you, Miss Foster."

"I love you, John."

He kissed her gently again, stood, then smiled at her, turned, opened the door, closed it softly behind him and almost smacked into Ruth White, who was walking from the kitchen.

"Oh, excuse me, Ruth."

"That's alright, John. You said you'd be bumping into me. I just didn't think you meant it literally."

John smiled and said, "I was just checking on Mattie. I've got to get back to my room. Is the sheriff still around?"

"I think he returned to his office."

"I need to talk to him again. Goodnight, Ruth."

'Goodnight, John."

THE DEBT

John walked quickly across the parlor, opened the front door and stepped onto the porch. After closing the door, he trotted across the porch and down the steps, then jogged down the road and had to wait for a rider to pass when he reached the main street before he continued his jog to the sheriff's office.

He opened the door, went inside and found Joe was still writing.

"Joe, about tomorrow. Why are we taking a wagon?"

"So, we can bring the bodies back for burial."

"Do we have to bury them here? They don't deserve any services or a proper gravestone. Why don't we just ride down there, you can identify them, and make your notes. I'll bury them on that abandoned ranch while the horses graze, get watered and we'll just ride back. We might do it in a day."

Joe sat back and said, "You know, there's really no reason to bring them all the way back here just to stick them in the ground. You're right. We'll need to bring a shovel, though."

"They already took care of that. There's a pickaxe and shovel down there. They were going to use them to bury Mattie, I think. It's only fitting we use it to bury them. I left a bunch of supplies down there, too. We could ride at a good pace, check them out, bury them and string the horses on the way back. They have three more horses down there somewhere, too."

"That sounds like a plan, John. I'll meet you at Murphy's at seven o'clock."

"See you in the morning, Joe."

John left the office, led Bolt back to the livery, brought him inside, unsaddled him, brushed him down and let him take care of his own needs as he patted his friend on the neck.

"We have a long ride tomorrow, big boy, then it's home, and you just have to walk behind a buggy."

He gave Bolt one more pat on the neck and left the barn, heading for the hotel.

CHAPTER 5

After they had eaten breakfast, Joe Wheeler and John were out of Green River and heading east at a medium trot riding into the bright morning sun. John had written his statement for the Abernathy shooting while he ate breakfast. It wasn't that long. Abernathy was in the jail with Deputy Lee Garrison and Doctor Spangler would check on him every three hours. His trial was set for tomorrow at ten o'clock.

They reached the southern turnoff to the ranch by mid-morning, and John found his supplies just where he had left them. He only took the pickaxe and shovel with him because of the lack of room. It was still awkward, but they reached the ranch before noon.

"Joe, the bodies and the horses are all in the tree line. Let's take the access road and cut over from the house. I'm kind of anxious to drop these damned things as soon as I can."

They turned down the access road and then angled toward the trees. Fifty yards from the tree line John finally could just drop the pickaxe and shovel to the ground. His arms were grateful, but stiff.

As Joe examined the bodies, John led the three horses out of the wooded area to the other side of the house. He brought them to the creek and let them drink. After he thought they had enough, he led them to a pasture and let them graze while he buried their previous owners. They'd have at least an hour to feed because John wasn't going to dig the grave to six feet. He hadn't promised Frank anything other than putting him underground.

He walked back to where he had dropped the pickaxe and shovel. Despite the temperature in the low forties, John stripped off his jacket and his shirt. It was chilly, but he knew he wouldn't be cold for long. He knew the hole would need to be bigger than the last one because the bodies were stiff and only one was straight and that was Big Ed, but his size didn't help.

John started with the pickaxe and worked quickly. He wanted to get this done.

It took him forty-five minutes of hard labor to get the hole big enough to get the bodies inside. He stepped out and saw that Joe had dragged all the bodies out of the woods. He had simply strung a rope around their chests and dragged them behind his horse, no fancy hearse necessary.

They dumped the bodies into the hole and John shoveled the dirt back on top, then tossed the pickaxe and shovel on the mound as their only marker.

"Get everything you need, Joe?" he asked as he quickly donned his shirt over his still wet torso.

"Yup. Got their gunbelts, too. Altogether they didn't even have twenty dollars. Go figure."

"Who says crime doesn't pay?" John said as he laughed.

They mounted their horses, left the gravesite and rode to where the saddled horses still grazed.

"Let's get those horses strung along and we'll head back. We can stop at the supplies and pick up what we need. I'd better make sure I take Mattie's clothes bag along. She'll need to do some more shopping tomorrow anyway if she's up to it."

"My wife can help if she needs it."

THE DEBT

"Maybe Ruth White will need some things too."

"Who's Ruth White?"

"She's Doc Spangler's sister-in-law. She's going to come down to Burnt Fork to teach."

"Have bigger plans for Mattie, do you?" Joe asked as he grinned.

"Much bigger," John replied and grinned back.

They had the horses trotting behind them as they left the Mitchell ranch just two hours after arriving and John never wanted to see that place again.

An hour later, the supplies were distributed among the three trailing horses after Joe and John had helped themselves to some ham and smoked beef.

It was mid-afternoon when they were leaving the site of Mattie's shooting, so they had made very good time.

Once underway, the sheriff said, "John, I forgot to tell you that we have Mattie's rewards in the office. You'll have some more coming for the other four. Did you want me to forward them to you down in Burnt Fork?"

"Just hang onto them for now, Joe. I'll need to come back here soon anyway. I'm going to try to find Mattie's real mother. It'll be tough, I think. She may have married someone else, so she'd have changed her name."

"What was her name?"

"It was Prudence Foster, but I have no idea what it could be now. She'd be forty to forty-five years old now."

"The only Prudence I know is Prudence Harper. She's married to Vance Harper about ten miles north of town. I don't think she's that old, though. I think she's only around thirty."

"I'll find her, Joe."

"I don't doubt that for a second, John."

They rode into Green River just ninety minutes after sunset, then stopped at the livery and dropped off the horses. Joe headed back to his office to check on his prisoner while John took Mattie's clothing bag and walked to Doctor Spangler's house, his stomach rumbling mightily as he walked, reminding him of its neglect.

He knocked on the door, and he wasn't surprised when Ruth White opened the door seconds later.

"Come in, John. Mattie didn't think you'd be back today."

"Neither did I until we decided to forget about transporting the bodies and skipped taking the wagon. We just buried them there."

Ruth nodded, then said, "She's still awake."

"Do you think she'll be able to walk tomorrow, Ruth?"

"I think so. She's gotten out of bed a few times today and she's getting stronger."

"What are you doing tomorrow?"

"Nothing special. Why?"

"I thought maybe you and Mattie could do some clothes shopping before you were sentenced to the wilds of Burnt Fork."

THE DEBT

Ruth laughed lightly, then said, "Honestly, John? My budget doesn't allow for a lot of clothing right now, but I'd be happy to help Mattie."

"I didn't ask you to pay for the clothes, Ruth. You pick out whatever you want, and I'll charge it to the town."

"I find that highly unlikely. You're paying. Aren't you?" she asked as she smiled.

"I'm a citizen, so it's the same thing. Besides, Mattie is now loaded. She has a couple of vouchers for rewards on two outlaws waiting for her. She can't spend that much money in a month, and she won't need to anyway."

"I could use some more clothes."

"Make sure you buy whatever you want, not whatever you need. Don't forget riding clothes, and warm jackets, scarves, hats, gloves. All the things you need to keep warm."

"You really are making me have to take the job, aren't you?" she asked, still smiling.

"That's the plan, Ruth. I'm a very selfish man. I'm trying to keep Mattie to myself and not share her with all the children, just my one boy."

"Then we'll do our shopping tomorrow."

"I'll go and visit Mattie."

Ruth waved him off and John stepped to the door and tapped again.

Mattie's voice echoed through the door when she said, "I heard you out there, John. Come in."

John opened the door and snuck a look around the door jamb, grinning at Mattie.

"And I can still come in after saying I was going to keep you all to myself?"

"Especially because you said you were going to keep me to yourself," she answered as she smiled back.

He stepped inside and closed the door, then took his seat by the head of Mattie's bed.

"I hear you've been up and moving."

"I'm getting much better, John. I hear my father's trial is tomorrow. Do I have to be there?"

"No. He's just being tried for the murder of Hap McDonnell and the man in the bar."

"Good. I didn't want to see him again. John. Just seeing him would remind me of what a fool I was."

"Mattie, you weren't a fool, I told you that. Maybe a bit naïve, but not a fool. Now, you know what he is. His character is so flawed he could simply send you away without a second thought. I think the only reason he didn't send you to an orphanage, or worse, was because he had killed Mrs. Mitchell. Maybe he did feel something for your real mother, too. I don't know. I can go and ask him right now, if you'd like."

Mattie asked excitedly, "Could you, John? Could you ask him about my mother? Maybe he'll know where she went."

"I'll go and do that in a minute. I brought your bag of clothes. You also have two vouchers waiting for you in the sheriff's office for Bill Nelson and Dick Pierce, but I don't know how much they are. Would you be able to join Ruth to do some clothes shopping tomorrow?"

"I may have to just pick things out and have the clerk package them, but I think so."

"Mattie, in all the excitement, I forgot to ask. What happened to your Bulldog?"

"Mrs. Spangler has it. She has all my things, and I'm wearing one of her nightdresses."

"I'm sure you'll buy her something to replace it tomorrow."

"I'll do that and much more, she and Ruth have been wonderful to me."

"You deserve it, Mattie. I'm going to go and talk to Russ Abernathy. He may spit in my face, but I'll try. I'll be back tomorrow and let you know what he says, if anything."

Mattie nodded and then said quietly, "Thank you, John. I love you so very much."

John smiled, then kissed her softly, turned and left the room, leaving a contented Mattie behind.

Three minutes later he was walking into the jail finding the sheriff talking to Deputy Garrison.

"How's the prisoner?" John asked as he crossed the office floor.

"He ain't doing so good, but he's awake."

"Can I talk to him?"

"Sure, if you can get him to talk. He hasn't said a word since we brought him back."

John nodded then headed for the cell and stopped outside the door.

Russ Abernathy was laying on his cot staring at him, not glaring, just watching.

"Abernathy, I need to ask you a couple of things."

He didn't answer but continued to stare.

"It's about Mattie's real mother, Prudence Foster. I just left Mattie in the doctor's office. While you were being treated, she was just twenty feet away. She was there because you shot her, Russ. You shot your own daughter and almost killed her. Tell me what you know about her mother. You owe her that at least."

Abernathy thought about it, and decided to answer, but not because of any sudden rush of paternal love.

"What do you want to know about Prudy?"

"You had a soft spot for her, didn't you?"

"Yeah. Kind of."

"Why did she leave? Frank said she just left while you were on a job and went back to her life as a prostitute."

"Nah. That's what I told them. She ran off with some cowhand from a ranch a few miles up the road. He'd been seeing her whenever we went off on a job. I kind of figured it out after the third job and I guess she told him I was onto him and he took her."

THE DEBT

"Do you remember his name?"

"Peterson. Jerome Peterson. I have no idea where they went, though. I had no reason to go looking for her because I found Jean Mitchell while she was seeing that cowhand."

"You felt bad about killing her. Didn't you?"

"It was a damned accident, but I did hit her. I found out she'd had Frank, and she smart-mouthed me when I asked her about it. I hit her, and she fell into the damned fireplace tools. It was an accident! That bastard Frank didn't even care that she died, either. That stupid woman thought he cared about her, but all he wanted was a night's romp."

"That's why you paid for Mattie all these years, wasn't it? You felt you had to satisfy that debt for killing Jean Mitchell."

"Yeah."

"Did it?"

Abernathy slowly shook his head and replied, "No. I wasted all that money for nothing. I should've just sent her to an orphanage."

"Why are you telling me all this? I expected you to spit in my face."

"I felt I owed you. You had me. You could've let me die there, but you tied off the arm. I don't think it was to see me hang, either. Was it?"

"No, it wasn't. I'm not even going to the trial."

"Why did you do that? I would've let you bleed to death."

"If I had killed you outright or shot you in the gut and couldn't do anything about it, then it wouldn't have bothered me at all. But I had it in my power to keep you alive, so I had to do it."

"That doesn't make a lick of sense to me."

"I know it doesn't."

"You said that was my daughter I shot. Is that the truth?"

"It is. That's why I'm here. She asked about her mother. She wants to find her."

Abernathy spat, "She never should've come to Green River."

"If she hadn't, I wouldn't have found her, and I wouldn't be marrying her."

"You're marrying Mattie?" he asked in surprise.

"I am."

"That's something, I suppose."

"She's turned into a very special young lady and I'm honored to be able to have her for my wife."

"Well, you take care of her now. I'm not going to be around."

John just looked at the outlaw, wondering if there was really any good at all in him, but just said, "Goodbye, Russ."

"What's your name? I know you must've told me at one time or another."

"John Clark."

"Okay. Goodbye, John."

THE DEBT

John stood up and walked past Joe and Lee, gave them a goodbye wave and headed for the hotel. As he walked, he thought about what Russ Abernathy had said. He had sent Mattie off to satisfy a debt he felt he owed to Jean Mitchell for killing her, but in the end, it hadn't. Mattie had returned to satisfy a debt she felt she had for Abernathy supporting her all those years and almost died in the process.

Mattie had eliminated her feeling of obligation when she found out the truth about her father, and in another two days, Russ Abernathy would die, having never satisfied his own debt for killing Jean Mitchell.

How would the feeling of guilt that he had for causing Nellie's death end? That irrational, nagging feeling that he now felt was just as much an obligation that either Mattie or Abernathy had felt. Would it ever leave him, or would he take it to his grave, as Abernathy would?

He went to his room and set down his saddlebags, took off his Stetson, his gunbelt and his boots and climbed into bed. He was still ruminating over his talk with Russ Abernathy when he slipped into sleep.

―――

John was in a better mood when he awakened. He rubbed his eyes and hopped out of bed, grabbed his new shave kit and walked down to the washroom, took a bath, shaved and combed his hair. He needed some new clothes, too.

But first, he needed to have breakfast, so once he was ready for the day, he walked to Murphy's taking long strides and arrived two minutes later, entered and found a table.

"Good morning, John," said an ebullient Nancy as she approached.

"Good morning, Nancy. You seem to be in a happier mood than usual."

"I am. Last night Lee Garrison asked to call on me. Isn't that wonderful?"

"Now that is great news. Lee is a good man."

"The usual this morning?"

"And a lot of coffee."

"I suspected as much," she said then left to get the coffee.

As more diners entered, they would see John and wave as if he was an old friend. John waved back.

Nancy brought his coffee, and as she was setting it on the table, said, "Lee said you shot Russ Abernathy in the dark last night."

"Yes, ma'am."

"And that you let him take the first shot, so you could aim at his gunfire."

"Also, true."

"That's amazing, John. I'll be right back."

She was, too. Nancy returned in less than three minutes with John's order.

She put his plates on the table as John gawked at the amount of food. So much for 'usual'. Six eggs, six strips of bacon, a thick slice of ham, four biscuits and some jam and butter.

THE DEBT

"Thank you, Nancy. I think you're trying to kill me with this much food."

"Just our way of saying thank you, John."

"I'll do my best on this breakfast feast."

Nancy disappeared, and John went to work on his breakfast. It took a while, but he finished it all, and thought he'd never have to eat again. He left a silver dollar on the table, then headed out the door, returning waves as he left.

He walked to the sheriff's office first, finding Joe and Lee in conversation as he entered.

The sheriff looked his way and said, "John, glad you're here. I need you to take these vouchers."

He handed Mattie's vouchers to him. They totaled four hundred and fifty dollars, which surprised him. He didn't think they'd be that much. Mattie could buy a lot of clothes for that much money. He folded the vouchers and slid them into his jacket pocket.

"The trial is at ten. I'll need you to be there. Can you make it?"

"Sure. I need to take care of a few things. Joe, can I ask a favor?"

"Anything short of my job. What do you need?"

"Can you send out a telegram to local law in the area asking if they know the whereabouts of a Jerome and Prudence Peterson? The woman is Millie's mother."

"I can do that. I should get the answers later today."

"I appreciate it. I've got to go down to Miller's Carriage Works and buy a buggy. Then I'm taking Mattie and Ruth White shopping. That will probably be after the trial, though."

"See you at ten, John."

"I'll be there."

John left and walked over to the livery to see how the horses were, and he'd need one for the buggy, too. He stopped short of the livery and looked at the stock out in the corral. There was a nice dark brown gelding that would probably work. For some reason, everyone seemed to want dark horses for buggies. Maybe because buggies were black, *and now that he thought about it, why were buggies always black?* Maybe it was time for a white horse and a white buggy, but not today.

He walked into the livery and shouted, "Fred! You in here?"

"In the back, John!"

John walked out of the livery to the back and found Fred brushing down a handsome gray gelding.

"Morning, Fred. Nice looking gelding."

"I figured you'd need him for that buggy you'll be buying."

"Now, how in the hell did you know that? I only told the sheriff a few minutes ago and came straight here."

"I was talking to Miss White last night when there was all the excitement. She said you were going to get a buggy and drive down to Burnt Fork. So, I figured you'd need a horse and this is the one you'd want."

"You're scaring me, Fred. How much for him?"

THE DEBT

"I won't even quibble this time, John. Just give me thirty dollars and you can have him. Newly shod, too."

"That's a good deal. Thanks, Fred."

John handed the cash to Fred then said, "I'll lead him down to Miller's and pick out the buggy. I think it's time for a trip to the bank as well. I'm getting low on cash."

"Chuck Miller already has your buggy picked out, too."

John just laughed, threw up his hands and took the gelding's reins from Fred who was laughing as well.

John walked the gelding down the street, admiring his gait and lines. He hadn't given Fred any profit on this one, he thought.

He stopped at the bank and cashed a draft for three hundred dollars before going to Miller's Carriage Works. He was going to write a draft for the buggy anyway, but the cash was for Mattie and Ruth's clothes and other things.

He led the gelding into the yard surrounding the Miller Carriage Works and looked at the carriages outside the building.

Chuck Miller saw him coming and walked out of his shop wiping his hands on a rough shop cloth.

"Morning, John. Thought I'd be seeing you today."

"Fred said you already had my buggy picked out."

"I did. I have one that I thought you'd like," he said, then looked at the gelding and said, "That's a mighty handsome horse."

"Fred had him picked out for the buggy."

"He'll look good pulling it, too."

John tied off the gelding and followed Chuck Miller into his shop.

"Here she is," Chuck said, pointing to the buggy.

"That is a nice buggy and looks sturdy, too."

"It's built out of hardwood like the carriage you bought last year. It's a little heavier than the pine ones, but it'll last longer. I even put a couple of blankets in there, figuring it'll be a chilly ride down to Burnt Fork."

John walked around in back and found a solid, wide folding parcel shelf.

"That's bigger than usual on a buggy."

"With the added strength of the hardwood, we could do that. It'll support four hundred pounds. I don't think the horse would like it though."

"I wouldn't think so. How much for the buggy and the harness, Chuck?"

"One hundred and sixty dollars."

"Let's go into your office and I'll write out a draft."

"I appreciate it, John."

"Can I leave the gray with you and pick up the rig in the morning after breakfast?"

THE DEBT

"That's not a problem. We'll take good care of that handsome boy."

John wrote out the draft and shook Chuck's hand.

This trip was costing him more every minute and he wasn't even finished.

He stopped down at the Western Union and sent two telegrams.

JACK CAMPBELL BURNT FORK WYOMING

SORRY ABOUT DELAY
RETURNING TOMORROW WITH TEACHER

JOHN CLARK GREEN RIVER WYOMING

WINNIE CLARK CIRCLE C BURNT FORK WYOMING

RETURNING TOMORROW WITH TEACHER
WILL ALSO BE BRINGING FUTURE WIFE
LOTS TO TALK ABOUT
LOVE TO YOU AND JAMEY

JOHN CLARK GREEN RIVER WYOMING

He smiled as he pictured his mother's face when she read her telegram.

He then checked the time on the telegraph office's clock. He had forty-five minutes before the trial, so he headed for McPherson's Jewelry.

After just a few minutes in the shop, he'd found a nice wedding band set easily enough, but he wanted something nice for Mattie. He doubted if she ever had any jewelry at all.

"Harvey, do you have anything special? I'd like to give Mattie something that would melt her heart."

"Like anything else, John. It comes down to price. If you really want to see something special, look at this."

He pulled out a necklace with a deep red stone that seemed to shimmer.

"What is it, Harvey?"

"It's called Alexandrite. Now watch this."

Harvey walked out from behind the counter and approached the window.

"Watch what it does when it gets more light."

John watched mesmerized as the gem shifted smoothly from a deep red to an equally deep green. As Harvey turned his back on the sunlight, the stone transitioned into a lighter red.

"That's spectacular, Harvey. Are they rare?"

"Very."

"How did you get one?"

"By accident, really. My order arrived from Chicago and they sent this along. It was on the bill, but I didn't order it. I was going to send it back, but it was too impressive. So, I mounted it in this gold necklace."

"How much is it?"

"Here's the pain, John. One hundred and eighty-five dollars."

"Wow! That is pricey. Can you put it in a nice case for me?"

"It has to be in a perfect case, and I have just the right one."

"I'll write you a draft."

John was almost giddy as he wrote out the draft. The Alexandrite was so incredible, just like Mattie.

He handed the draft to Harvey who gave him a suede bag with the case inside.

"Thanks, Harvey. She's going to love this."

"She's a lucky woman, John, and not just for the necklace."

John shook Harvey's hand and left the shop with a huge grin on his face, slipped the bag into his pocket and headed for the county courthouse for the trial.

John took a seat in the back of the courtroom and doubted if he'd be called as a witness. He hadn't been there when either victim had been murdered.

The seats filled up rapidly and soon they were standing in the hallway with the doors open. Russ Abernathy was brought into the courtroom amid jeering and hissing. John was surprised, but he shouldn't have been. Abernathy's name had been at the center of a lot of rumors and bona fide crimes in the area since his gang had arrived.

Joe Wheeler and Lee Garrison escorted him into the courtroom. John noticed the folded sleeve over Abernathy's right arm, and almost felt sorry for the man until he remembered that he had shot Mattie.

They were all told to rise when Judge Gerald Wright entered the courtroom and took his seat.

The prosecutor made his opening remarks, and John watched the jury as he spoke. *Why have a trial?* Those men were nodding their heads at every oratorical condemnation made by the prosecutor, while the defense attorney's opener was met with glares of disapproval.

The foregone conclusion was even more evident when they began calling witnesses. The men in the saloon were called and pointed out Russ Abernathy as the man who shot Ben Chambers. Joe Wheeler was called and described how Hap McDonnell had been found and how boot prints on his neck showed how the prisoner had broken his neck even after he was down.

As he had expected, John hadn't been called and wondered why Joe had needed him there. The jury returned their verdict so quickly that it appeared as if they went into the jury room, walked around the table once then walked back out the still open door.

Russ Abernathy was found guilty of two counts of first-degree murder and sentenced to hang the next morning at nine o'clock.

They led Russ Abernathy from the courtroom to a new chorus of catcalls and hissing. The courtroom was clearing and people he didn't even know came by to shake his hand, but knew most of them. What did please him was that most people didn't say 'thank you for shooting him' or 'thanks for bringing

THE DEBT

him back to hang'. Most said something akin to 'thank you for keeping our families safe' or 'we can sleep better now'.

He finally left the courthouse and asked a passerby if he knew where they'd build the gallows and was told there already was one behind the courthouse. He had never noticed it before.

It was time to take the ladies shopping, so he headed for the doctor's house and arrived two minutes later.

Not surprisingly, his knock was answered by Ruth White.

"Is the trial over?" she asked as he entered, removing his soon-to-be-replaced hat.

"It is. He'll hang tomorrow morning at nine o'clock."

"We'll be gone by then, won't we?"

"We'll be on our way."

"That's good. Come on in. Mattie is already dressed. I believe that she's more than anxious to get out of the house."

"She'll need a new jacket."

"I washed her old one, but there are still some stains. I think a new one would be a good idea."

Mattie heard John enter and walked out of her room, smiling.

John smiled, walked close to her and asked, "Is it safe to give you a gentle hug?"

She replied, "If it isn't, I wouldn't tell you."

John wrapped his arms carefully around Mattie and kissed her softly.

"Are you up to shopping?"

"I'm always up to shopping, although I've never been able to spend much."

"That, Miss Foster, is about to change," John said, then smiled and asked, "Shall we go, ladies?"

John escorted Mattie and Ruth down the porch steps and across the street. They turned the corner onto the main street boardwalk and then only had another hundred yards to the clothing store. It had only been built two years earlier and was a welcome addition to Green River.

As they walked, Mattie asked, "Did my father talk to you last night, John?"

"Surprisingly, he did. If it makes you feel any better, he didn't know it was you he was shooting, but it shouldn't. He still knew he was shooting at a woman. He gave me some leads about your mother that I'm following, but I don't want you to get your hopes up. I'll tell you more when I get a better idea."

She asked quietly, "Do you think she's still alive, John?"

"I really don't know, Mattie. I know you are really hungry for more information, but please don't fall into the same trap you did about your father. Can you let me be the judge about what to tell you?"

Mattie squeezed his arm and said, "I trust you, John. If you find out more, you can decide if I should know."

John smiled at her as they neared the store, having accepted the responsibility for making Mattie either extraordinarily happy when she discovered a loving mother or

THE DEBT

not knowing if her mother had abandoned her and never wanted to see her again or had died in some brothel.

After entering, Ruth wandered off on her own as John kept Mattie on his arm, so he could act as a crutch.

"John, would you be embarrassed if I gave you things to carry for me?"

"That's why I'm here, Mattie."

Mattie smiled and began showing John what she wanted. He didn't really mind the dresses but some of the other, more intimate items, did cause his ears to redden. Mattie noticed and didn't say anything, but had a hard time containing her desire to giggle.

"Don't forget a new jacket, Mattie. You'll really want some heavy socks, too. Especially for tomorrow's long ride. I don't want you getting cold tomorrow."

"I'll be ready."

"I'm going to take these to the counter. I'll be back shortly."

John carried his heavy load over to the counter and left them, telling the clerk he'd be back with more items in a little while.

Meanwhile, Ruth was doing her own damage. John had advised her to get riding clothes and boots, and she added winter clothing as well. She had some, but not enough.

It took several more trips, and when they said they were done, John had the store put the clothes tightly into large bags. Mattie and Ruth had already taken out what they would be wearing on the long buggy ride tomorrow and had put them in a different bag. Mattie had also separated the things she'd bought for Mrs. Spangler. That made three large, heavily packed bags for the trip and two lighter bags for John to carry.

The ladies sat and waited while John quickly added two new shirts, pants, a union suit and heavy socks to the order, and finally, a new Stetson, making his own bag to carry.

John paid for the order and checked to make sure Mattie wasn't too tired before he asked, "Lunch, ladies?"

Mattie nodded and replied, "I wouldn't mind."

The ladies rose, John took his bag and the bags with the clothes they'd be wearing tomorrow and Mrs. Spangler's clothes, then escorted them out of the store and walked to Murphy's wearing his new hat.

An hour after leaving the store, John returned them to the doctor's house.

"I'll have the big bags with most of your new things sent over to the Carriage Works and have Chuck Miller mount them on the back of the new buggy."

Mattie was tired, so she simply nodded, accepted a soft kiss and returned to her room.

Ruth smiled, thanked John for all the things and went to look after Mattie, carrying the two bags with her. Once she was sure that Mattie was back in her bed, Ruth took the bag of clothes to her unsuspecting sister.

As John watched the women leave, Doctor Spangler came out of his examination room, spotted John and walked over.

THE DEBT

"How did she do?" he asked.

"She did better than I expected. She's tired now, though."

"She is doing very well. Young people are like that. She should be fine for the drive tomorrow."

"Thanks, Doc. What do I owe you?"

"Forget it, John. We owe you a lot more."

"Nonsense, Doc."

John pulled out twenty dollars, gave it to Doctor Spangler and said, "You're a good man, Doc. I'll come by and see Mattie again before dinnertime. I don't think she should take another walk."

"No. I think she's had her exercise for the day."

"Thanks again, Doc."

John left the doctor's house carrying his one bag of clothes and walked down to the livery to make sure the horses were all ready to go in the morning. They'd trail all three horses behind the buggy.

After leaving the livery, he was walking back to the hotel and decided he'd stop in at the jail and ask the sheriff why he'd wanted him at the trial.

When he stepped inside, the sheriff waved him in.

"Afternoon, John. Come on back to my office. I've got some things for you," said Joe Wheeler.

John stepped back to Joe's office, thinking that was mighty fast response time for reward money. Usually it takes two or three days.

When he walked in, Joe was sitting at his desk holding a telegram.

"I got four negative responses right away from my inquiry about Jerome and Prudence Peterson. Then I got this one from the sheriff at Lone Tree."

"Lone Tree? That's only eight miles west of Burnt Fork. I know most of those ranchers."

"That's why you may not know this couple. Jerome and Prudence Peterson aren't ranchers. Here, you read it."

He slid the yellow sheet across the desk to John.

SHERIFF WHEELER GREEN RIVER WYOMING

JEROME AND PRUDENCE WHEELER
LONG TIME RESIDENTS
AGE IN FORTIES
JEROME PASTOR OF LUTHERAN CHURCH
GOOD PEOPLE

SHERIFF INGERSOLL LONE TREE WYOMING

"Now I didn't see that coming," John said quietly as he stared at the telegraph operator's scrawl.

"I almost fell off my chair reading that one. I don't know how a minister's wife will react to hearing the news that her past is going to come back to haunt her in the form of a grown daughter," the sheriff said.

THE DEBT

John continued to stare at the message as he said, "I think I'll have to play this one by ear. I'll take a ride over there one day and meet with her privately. If she doesn't want to see Mattie, I can't do anything about it. But if they're good folks like the sheriff says, maybe it'll work out. Can I keep this?"

"I sure don't need it. But you do have to take this, per the judge's order," he said as he held out Russ Abernathy's saddlebags.

"The judge said it should go to his next of kin or you but was pleased to learn that it was going to the same place. It's Abernathy's money. It's more than thirty-five hundred dollars."

Joe took the set of saddlebags and hung them over his shoulder and said, "Thanks, Joe."

"Oh, in case you're interested, the rewards on the other four come to eleven hundred and fifty dollars."

John was surprised again by the amount, but downplayed it when he said, "That'll just about cover the cost of the trip. Can you have them forwarded to my ranch?"

"I'll do that. I also checked with the land office. Your application for adding those canyons to your current ranch was approved by the board unanimously. I think if you'd asked to add the rest of the state, they would have approved it."

John grinned and said, "That's great news."

"John, I know you're leaving tomorrow, but before you go, I really do want to thank you for all the tough things you did for the whole county. You weren't here when we got the telegram about the failed stage robbery in Hopkins. They killed three men in that botched attempt. If Frank Lewis had taken over and added some more men, there would have been a lot more bloodshed. I don't have the manpower to cover the whole county. You know that. What you did just can't be put into words."

"Sure, it can, Joe. A simple 'thanks' is good enough."

"Then thanks, John," Joe replied as he stood and offered his hand.

John stood and shook his hand. He then folded the telegram and put it in his other jacket pocket away from the vouchers.

"I'm sure I'll be stopping by again soon, Joe."

"Don't be a stranger, John. And congratulations on your upcoming wedding. Mattie is special."

"Thanks again for all your help, Joe. Hire yourself a good deputy," John said as he left his temporary deputy badge on the desk.

Joe waved, and John left the office. The land approval was great news, but the discovery of Mattie's mother living so close to Burnt Fork was astonishing, and she was the wife of a preacher, too. That could either be really good news or really bad.

He wondered how you go from a ranch hand to a Lutheran minister. That would be an interesting story if he ever got a chance to hear it. He wondered if the minister knew of Prudence's past history. He surely must have known about Mattie, and that brought up all sorts of other issues. She had abandoned her own daughter to run off with the man.

John really needed to get the whole story before he could make his own judgement about whether to tell Mattie what he'd found.

THE DEBT

It was only mid-afternoon, so after dropping off his own bag of new clothing in his hotel room, he headed back to the clothing store and asked that the enormous bags be sent to the carriage works, then swung by Miller's Carriage Works and informed Chuck Miller of their imminent arrival.

He then walked back to Dr. Spangler's to see Mattie. He hoped Mattie would stick with her decision to let him decide to tell her what he'd found. He knew he couldn't lie to her if she asked and thought about deflecting the possible question by giving her the necklace but knew it would only be a delay. Besides, he really wanted it to be a special moment to give her the unique piece of jewelry. John was going to have to find a way of lying to Mattie without lying if she asked about her mother.

Tomorrow was Thursday, so they when they arrived in Burnt Fork, they'd stop to tell Jack Campbell that school would start on Monday and introduce him to Ruth White. Then they'd continue to the Circle C and settle in for the weekend. He couldn't wait to see his mother and Jamey again. It seemed like it had been a long time, but it had been less than two weeks.

He stopped and paused to think about it. It had been less than fourteen days. Two weeks earlier, the name Mattie Foster had just been an unidentified schoolmarm that needed to be rescued. In a few more days, she'd be his wife and they'd spend the rest of their lives together. It was just an extraordinary amount of change, but it was the best change he could imagine.

He began walking again, stepped up to the doctor's house, knocked and was surprised when Mattie answered the door.

"Mattie! I thought you'd be in bed."

She smiled and said, "Come in, sir. I've been waiting for you."

John stepped inside as Mattie closed the door behind him.

"I had to feel useful, John. Is everything ready for our trip tomorrow?"

"Yes, ma'am. I had yours and Ruth's bags sent over to Miller's Carriage Works and put on the back of the buggy and checked on the horses. We're all set."

She took his arm, then they walked to the sitting room and sat on the couch.

"I have your vouchers in my pocket. You're getting four hundred and fifty dollars, Miss Foster."

"No, I'm not. I'm getting a husband who's going to deposit them into the family account."

"Then you'll be pleased to know there's another eleven hundred and fifty dollars coming."

Mattie smiled and said, "This makes me out to be a regular gold digger."

"You're worth every bit of gold in Wyoming Territory, Mattie, if not the entire planet."

Mattie blushed at the compliment, and said, "Now, you're just getting extravagant, mister."

John chuckled and said, "Oh, and the land office board approved my request to have those three canyons added to our property holdings."

THE DEBT

"That's wonderful news, John. When will you be able to show me the ranch?"

"When you can ride Honey without discomfort, Mattie. When did the doctor say to remove your stitches?"

"He said you did such a good job putting them in, you could take them out in eight days."

"Isn't that asking for trouble, almost wife?" he asked as he grinned.

"Define trouble," she replied with a knowing smile.

"The kind of trouble that we'll be having for the rest of our lives, Mattie."

Then she asked quietly, "John, when can we get married?"

"Today is September 11th. How about the 20th, the last day of summer?"

"I don't know if I can wait nine days, John. I want to be with you all the time, not just the daytime."

"I know. It's tough on me, too. Ever since I met you, Mattie, I've wanted to be with you, but I had to avoid saying anything because I thought there was a chance that I'd be losing you if you went back to Missouri."

"That didn't work out too well, did it?"

"No. But we will work out well. I enjoy every second I spend with you, Mattie."

"I'll admit to a bit nervousness about meeting your mother and Jamey."

"That's only because you don't know them. Once you meet them, you'll be as comfortable with them as you are with me. Just remember that my mother isn't some mother figure, meaning she expects deferential treatment because of her age or position as a mother. We get along because of who she is as a person. Jamey, as I've told you before, is the best boy I know. If you want to get on his good side quickly, ask if you can come along on our next fishing trip."

"I've never been fishing before."

"It's a lot of fun for us, but not just because of the fishing. We get to spend time out on the ranch and enjoy nature. We enjoy being together. I'll buy you some long johns and some britches along with some waders to stay dry. When it gets cool like this, we have a tent."

"That does sound like fun."

"Mattie, the world you'll be entering is special, just as you are. I can't wait for you to officially join our family. You're part of me already."

Mattie teared up just a little before trying to reach over and hug John but had a twinge in her side and pulled back. John took the hint and leaned over and kissed Mattie. It was a long kiss, and Mattie felt her toes curl as John held her softly.

"John, remember when you had to lift me from the horse because of the cramping in my legs."

"Every second."

"I didn't want to touch the ground. I wanted to stay suspended while you held me."

THE DEBT

"I didn't want to let you go, either. I had my face so close to yours. Even then, I wanted to kiss you and that was only one day."

"Then we do think alike," she said as she smiled.

"I'm going to go back to the hotel and get things ready. I'll talk to the folks at Murphy's and have a basket of food prepared for our trip tomorrow, but it'll probably be too cold for a proper picnic. I'll be by early in the morning to pick you and Ruth up in the buggy. We'll drive down to Murphy's, have breakfast and then stop by the livery on the way out and pick up Bolt, Honey and the packhorse, then we'll finally get to head for Burnt Fork."

"How long will it take? I know the stage took four and a half hours."

"We'll go a little slower than that. It'll take us about five and a half hours or so, which will get us there in the mid-afternoon."

"I'll see you in the morning, then."

John leaned over, kissed her one more time, then stood to leave. He picked up his new Stetson and headed for the door, waved at Mattie, opened the door and stepped outside. He hoped the weather stayed like this for at least one more day. It was over fifty degrees, and the sun was shining making it feel even warmer.

John had intentionally not told her about the large amount of Abernathy's cash in the saddlebags. It was too close to his hanging and the thought of getting his money might make her feel some sense of obligation again. He'd tell her when he knew she was ready.

He walked to the dry goods store and bought a picnic set for the food tomorrow. It came with knives, forks and spoons, four napkins and four cups in a bag that could be pulled out, so the food could go in. It was an ingenious use of space.

He carried the picnic basket to Murphy's, explained what he needed to Nancy and asked that they include two large Mason jars full of a fifty-fifty mix of milk and coffee with sugar. She took the basket and said she'd make sure it was perfect.

He had his dinner and tried to think of anything he missed, decided he hadn't and returned to the hotel and just relaxed. Tomorrow was going to be an exciting day.

Winnie reread the telegram she had just received from John. *He was bringing a teacher and his future wife?*

John wired that he had a lot to tell, and she concluded that it was an understatement. Lots of stories about her son and the Abernathy gang had been filtering down to Burnt Fork and some were so outlandish as to reach the level of fairytales.

But if he was bringing his future wife tomorrow, she'd better be prepared.

Jamey came in from the back yard and saw his grandmother reading the telegram.

"Is it from papa, Grandma?" he asked.

"It is. It appears your days of hooky are over. He's bringing the new teacher back tomorrow."

"Maybe she'll be nice," Jamey said as he trotted over to his grandmother.

"I hope so. He is also bringing someone else with him."

THE DEBT

"Who?"

"It seems he's bringing your new mother."

Jamey lit up and exclaimed, *"Papa's getting married?"*

"He says he's bringing his future wife."

"I hope she makes him happy, Grandma."

"I don't think your father would bring her home if she didn't. As many women around here and up in Green River that have unsuccessfully tried to rope him into marriage, this one must be pretty special to win him in such a short time."

"Do you think that I can call her mama?"

"I think she'll be thrilled, Jamey."

"Can I help to make it ready for her and papa?"

"I hope so. We have a lot to do."

CHAPTER 6

John barely slept. He finally got out of bed around six o'clock and headed to the washroom, took a bath, shaved and dressed in his new clothes. He returned to his room, packed his old clothes into the bag and strapped on his gunbelt. After he pulled on his gloves and jacket, he snatched his money-laden saddlebags and hung them over his shoulder, grabbed his Stetson and tugged it on. He picked up his bag and walked out the door, left his key at the desk, crossed the lobby and walked outside.

The sun was already up, and the sky was clear. It was crisp, but not cold. He thought it would be a warm, late summer day which suited his needs and his mood. He trotted down the street, walked into the Carriage Works and found his buggy already harnessed and the clothes securely tied on the back, then tossed his clothing bag and saddlebags into the buggy and sought out Chuck Miller.

"Chuck! Am I ready to go?" he asked loudly unable to find the carriage maker.

Chuck Miller slid out from under a nearby carriage and replied, "No use shouting, John. You're all set. The blankets are in there to keep the ladies warm."

"What, so I can freeze?"

Chuck smiled before sliding back under the carriage, saying, "You've got two ladies to keep you warm."

John laughed and replied, "Thanks, Chuck."

THE DEBT

Chuck was still laughing under the carriage as John left the shop and climbed into the buggy. He drove it out of the yard and onto the street, impressed with the buggy's smooth ride, and arrived at the doctor's house just a minute later. He stepped out of the buggy and put his saddlebags and clothing bag on the back shelf on top of the other bags, then used the supplied cord to tie them down.

He trotted up the porch steps and knocked on the door, which Ruth opened just seconds later. She must be almost as anxious as he was to go to Burnt Fork, but he found that hard to imagine.

"Come in, John. We're both ready to go."

John stepped in as Ruth closed the door and then saw Mattie sitting in a brocaded chair in the parlor smiled broadly. She stood, and John picked up the two clothing bags.

"Ready, Mattie?"

She nodded, and John could see the nervousness in her smile.

"Let's go and get some breakfast and lunch," he said.

John's hands were full, so Ruth handled the door as they all exited Doctor Spangler's house. He walked behind the buggy and secured their bags. It was getting messy back there, but he knew it was only temporary until they got the packhorse and he could transfer some of the bags. He was still grateful for the large parcel shelf.

He assisted Mattie into the buggy and got in himself. Ruth had to fend for herself as she boarded on the opposite side.

"There are blankets in here, too," said Maddie as she discovered the heavy woolen blankets on the red leather seats.

"Chuck Miller said it was to keep the ladies warm on the trip and when I complained, he said the ladies would keep me warm."

Both women laughed as expected before he turned the buggy and headed for Murphy's.

Thirty minutes later, just as they were finishing their breakfasts, Nancy brought the heavy basket and the bag of utensils.

"Thank you for everything, Nancy," John said.

She just smiled and waved as John left a five-dollar gold piece on the table. She had told him that the basket was no charge, but John knew it cost them some time because he doubted if there were just bacon and eggs in the basket. The thing was pretty heavy, especially with those two quarts of coffee milk.

John and the ladies stepped out to the buggy where John helped Mattie into the buggy and set the basket on the floorboard near her feet then placed the bag of utensils beside it, grateful for the ladies' smaller feet. There wasn't much room in front of his much larger boots.

"This is just until I straighten out the mess in back," he said as Mattie pulled a blanket over her lap.

The buggy was soon rolling to the livery where Fred had all three horses ready to go.

After he pulled it to a stop, John and Fred quickly rearranged the back of the buggy and moved the clothing bags to the

THE DEBT

packhorse and his saddlebags to Bolt. John pulled the shotgun out of Bolt's scabbard, checked the load and when he climbed back in the buggy, slid it under the blanket between him and Mattie, who glanced at the scattergun, wondering if John expected more trouble. Ruth climbed aboard, and they were off, leaving the town just after eight-thirty.

"Expecting trouble, John?" asked Ruth.

"Always. You don't want the trouble to arrive when you're not ready."

The buggy rolled effortlessly along as they crossed the railroad tracks and left Green River behind.

"This is really comfortable, John," commented Mattie.

"You're not giving up on Honey, are you?"

"Never in a thousand years," she said as she grinned, then snuggled closer to John.

She had made sure to keep her wounded side on the outside of the buggy for just that purpose.

―――

They were three miles south of Green River when Russ Abernathy dropped six feet and his neck snapped, ending that chapter of Mattie's life.

―――

They rolled along easily for three hours with the talk mainly about the Circle C and Burnt Fork. John had to describe his ranch in detail, and Mattie wanted to hear it again because it sounded almost magical and it was going to be her new home.

They were only fifteen miles out of Burnt Fork when John pulled the buggy over for lunch. The weather had cooperated as the temperature was above sixty and the wind was just a whisper.

"Ladies, did you want to get out and stretch your legs?"

"That sounds good," agreed Ruth, as she stepped out of the buggy and arched her back.

John slid out the same side and walked around the buggy to assist Mattie. As he crossed in front of the horse, he looked south and saw a dust cloud in the distance, stopped for a minute and watched as the dust cloud grew larger and he could make out riders. He had no idea who would be on the road north this late in the day but didn't want to take chances, not with Mattie and Ruth here.

John trotted around to Mattie's side and asked, "Mattie, are you wearing your Bulldog?"

"Yes. Why?"

"Take it out of the holster and slip it into your pocket."

"Alright, John. Is it because of that dust cloud?"

"Uh-uh. It's probably nothing, but I'd rather play it safe."

Ruth walked behind John and asked, "What's going on?"

"I'm just taking precautions. Those riders will be here in ten minutes," then he looked at Mattie and said, "Mattie, give me the shotgun."

Mattie slid the scattergun out of the buggy and handed it to John.

THE DEBT

"John, what can I do?" asked Ruth.

"Get back in the buggy. Mattie, take the reins. If this gets ugly, just go. It's only a couple of hours to Burnt Fork. Just drive and keep going."

"Okay," Ruth replied as she stepped back into the buggy.

"And it was such a nice day," thought John, as he moved his left-hand Colt to his jacket pocket. He counted three riders in the distance. This could be a serious problem.

John continued to watch them approach at a medium trot, but when they were within a half mile, he handed the shotgun back to Mattie.

"Never mind. I know who they are," he said as he returned his Colt to his holster and turned toward the riders.

John waved, and all three men waved back.

"Who are they, John?" asked Mattie.

"Pete Harris, my foreman, Tex Elliott and Joe Freeman. They all work for the Circle C."

Mattie and Ruth both relaxed as the men drew to a stop close to the buggy.

"Afternoon, Pete. Heading for Green River?" John asked loudly.

"No, sir. The boss said to come and meet you. We were all curious to meet your lady anyway, so she really only had to suggest it," he replied.

"You do know that technically, I'm the boss, don't you?"

"You don't really believe that, do you, John?" Pete asked with a grin.

John grinned back and answered, "No, I suppose not. Did you guys have lunch before you left?"

"No, sir. We figured we could have something when we got back. Your mama is making quite a big deal about your return. We've been hearing all sorts of far-fetched tales about gunfights, kidnapping and night shots."

"I'll tell you about everything later. Why don't you all step down. I think there should be enough food for everyone, and I'll introduce you to my future wife and Burnt Fork's new teacher."

They dismounted and led their horses to the back of the buggy and hitched them to the three trailers making a small herd behind the conveyance.

"Fancy new rig, Boss," said Tex Elliott as he examined the buggy.

"It has a nice, smooth ride, and I needed the room," he said before continuing, "Okay, now for the introductions. Ladies, this is Pete Harris, my foreman. That's Tex Elliott and that ugly face belongs to Joe Freeman."

Ruth and Mattie both acknowledged the three men with 'hellos', as the three tough ranch hands nodded and tipped their hats like schoolboys.

"Now, Pete, Tex and Joe. This is my fiancée, Mattie Foster. She's the lady I had to go and chase down in the first place. I not only chased her down, I caught her, too. The other lovely lady is Ruth White. She's coming to Burnt Fork to teach school."

THE DEBT

The three men removed their Stetsons and mumbled 'howdy, ma'ams'.

John couldn't help noticing that as pretty as Mattie was, Pete Harris was watching Ruth White closely, and she seemed to be paying attention to Pete as well. This might be interesting.

John followed the introductions by saying, "Let's see what they packed."

John opened the basket and found what looked like two whole chickens' worth of fried chicken, a large tub of potato salad and an apple pie. There were the Mason jars of the coffee milk as well. John then made plates of food for Mattie and Ruth.

"Gentlemen, we are going to share. Grab some chicken and we can eat the potato salad out of the bowl."

As they began eating, John took one of the coffee milk jars and poured some into two of the cups, handing one to each lady.

When they tried it, Mattie seemed positively enthralled and said, "John, this is delicious. It's coffee and milk with sugar. Is that right?"

"Yes, ma'am. Jamey wanted to try coffee, and my mother made it like this. He really liked it, so I tried it and found out it was better when it was cold."

"Boss, that is one gorgeous buckskin mare you're trailing," said Pete.

"That's Mattie's horse. I couldn't pass her up when I found her in Fred's corral."

They chatted as they ate, and soon were finishing their roadside meal with slices of apple pie before Mattie and Ruth packed the remaining food back into the basket.

"Let's go home, ladies," John said before he assisted Mattie into the buggy and noticed that Pete quickly hustled over to aid Ruth's entry on the opposite side.

The buggy, now escorted by three riders, made good time into Burnt Fork.

John had them stop at Campbell's Dry Goods, then had to have Ruth step out as he trotted inside and saw Jack Campbell.

"You're back! How are you, John?" the mayor asked.

"I'm fine, Jack. Come on out and meet your new teacher. School will start on Monday."

"Wonderful. You brought Miss Foster back."

"Well, I stole Miss Foster, Jack, and I'll be marrying her soon. Miss White will be your new teacher. She's really a good person and had been a teacher in Cheyenne before moving out here."

"You'll have to explain everything later. I'm right behind you."

John led Jack Campbell to the boardwalk where Ruth was waiting and already talking to Pete. When she heard John and Jack approach, she turned and smiled.

"Ruth, this is Jack Campbell. He's the mayor."

"Nice to meet you, Mister Campbell," she said as she continued to smile.

THE DEBT

"The pleasure is all mine. We are really happy to see you."

John then said, "Jack, we've got to get back to the ranch. I just stopped by to let you know that school would be ready to start on Monday."

"Oh, of course. Nice to meet you, Miss White. Good to see you again, Miss Foster, and congratulations on your upcoming nuptials. We never thought we'd get that big galoot married again."

Mattie smiled and blushed slightly as she said, "Thank you, Mister Campbell."

John crawled back into the buggy and had them moving quickly again after Pete helped Ruth back inside. The closer they moved to the Circle C, the more nervous Mattie became, while Ruth was just excited.

Ruth thought that John made the ranch seem like a western paradise, and Pete Harris seemed awfully nice. She remembered what John had told her about being able to marry when they'd first met, and hoped it wasn't just some empty sales pitch to get her to accept the teaching position. She would have accepted it anyway, but suddenly, it seems to have taken on greater significance.

An hour later, they crossed under the Circle C ranch sign, but no house was in sight.

"Where is the house?" asked Ruth.

"The original house is about another mile down on the right. The new house is another half mile on the left. You'll see both when we pass that line of trees.

"Why are they so far apart?"

"The first house was built to be close to a creek for water, but my father wanted a more picturesque location for the new house once he had the money to drill a well."

Five minutes later, the old house came into view and both Mattie and Ruth were surprised how large and well-crafted it appeared.

"John, that's a very nice house," said Ruth.

"We have to keep it up because it means a lot to us."

When the new house appeared, even Mattie was surprised. It was a big house, with two stories and two chimneys with other heat stove pipes. There was a water tower about a hundred yards behind the house that was almost hidden by a stand of tall pines that John pointed out to them.

As the buggy approached John could see his mother and Jamey on the front porch waving. John waved back with a massive grin on his face.

Mattie thought she might be sick which would be an embarrassing introduction to say the least. She had only known Winnie's son for two weeks and hoped that his mother didn't think that she was a gold digger.

John glanced over at her and said, 'It'll be fine, Mattie."

She smiled weakly and nodded as the buggy pulled up to the front of the porch and John brought it to a gentle stop.

Ruth was getting ready to step down, when Pete Harris slipped down from his horse and jogged over to help her exit.

THE DEBT

John stepped out and walked around the horse to help Mattie down. He took her arm and walked her up the stairs to see his mother and son and could feel her shaking.

"Mama, Jamey, this is Mattie. She's going to be your mother, Son. Now you both be careful when you try to hug Mattie. She was shot a few days ago, so she's still sore."

The first words Mattie ever heard from her future mother-in-law were, "What kind of bastard would shoot such a pretty young lady?"

It said so much to her that her fear and anxiety washed away instantly. This was an honest, straightforward woman, just as John had described her.

When Mattie and John reached the porch, Winnie gave her a gentle hug and a kiss on the cheek.

"Welcome home, Mattie," she said softly as she smiled at her future daughter-in-law.

"John has talked about you so much, I feel as if I know you already," Mattie replied.

"Well, he hasn't told me anything about you, but for you to win his heart, you must be very special."

If Mattie had felt immensely better about her new mother-in-law, it was nothing compared to meeting her new son.

She looked down at Jamey, who asked, "Can I call you mama now, or do I have to wait until you and papa get married?"

Mattie smiled, and replied, "I'd like it very much if you called me mama."

Jamey grinned and said, "Thank you, Mama. I'm glad you're marrying papa. You're very pretty."

"Your father kept telling me what a wonderful son you were. I'll be proud to be your mother. Maybe you'll even let me come fishing with you and your father."

Jamey's grin grew wider as did his eyes as he exclaimed, "You want to come fishing with us! Wow!"

"Mama, Jamey, this is Miss Ruth White. Jamey, she's going to be your new teacher."

Jamey walked solemnly to Ruth, nodded his head deferentially and said, "Good afternoon, Miss White."

Ruth couldn't help smiling, as she replied, "Good afternoon to you, Jamey."

Winnie gave Ruth a hug and said, "Enough of these outside greetings. Let's go inside where it's warmer."

John turned to Pete Harris and said, "Pete, can you have all of the bags brought into the house, including my saddlebags and guns?"

"I'll take care of it, boss. We'll get the buggy and horses put away, too."

"Thanks, Pete."

John followed the women and Jamey into the house, and once inside, he found Jamey waiting for him, as expected.

John put his hand on his son's shoulder and said, "I missed you, Jamey."

"I missed you too, Papa. What happened?"

THE DEBT

"Well, I rescued your new mother from the two men who kidnapped her."

"Did you shoot 'em?"

"Yes, sir. I buried them both."

"Then what?"

"Well, I hunted down the rest of the gang and they're all gone, too."

"Wow! Can you tell me about it later?"

"You can listen when I tell your grandma."

"Okay. Papa, I really like my new mother. She seems really nice."

"She's very nice. She's smart and a lot of fun, too."

"Thank you for saving her, Papa. I can't wait to have a real mother. Grandma is nice, but I always wanted a mother."

"She's worth the wait, Jamey."

Everyone had removed their jackets, hats, scarves and gloves and Jamey was impressed that his new mother packed iron. Winnie didn't comment as Mattie removed her Webley, knowing that a lot of stories were forthcoming.

Winnie led Ruth upstairs to her room and John followed, taking Mattie's arm. Winnie and Ruth continued down the hallway, but John stopped at the large first bedroom.

"Mattie, you'll be staying in what will be our bedroom. I'll sleep in another bedroom down the hall."

Mattie looked at John and was hesitant to ask but didn't want to start out their married life by holding back something that bothered her.

"John, can I ask something that might be difficult?" she asked quietly while Winnie was showing Ruth her room down the hall.

"Don't worry, Mattie. Nellie and I were living in the old house when she died. I only moved in here when I returned to the ranch."

Mattie sighed and said, "I know it was a terrible thing to ask."

"No, it's perfectly understandable. That's why I answered it before you asked."

They stepped inside the large room and Mattie said, "It's a beautiful room, John."

John walked behind her and put his arms around her. He leaned close to her ear and whispered, "It'll be our private sanctuary, Mattie. I'll make love to you here and show you how much I love you."

He kissed her on the back of her neck sending a shiver down her spine.

"It's going to be a long nine days, John," she answered hoarsely.

"It'll be worth the wait, Mattie."

He took her hand as they left the bedroom and met Ruth and Winnie walking back down the hall.

THE DEBT

"I suppose I owe you and Jamey all the details about how this all happened."

"You do. I've gotten snippets and rumors from the boys that sound like you've been up to your usual mischief, but honestly, John, most of them sounded too incredible to be true."

"This was much more than just usual mischief, Mama. Trust me."

Winnie laughed, and they all walked down the stairway to the main room.

"You can tell us the tales while we're eating dinner. I've got everything almost done."

"I'll help," volunteered Mattie.

"Me, too," added Ruth.

"I'll be in the main room with Jamey," said John.

The ladies adjourned to the kitchen while John and Jamey sat and talked about father-son things, which included shortened versions of the gunfights.

During dinner, John and Mattie told the full stories about the past two weeks. Ruth, although aware of most of them, was still astounded when she heard the details.

After dinner, Ruth had gone to her room to rest, and Winnie had advised Jamey that his father and new mother needed some private time together, but Jamey didn't mind. He was just glad that his father and new mother seemed to be so happy together, and he was getting a mother who wore a pistol and wanted to go fishing.

John and Mattie were curled up together on the couch in front of the fire and Mattie was so content and comfortable she felt she belonged here.

"Mattie, did you buy a dress to wear on our wedding?" John asked.

"I did, why?"

"Well, I thought you might need something to accent the dress," he said as pulled the fancy box out from his jacket pocket that was hanging over the next chair and handed it to her.

Mattie had never had any jewelry before but had friends in college who had shown her theirs, so she recognized the felt-covered jewelry box.

She opened it slowly and saw the deep red stone and simple gold chain.

"John, it's beautiful! Is it a ruby?" she asked barely above a whisper.

"No, Mattie. It's much more special. Here, let me show you."

John reached over, picked up a nearby lamp, and as he brought it closer, the Alexandrite began to change color. It achieved a purplish blue before he returned the lamp to the table.

Mattie was astonished as he said, "In the sunlight, it looks like an emerald. It changes color with the changing light. It's very rare, Mattie, just as you are."

THE DEBT

She asked, "May I try it on? I've never worn jewelry before."

"I know. That's why I wanted your first to be so special."

He hung the necklace around her throat, as Mattie was overwhelmed with its beauty and John's thoughtfulness for giving it to her.

She pulled John closer and kissed him, then said, "Thank you, John. Not just for the necklace, but for being you."

John just held her softly as she snuggled in closer and felt the heat from the fire, but more warmth inside.

They stayed sitting closely together in silence for another thirty minutes, before John escorted her to the big bedroom, kissed her softly, and as he stepped back, she began to close the door, but held the necklace in her right hand and smiled at him before the door closed quietly.

John exhaled and walked to his own bedroom. As Mattie had said earlier, it was going to be a long nine days.

―――

Friday morning was noticeably chillier. There was a heavy frost covering everything, but it was a working ranch and things needed to be done.

Winnie made breakfast while John and Jamey saddled their horses to go out to the pastures with the boys. Mattie wished she could take Honey along, but knew she had to have her stitches removed before she did any riding and was looking forward to having them out beyond being able to ride again.

After they rode to the western pastures, John pulled Jamey aside and said, "Jamey, I'm going to tell you a secret. This is between you and me. Alright?"

"Yes, sir," Jamey said, knowing it must be important and probably involved his new mother.

"I want you to stay out with the men. I have to go and ride to Lone Tree. Mattie never met her mother just like you never met yours. I think she's living in Lone Tree, and I can be there and back before lunch. It's important that I see her alone in case she doesn't want to see your new mother."

"Why wouldn't she want to see her?"

"Because she abandoned her when she was very young and might feel too guilty to see her now."

His father's reply inspired many new questions in Jamey's mind, but he was sure his father would explain everything to him when he had the time, so he just replied, "Oh. Alright, Papa. I'll be here."

"I'll be back as soon as I can. I've already told Pete that I have to go to Lone Tree and that only the men can know."

"Okay, Papa."

He smiled at Jamey, then waved and set off west northwest toward Lone Tree at a medium trot. From this pasture, it was almost the same distance to Lone Tree as it was to Burnt Fork, approximately seven miles.

He knew the route well. There wasn't a road, but there was a path. He kept Bolt to a medium trot and the outline of Lone Tree came into view before mid-morning. John wondered what reaction Mrs. Peterson would have over the news, and just as

THE DEBT

importantly, he wondered what his own reaction would be when he met her. She had abandoned Mattie with a band of outlaws when she was just a baby to run off with a cowhand.

There was the possibility that she wasn't Mattie's mother, too. Russ Abernathy could have lied to him for some reason, but John didn't think he had. He had seemed resigned to his fate and had nothing to gain by lying.

John arrived in Lone Tree five minutes later. He knew where the church was with its attached presbytery, so he turned toward the church and was soon stepping down. He tied off Bolt's reins and removed his Stetson as he entered the church, finding no one there, so he left, pulled his hat back on and walked around the north side to the front of the presbytery. John stepped up on the small entrance porch and knocked on the door.

A minute later a middle-aged woman opened the door, and he instantly knew she was Prudence Peterson, because there was no doubt that she was Mattie's mother. She had the same oval face and soft brown eyes.

"May I help you?" she asked in a soft, melodious voice, much like Mattie's.

"Mrs. Peterson? My name is John Clark. I own the Circle C ranch south of Burnt Fork. I was wondering if I could have a few minutes of your time?"

"Do you wish to speak to my husband?"

"No, ma'am. I need to speak to you. In fact, you may prefer it to be in private at least until I've had a chance to explain."

"Come in, please, Mister Clark."

John stepped in, removing his Stetson as he did.

Mrs. Peterson led him to a small sitting room, then asked, "Won't you have a seat, Mister Clark?"

"Thank you, ma'am."

John sat down, and Mrs. Peterson took a seat in the couch across from him.

"My husband is talking to the mayor right now, so what do you have to tell me that is so secretive?"

"Mrs. Peterson, I'm getting married in eight days."

"Well, congratulations, but I can't see why that would affect me."

"I'm marrying a wonderful young woman named Mattie Foster."

Suddenly, Prudence Peterson did see how it would affect her as she froze and stared at John without breathing for ten seconds.

Finally, she stammered, "Did you...did you say...did you say Mattie Foster?"

"Your daughter, I believe."

"No, no, you must be wrong!" she exclaimed as she shook her head rapidly.

John kept his eyes on her to watch her Mattie-like eyes as he said, "Mattie was born to a woman named Prudence Foster almost twenty-three years ago. Her father was Russ Abernathy. The woman that raised her until she was seven was named Jean Mitchell. Russ Abernathy killed Jean Mitchell and sent

THE DEBT

Mattie away to Missouri. She graduated from college in June and came to Green River to find her father, believing him to be a rancher, but he was the leader of a gang of thieves and killers.

"There was a power struggle in the gang and some members kidnapped Mattie to force Abernathy out. I caught them and killed the kidnappers in a shootout and rescued Mattie. After another gunfight, the only surviving member of the gang was Russ Abernathy. I captured him, but he escaped from jail, so I went after him again, shot him, and he was hanged yesterday. Before he died, I asked him about you. He told me you had married a ranch hand named Jerome Peterson. That's how I found you."

She stood and began to pace around the small room as John watched. She continued to pace, wringing her hands for another three minutes before returning to her seat.

She looked at John and said softly, "I'm so ashamed. I've lived with my shame all my life. I was so young and foolish. I loved my little Mattie, but I had to get away from there. I felt so helpless. I met Jerome when he chased a loose steer to the front of the house while the gang was away on a job. We fell in love, but I never told him about Mattie because I was getting desperate to leave.

"Then when they were gone on another job, Jerome came with an extra horse and supplies. He had been saving his money, so we ran. I convinced myself that Mattie would be all right but should have taken her with me. Who would hurt a little girl?

"But no matter how happy Jerome and I were, I felt so guilty about abandoning my daughter. Now, I feel like God has punished me for leaving her by denying me another child with Jerome. She must hate me now."

"She doesn't know you're here."

"It has to stay that way. Please. She can't know. I couldn't face her."

"Mrs. Peterson, let me tell you about your daughter; the woman I love and will make my wife in eight days. She found out that her father was a criminal, yet still wanted to meet him to ask him to return with her to Missouri.

"Then, even after finding out that he didn't seem to care about her at all, still chased after him to simply find out if he cared for her just a little. She was so starved for love, Mrs. Peterson, because she'd grown up with no one to really love her.

"Do you know what she earned for trying to catch him? He shot her. Her father cared so little for her that he put a bullet into her. This was even after she knew how little she mattered to him. Mattie is a forgiving, beautiful young woman. She's as beautiful in her soul as she is in every part of her. She craves the parental love that had been denied her for her entire life. I can and do love her completely, but it's not the same."

Prudence looked into his eyes and after a pause, asked, "Do you honestly believe she would forgive me for abandoning her for such selfish reasons?"

"Yes."

"How can I tell Jerome? He'll be so disappointed in me for doing such a horrible thing."

"Doesn't he love you?"

"Of course, he loves me."

THE DEBT

"Then it shouldn't a problem. You explain to him just as you did to me. You were young and made a horrendous mistake, as we all do, and young people make more often. But unlike most of those early mistakes, you'll have the opportunity to correct it and soothe your guilt. This is your chance to make everything right, Mrs. Peterson. You can erase that guilt that's haunted you for twenty years. You owe Mattie the chance to make things better for both of you."

Prudence sat there chewing her lip. She never said how she still had dreams of Mattie and often nightmares as she imagined bad things happening to the only baby she'd ever carried.

John continued, saying, "Mrs. Peterson, this is a chance to regain the love of your only child. You'll be able to play with your grandchildren. Don't pass this up because of the fear of disclosing a past mistake to your husband. If you don't want her to know, I'll honor your wish, but I think it would be making a bigger mistake than you made twenty years ago."

Prudence knew John was right. If she knew that Mattie was here, denying her would make her nightmares worse and Mattie would never know her.

"Alright. I'll tell Jerome. Can you wait until he returns? He'll be back shortly."

"I can. What would you like to know about Mattie?"

Prudence finally smiled as she answered simply, "Everything."

John smiled and began telling Prudence about her daughter. John could see her mother's pride in Mattie taking hold. He could see the long-hidden mother's love emerging from its cocoon as well. Prudence was becoming a mother again.

John talked for twenty minutes non-stop when the door opened.

"Prudy, whose horse is out front?" her husband asked as he entered the room. Then he saw John, who stood.

"Oh. Hello, I'm Reverend Jerome Peterson," he said, extending his hand.

John shook his hand and replied, "I'm John Clark. I own the Circle C ranch seven miles east of here."

"I wondered who owned that spread. It's very impressive."

"It is. I just stopped by to tell your wife about my upcoming marriage."

"Congratulations. Did you need someone to perform the ceremony?"

"Perhaps. Can we sit?"

"Certainly. Who's the lucky bride?" he asked, taking a seat next to his wife.

"Mattie Foster."

"That's a coincidence. Prudence's maiden name was Foster."

Prudence then said quickly, "No, Jerome, it's not a coincidence at all. Mattie Foster is my daughter."

Jerome slowly turned to Prudence and asked quietly, "Your daughter?"

Prudence began to weep softly as she confessed, "Jerome, I'm so ashamed of myself. I should have told you, but I was so afraid you wouldn't take me away from that horrible place twenty years ago that I abandoned my little girl. I've hated myself for all this time for what I did. It consumed my very soul. I've wanted to tell you for so long, but the longer it went, the harder it became."

John wondered if Jerome knew about her previous life as a prostitute but wasn't about to bring that into the discussion. It meant nothing to him anyway.

Jerome looked at Prudence with soft eyes and took her hands as he said, "Sweetheart, you could have told me. I would have loved to have your little girl with us. How could I not forgive you for a young woman's mistake? God must have been looking out for her and now He has returned her to you."

"You don't hate me?" she asked softly as she looked at him with wet eyes.

"No, my love. I don't hate you. Did you want to meet her?"

Prudence turned to John and asked, "Could I meet her?"

"I'm sure she would be thrilled, but I have a better idea for the introduction. Reverend, would you like to perform our marriage ceremony?"

He smiled and replied, "I would enjoy nothing more."

"Then why don't we set up a meeting? Mattie can't ride right now because she's still recovering from being shot by her father."

"What?" exclaimed Jerome.

"Your wife can explain after I'm gone. I have to get back quickly. Can you perform the ceremony at the Burnt Creek church on the twentieth of September at eleven o'clock?"

"I can."

"If you can meet us there tomorrow at ten o'clock, I'll bring Mattie in our buggy, then we'll see how it goes. I won't tell her who you are until we're there."

"We'll see you tomorrow morning at ten."

"Before I go, I have to ask one question that's been just buzzing around in my head. How does one go from being a cowhand to a Lutheran minister?"

Jerome smiled, and replied, "I grew up on a ranch before I went off to seminary. After I was ordained, returned to work on the ranch until I was assigned. I received my assignment to Lone Tree and took Prudence with me."

"That mystery is solved then."

John stood and shook the reverend's hand. He was going to do the same to Mrs. Peterson, but before he could, she leapt forward and hugged him.

She then stepped back and said, "Thank you, Mister Clark. I can't wait to meet my Mattie again."

"No matter how wonderful you think she may be, Mrs. Peterson, you'll discover that she's even better, and just to let you know, when I first saw you, there was no doubt in my mind that you were her mother. She has your face and eyes."

Prudence glanced at her husband, smiled, and then looked back at John but couldn't speak.

He smiled back, then pulled on his Stetson and left the presbytery. He mounted Bolt and was back in the pasture with the men and Jamey before lunchtime.

Jamey trotted over to his father and asked, "Did you find her, Papa?"

"I did. I'm taking your new mother to the church in Burnt Fork tomorrow morning to meet her own mother."

"I wish I could see it."

"I know, but this will be a very private moment between a mother and her long-lost daughter."

"I understand, Papa. My new mother will be even happier, won't she?"

"She will."

The men and one boy all returned for lunch an hour later.

That evening as they sat around the dinner table, John said, "Mattie, we need to meet with the preacher tomorrow morning at ten about the wedding. We'll take the buggy. Okay?"

"I'm already getting excited, John. A week from tomorrow I'll be your wife."

"It'll be a long week, won't it, Mattie?"

"It'll seem like seven years, not seven days."

"When can we see the ranch, John?" asked Ruth.

"It has to be done on horseback, so I have to wait until Mattie can ride. I'm sure Pete Harris would love to show it to you tomorrow."

Ruth blushed but replied, "That was my impression, too."

"I'll let him know that you'd like a tour. Mattie, can she borrow Honey?"

"Of course, she can. I was going to suggest that."

"Good. Then tomorrow, we'll set off to Burnt Fork at nine o'clock and Ruth and Pete can see the ranch. Jamey, after dinner, I want you to show your new mother your fishing pole and tell her how it works. We'll be going fishing once more before the snows arrive and I'll buy her a pole when we're in town tomorrow."

"Okay, Papa."

When dinner was finished, John suggested that Mattie might want to take advantage of the bath before meeting the minister tomorrow, and she readily agreed.

He escorted her up the stairs, opened the door to the big bedroom, then gave her a quick kiss before she closed the door.

John trotted back down the stairs and waved his mother and Ruth over.

Once they were close, he said quietly, "This will be short. Tomorrow, I'm taking Mattie to meet her mother she hasn't seen in twenty years and had believed was dead until a few days ago. Her mother is married to the reverend who will perform the ceremony. I went over there to Lone Tree today to meet with her and arrange the surprise. I'll tell you both the long story later, but she won't know until I introduce her tomorrow."

Both women began to smile as tears arrived in their eyes.

Winnie said softly, "No man ever gave a greater gift to his bride."

Ruth just nodded as she dabbed at her eyes with her handkerchief.

"Let's get going on these dishes," Winnie said before she and Ruth disappeared into the kitchen.

When Mattie finally returned from her bath forty minutes later everything seemed normal, but Ruth and Winnie had to limit themselves to short comments, so Mattie wouldn't grow suspicious as they tried to keep the secret.

John had no such problems, as he had spent hours playing poker with the boys and had developed an outstanding poker face that rivaled his scary face.

Later, when John and Mattie had their private time on the couch in front of the fire, Mattie curled in close to John and said, "John, I couldn't be happier. My life is so complete now. You can't imagine how happy you've made me."

"Just as happy as you've made me, Mattie, but it'll only get better."

"You keep saying that, but I don't see how that's possible, except for the popcorn and hot cocoa."

"It's not nearly cold enough. You'll know when the time is right."

"The worst weather we had in Missouri was the ice storms. We'd get heavy snow and tornadoes, but the ice storms were the worst."

"We get those and some really nasty blizzards too, but the spring and summer make up for it. When the wildflowers are all over the hills and the sun is warm, there's no better place to be."

Mattie whispered, "I'm home, John."

John leaned over and kissed the top of her head, while trying to imagine how much happier she would be tomorrow.

―――

Saturday morning began routinely. They all ate breakfast with Ruth taking some well-deserved barbs for her upcoming 'tour' of the ranch with Pete Harris.

As long as she was taking the hits, Ruth asked, "John, remember you said that married women should still be able to teach? How could that happen?"

"I'll go and talk to Jack Campbell and the councilmembers tomorrow and bring that subject up. It's a silly thing, really. You're still the same person the day after you're wed as you were the day before, so why should that disqualify you from teaching?

"I know they're all worried about the whole pregnancy issue. The children must be protected from such a blatant display of creation. Really? Don't they even know where they come from? Anyway, I'll talk to them and see if that rule can go away. If not, we set up our own school."

"You can do that?"

"Sure. There are thousands of private schools. If we fund it, we do what we want."

"Let's hope they listen."

"They will," he replied, then turned to Winnie and said, "Oh, Mama, in all the other news I forgot to mention that the land office board approved the addition of the canyon property. Our taxes went up, but it's worth it, don't you think?"

"John, those canyons are gorgeous. I have a feeling there are some minerals worth finding in there as well."

"The plateaus above the canyon are rich ground as well. There is a lot of grass in those canyons and I think we'll have to add at least two more hands in the spring."

"Will Pete show me the canyons, too?" asked Ruth.

"I'm sure he will. I don't think I told him yet, so you get the honor of telling him that the canyons are now part of the Circle C and he'll be hiring two more men in the spring."

"I'll do that."

"Well, we'd better get ready to go, Mattie. The weather looks good."

"I'll dress warmly anyway. I don't have a beard to protect my face."

"I shaved this morning, lady. One of these days, I'll skip shaving and get really friendly with you to let you appreciate a smooth-shaven husband."

"Then I'll shave you myself. Do you trust me with your razor?"

"Never mind. I rescind my previous threat."

She laughed, then waltzed from the kitchen. Mattie was going to practice for her wedding and was so ecstatic that she couldn't imagine a happier day.

Just before ten o'clock, the buggy arrived at the Burnt Fork Church and John noticed another buggy already present.

"Looks like Reverend Peterson is already here," he said.

"Who's Reverend Peterson?"

"Reverend Jerome Peterson from Lone Tree. I asked him to perform the ceremony. You'll like him. He's a good man."

John stepped out of the buggy and tied the reins on the hitch rail, then walked around the buggy and helped Mattie out.

"How is your side?" he asked.

"I hardly notice it anymore."

"I'll take those stitches out on Thursday. That way we can have a fun wedding night."

"As if that would stop you," she said as she laughed and held his arm closely before they began walking to the church.

Inside the church, Prudence was more nervous than she had ever been before. She was wringing her hands and pacing, just as she had when John had first told her about Mattie.

Jerome watched his wife and hoped that this all worked out. She had been an emotional disaster after John had gone, with guilt, love, shame and pride making a volatile mix.

THE DEBT

The door opened, and mother and daughter saw each other for the first time in twenty years, but only one knew of their relationship. Jerome saw the resemblance immediately, just as John had when he first saw Prudence.

"Looks like the reverend brought his wife," John said, then added, "Good morning, Reverend and Mrs. Peterson."

"Hello, John, and this is your fiancée?" Jerome asked as the couple approached the front of the church.

John and Mattie reached the first row of pews and stood before Jerome and Prudence.

Prudence tried not to stare at her daughter but couldn't help herself, but Mattie didn't notice.

"Mattie, I'd like you to meet Reverend Jerome Peterson and his wife."

"Hello. It's so nice to meet you both," Mattie said as she smiled.

John couldn't hold the secret any longer as he looked at his fiancée and said quietly, "Mattie, Mrs. Peterson's name before she married the reverend was Prudence Foster."

Mattie almost fell as her knees weakened and they lost their ability to support her. John expected it and caught her before she fell.

Mattie stared at Prudence, whose eyes were welling with tears and whispered, "Mama?"

Then the dykes burst as both women clutched each other, and their faces were flooded in tears, Mattie totally forgetting about her gunshot wound. John glanced at a smiling Jerome Peterson and grinned himself.

Prudence was sobbing and begging forgiveness from Mattie, as she managed to say, "I'm so sorry, Mattie. I abandoned you. I was young. I was young, foolish, stupid and selfish. Can you ever forgive me, Mattie?"

Mattie's choking voice was offering only forgiveness and love as she replied, "You're my mother. That's all that matters to me. I'm so happy to have found you. Nothing else matters. Nothing. I love you, Mama."

John had thoughtfully stashed four handkerchiefs in his pockets and handed one to each woman. They quickly began wiping their faces as he handed one to the reverend, which was gratefully accepted and kept one for himself.

"Mama, you live near here?" asked a breathless Mattie.

"I live in Lone Tree. John can reach it in forty-five minutes from his ranch."

Mattie turned to John and hugged him gently as she whispered, "Thank you so very much, John. And I thought I couldn't be any happier."

John hugged Mattie carefully and had to use his handkerchief after all.

They had to do a rudimentary rehearsal for the wedding, but it was a basic ceremony, so it didn't take long. The real goal for the trip had been met.

After the rehearsal, John said he needed to go to talk to the mayor and council members and also had to explain to

THE DEBT

Reverend Davenport why he wasn't performing the ceremony to smooth any ruffled feathers.

He left knowing that Mattie and her mother needed time to talk, a lot of time.

His visit with Mister Davenport didn't take long. He was touched by the story John told him and asked if he could attend the ceremony. John said he could, so he was happy about the situation.

He found Jack Campbell in his store and told him that his new teacher might not be unmarried very long. He was getting tired of trying to find teachers for the town, so he was amenable to John's idea. They corralled the council members and two endorsed the idea, the third agreed but grumbled. John even remembered to buy Mattie's fishing pole before he left the store, which surprised him.

His jobs for the day completed, John returned to the church. When he entered, he heard female laughter echoing in the building, which was a good sign. By the time his eyes adjusted to the darkness, he could see Mattie and her mother sitting side by side in a pew chatting as if they had never been separated. Jerome was sitting at the end of the pew letting the women talk.

Mattie heard John enter and turned to see him walk down the aisle. Her turn to make that walk would be coming soon. She thought he'd only been gone a few minutes, not an hour.

"Back so soon, John?" she asked as she grinned. It was hard for her to have any other expression.

"I took care of the married teacher issue and talked to Reverend Davenport to smooth any ruffled feathers."

"You did that quickly."

"Actually, I kind of dragged it out so you and your mother could talk for a while."

"How long were you gone?"

"A little over an hour. Surprised?"

"Very. I thought you were gone for just a few minutes."

"What's next on the agenda?"

"Mama and Jerome are going to go back to Lone Tree. Can they stop by the ranch sometime?"

"Anytime. They're always welcome. If they ride a horse, they can cut the distance in half. There's a path that I follow that enters Lone Tree near the church. Just look for the white painted boulder. It'll take you right to the ranch."

"That will save time," said Prudence.

Jerome, seeing that the reunion was finished, wandered over as Mattie and Prudence stood and hugged one more time.

"See you next week, Mattie," said Prudence.

"I'll see you at the wedding, Mama," she said as she smiled. Mattie flushed just saying 'mama'.

Jerome and Prudence walked back down the aisle and left the church, waving once more before the door closed.

"How did you do that, John?" asked a very contented Mattie as she held his hand.

"Before the trial, I talked to Russ Abernathy in his cell. I think he'd resigned himself to his upcoming death and told me what had happened to your mother and who had taken her away. I

THE DEBT

asked Joe Wheeler to query surrounding law enforcement asking for the whereabouts of a Jerome and Prudence Peterson, and he received a response from Lone Tree.

"I rode over there yesterday to talk to her because I wanted to make sure that she would see you. The worst thing for you would be if I had told you about her and you decided to meet her yourself, then she refused to talk to you. That would be like you'd experienced with your father all over again, and maybe worse."

"But it didn't. You made this happen, John, and I believe I'm the luckiest woman in the world," she said as she clutched his arm.

John wasn't sure if she was referring to their upcoming marriage or finding her mother, but it wasn't important. Mattie was happy and that was all that mattered.

Then John said, "Mattie, after your father's trial, I met with the sheriff and he gave me a set of saddlebags. The judge decided that the contents should go to either you or me. Inside was over thirty-five hundred dollars."

Mattie said quietly, "I don't want the money, John."

"I knew that you probably wouldn't, Mattie, and I'd been trying to come up with something appropriate to do with it, and I think that maybe if we added a donation to tomorrow's service at the Lutheran Church in Lone Tree would be the best place for it. Reverends in small towns don't make much money."

Mattie brightened and exclaimed, "That's wonderful idea, John!"

"So, we'll meet with my mother, Pete, Ruth and Jamey and we'll attend services tomorrow."

Mattie felt like dancing when she took John's hand as they left the church, stepped into the buggy and drove back to the ranch with Mattie chatted continuously about her mother, telling John everything that Prudence had told her.

When they reached the house, he helped Mattie out of the buggy and escorted her inside while he returned to put the buggy and horse away. He was smiling as he walked back down the porch steps because he could hear the excited conversation between Mattie and his mother. He didn't doubt that tears were being shed, either.

Ruth and Pete returned two hours later and before she could ask how the reunion went, John told her about the mayor's decision, which had the expected effect. Why it had such a positive impact was no mystery either. For Ruth, it was having her cake and eating it too. She could teach and be married, a situation she never thought was possible.

Then he told them about his plan to attend services tomorrow morning and make a generous donation to the church. He'd split up the cash, so each of them could contribute.

An hour later, while everyone else was in the house, John left and walked the half mile to the old house and went inside. He stepped slowly toward the first bedroom and after entering, sat on the bed then turned his head to the pillow.

"Nellie, what are you thinking? I still have that nagging sensation that I'm missing something. I don't believe that it's guilt anymore for what happened to you, but is it an obligation? Is it like the debt that Mattie or her father felt? If so, how can I satisfy it? What do I have to do to be fully at peace after that terrible night nine years ago?"

THE DEBT

John then sat in silence for almost a minute before standing, then blew out his breath, turned slowly on his heels and left the room and then the house. He picked up the pace and returned to the big house, not really expecting an answer.

CHAPTER 7

The week before the wedding flashed past, the surreptitious donation of Russ Abernathy's cash being not so stealthy when the cash was spotted in the baskets. As welcome as the donation had been, Prudence and Jerome were more pleased about seeing John and Mattie along with the rest of the family. They spent another two hours in Lone Tree before returning to the ranch.

Ruth began teaching the next day and Jamey reported that the students were all tickled pink about the difference between Miss White and Miss Hall. They were actually enjoying going to school, or at least they didn't complain as much.

John removed Mattie's stitches on Thursday and couldn't resist kissing her healed wound after taking out the last thread, giving her a majestic rush as she felt his lips on her skin and creating a massive arrival of goosebumps.

Mattie surprised herself when she put her hand on his neck and asked John not to stop, which wasn't difficult. John moved his lips along her body, and she thought she'd faint from the experience, but John told her he had to stop. He said as close as it was to their wedding, he could hold off but barely.

The wedding preparations weren't as horrible as some. It was going to be a simple affair with just the ceremony and then the departure of the newlyweds to their home.

Pete volunteered to drive the carriage with Mattie, Winnie, and Ruth. John would take the buggy, so Pete and Ruth could

THE DEBT

ride back together. Jamey and Winnie would accompany the bride and groom back to the house in the carriage.

The day of the wedding, the last day of summer, was more summer-like than it had been for three weeks, which allowed everyone to forgo the heavy jackets. John left first driving the buggy with Jamey. John was wearing his only suit and had not been allowed to see Mattie after she went into her room to change. Winnie and Ruth had told him originally that he couldn't see Mattie all that morning, but that proved to be difficult as they lived in the same house.

He arrived at the church and tied off the buggy behind the church, then he and Jamey went inside, took a pew and waited.

"Papa, how long is this going to take?" he asked.

"Not long, Jamey. What do you think of your new mother?"

"She's great, Papa. I can see why you like her so much."

John smiled and said, "That is an understatement, Jamey."

Guests began filtering in as the time passed. No invitations had been sent, but many townsfolk showed up.

Reverend Peterson and Prudence arrived fifteen minutes before the ceremony, and Prudence walked to the back of the church as John stood and walked to the altar near Reverend Peterson. Pete Harris was going to be his witness and Ruth was going to be Mattie's.

"There's some significance there," John thought.

The carriage with Mattie, Winnie and Ruth arrived just after the reverend had entered the church. Pete tied it off and assisted each lady from the carriage before trotting inside to join John at the altar.

Mattie wasn't nervous at all, which surprised her. She was anxious, though. After the removal of the sutures, she couldn't wait to be John's wife completely. She walked up the four steps into the church and was met by her mother as Winnie and Ruth hurried past and found their reserved seats in the front pew recently vacated by John.

Mattie hooked her arm through her mother's and began to walk quietly down the aisle, holding back her tears because she was so absolutely content and happy. She was walking down the aisle holding her newly discovered mother to be married to the man who made this and everything else possible.

John watched Mattie approach and tried to slow down his pounding heart but failed. Mattie was wearing an ivory satin dress that had a hint of gold. She was wearing her Alexandrite necklace and it had already transitioned to its ruby-like appearance.

It was her eyes that captivated his attention. He couldn't stop looking into her eyes because there was so much there. But what pleased him the most was her glowing, joyful face. She had been through so much in the past month. She had experienced so much fear and worry, had been lost and had nowhere to go. She had learned so many terrible things about her past and had no future, until that day when he had found her on the dirty floor in that dilapidated house. Since then, things had changed for each of them. Now they would share a very bright future, and there would be no more lonely nights for Mattie.

Mattie reached the altar and took John's hand.

THE DEBT

Reverend Peterson began the marriage ceremony. Both mothers were already tearing as John and Mattie exchanged vows and were soaking their handkerchiefs by the time the couple placed the gold bands on each other's fingers and totally lost control when John took Mattie in close and kissed her to seal the marriage.

John and Mattie left the church without noticing the smiling faces on either side of the aisle. As they approached the door, Mattie's necklace changed quickly to a deep green and John led her down to the carriage and helped her inside.

"I suppose we have to wait for our mother and son, Mrs. Clark," he said as he smiled at his bride.

Mattie flushed and replied, "I think so, husband."

Winnie and Jamey stepped down from the church and entered the carriage, then John stepped up onto the driver's seat and turned the carriage back toward the ranch. Not surprisingly, John had the carriage moving at a brisk clip on the return, a fact commented on by Winnie.

The carriage arrived just forty minutes later, and John parked it in front of the house. Tex Elliott was waiting with a 'I know what you're gonna be doing later' grin as he took the reins of the team and let John help his new bride and mother down from the carriage while Jamey popped out of the other door.

"Thanks, Tex," John said as he held Mattie's hand.

"Anytime, boss," he replied, doing everything short of winking.

The newlyweds entered the house where Winnie and Ruth had already prepared a big lunch.

John and Mattie kept exchanging glances as they moved among the family and guests, each anxious for their first private moment together as husband and wife. It was only noon and the clock didn't appear to be moving.

Pete and Ruth arrived twenty minutes later. They must have taken the circuitous route.

After lunch, Mattie had an unusual wedding day request.

"John, now that I don't have any stitches, can we take a ride to see the waterfall?"

John was pleasantly surprised and said, "Mattie, that's perfect. I'll go and saddle the horses."

"I'm going to get changed and I'll meet you in the barn."

John smiled and went upstairs to change quickly as well and was soon quick stepping down the stairs and out the door.

Before she walked up the stairs to her room, Mattie turned to her new mother-in-law and said, "Since we've been together, John has talked a lot about the ranch and the trout streams and the lake and the waterfall. I've never seen a real waterfall. I can't wait."

"It's not a big waterfall like Niagara Falls, but it is impressive," said Winnie.

"Can I come?" asked Jamey excitedly.

Before Mattie could answer, Winnie replied, "No, Jamey. Not this time. You stay here with me."

"Okay, Grandma," a disappointed Jamey replied.

"We'll be back. John said it took almost an hour to get there."

"It does, but it's a beautiful ride," said Winnie.

Mattie walked quickly down the hall and up the stairs to what was now their bedroom as John had moved his clothes in earlier. Ten minutes later, Mattie returned wearing her riding skirt, a white blouse, light jacket, her boots and her Stetson. She had thought of taking her Bulldog but thought John would be more than well enough armed for both of them.

She waved at Winnie as she left the house, trotted down the porch steps and saw John walking Honey and Bolt in her direction. She smiled and jogged to meet him.

"Need help getting mounted, Mattie?" he asked.

"Only to inspire you, my husband of one hundred and forty-two minutes."

"Like I need more inspiration," he said as he grinned at her.

"Let's go see the waterfall," she said after she had boarded Honey.

John wheeled Bolt to the southeast and set off at a trot as Mattie joined him and soon, they were both riding comfortably across the open ranch land.

"Where's the herd?" she asked.

"Right now, most of them are in the southwestern pastures. They'll need to be moved to the northeastern pastures pretty soon."

"When will you move them to the canyons?"

"In December. Those three canyons are perfect. They have a lot of grass and water and the cattle will be protected from the wind and snow. We won't lose as many if the winter is a bad one."

They reached the first trout stream and followed it due east. Occasionally, a large trout would leave the water making Mattie laugh.

"This really is beautiful, John."

"It is. But I'd rather look at you, if that's alright."

"You're no longer limited to just looking, you know."

"Trust me, I know."

After another thirty minutes, Mattie spotted the waterfall. It was almost eighty feet high and could be heard for miles. They reached it five minutes later and they stepped down. John hitched the horses to a post he'd driven into the ground himself years ago.

He took her hand in his as they strolled closer to the thundering water.

"John, it's magnificent. That pool is so enticing. It makes me want to dive in."

"It stays cold all summer, but it is invigorating."

"You've swum in it?"

"Since I was a boy. I'm the only one I know that has except for Jamey. We come here and fish about a mile downstream. See the top of the waterfall? That's the plateau that the four canyons go into. That fourth one doesn't have much grass, but it may be the most interesting. I'll show it to you one of these days."

Mattie put her arm around John's waist and John put his arm across his wife's shoulders.

She turned to look at him and said quietly, "John, make love to me now. I don't want to wait until we're in a dark bedroom. I want you to love me now. Here."

John turned to Mattie and kissed her in reply to her request. They walked back to the horses and John took a bedroll off and let it unfurl.

Mattie watched as he prepared their marital bed and was much more excited than nervous. She had heard all the stories and talk about it from her friends in college, but she knew her husband would do everything he could to make her happy.

An hour later, they were snuggled together in the bedroll. Mattie was more contented than she could have thought possible. She felt like a woman now, not some innocent girl. John had been everything she had hoped for only so much more. He had talked to her, made her feel alive and wanted.

By the time they had consummated the marriage, she had wanted him more than she had wanted anything in her life, and now they were together closely entwined with the roaring waterfall a few dozen yards away, throwing up a mist that they could feel if the wind shifted.

"John, does this pass for a wedding night even though it's the afternoon?"

"No, ma'am. You're not getting away that easy. This was a preliminary to our wedding night. I fully expect to entertain you again in our bedroom."

"Will you curl my toes again?"

"Every time, Mattie. I can't tell you how exciting you are to me. I'll never get enough of you, Mattie."

"Good. I can't wait until our wedding night, then."

"Do we have to wait that long, Mattie?"

"Not unless you need to rest."

He kissed her again and she knew he didn't need the rest.

―――

They returned to the house just before dinner, and Winnie and Ruth had no doubt that the marriage had been consummated by the looks on their faces. That and the missing buttons on Mattie's blouse.

Later that night, Mattie enjoyed her wedding night as it was intended.

―――

Things quieted down for almost a month after the wedding. Normal ranch operations were conducted, and Jerome and Prudence paid two visits to the ranch. On their first visit John and Mattie showed them the waterfall. John took Jamey and Mattie fishing and Mattie enjoyed her first trout dinner.

No one was surprised when Ruth and Pete announced that they were going to get married. Then it was all hectic again until they were wed on the last day of October.

THE DEBT

John was immensely happy with Mattie and she grew to know him so much better as they spent so much time together.

It was Christmas Eve. As expected, there were three feet of snow outside, but a roaring fire inside. They had just had popcorn and hot cocoa and Jamey and Winnie had turned in.

Mattie was in her accustomed position with her left shoulder under John's right arm.

"John, are you happy?" she asked softly.

"Happier than I've ever been, sweetheart."

"Do you still have that feeling about Nellie?"

"It's just always going to be there, Mattie."

"Would it go away, you think, if I told you that I was carrying our child?"

John looked at Mattie and smiled softly as he laid his hand on her stomach.

"It doesn't matter if it does or not, my love. What matters is that you're going to be having our baby and you've made me so very happy."

He kissed Mattie, then stood and led her to their bedroom.

John didn't tell Mattie that the nagging feeling was still there because she was more important than his guilt, or debt, or whatever it was.

The winter wasn't a particularly bad one for Wyoming Territory, but they still had a hard time moving the herds to the canyons. One of the two new ranch hands died when he fell off his horse and was trampled in February, casting a pall over the ranch.

Spring arrived, and Mattie's tummy began to show her status as an expectant mother. She was doing well and hadn't even suffered morning sickness, which was more than could be said for Ruth, who was two months behind Mattie.

Despite her increasing girth, Mattie still joined Jamey and John on their occasional fishing trips, and Jamey found he missed his new mother when she finally couldn't join them in the late spring as her time was too close.

On June 21st, in the middle of the afternoon, John sent Tex to Burnt Fork to fetch Mrs. Rider, the midwife. Winnie took over preparing Mattie's birthing room which had been set up next to the big bedroom.

By the time Mrs. Rider arrived, she'd been in labor for four hours and John sat with Pete down in the kitchen listening to her cries of pain and grunts as the sun fell.

Prudence arrived and went to the birthing room to help Winnie and Mrs. Rider while Jerome joined John and Pete in the kitchen, knowing they were all useless appendages to what was happening upstairs.

John tried to make small talk but couldn't finish his stories as he was distracted by the wails and cries from his precious wife. Finally, he stopped talking and let Pete and Jerome fill in the kitchen's silence to try and mask the horrendous sounds of pain that filled the house.

John couldn't eat as the sun set and Mattie continued in her labor. He was pacing from the kitchen all the way to the front door and back again, but he couldn't leave the house. He felt

THE DEBT

he owed it to Mattie to endure his own emotional pain as she suffered the tortured pains of childbirth.

The night wore on and he'd get periodic reassurances from Winnie, Mrs. Rider or Prudence, as they took much-needed breaks, but his mind couldn't help to drift back to that night more than nine years ago when he'd lost Nellie.

He kept trying to push away those morbid thoughts and tried to picture Mattie as they made love that day by the waterfall, but he kept failing as the memories of Nellie kept driving deeper into his mind.

"Was this what you want, Nellie?" he whispered, "Do you want to take away my Mattie because I caused you to lose your life?"

He was so immersed in his feelings of guilt for causing not only Nellie's death, but now Mattie's that he didn't hear the sudden cry of a newborn infant from upstairs until Pete shook him from his dark reverie and exclaimed, "You're a papa again, John!"

John knew he should be bouncing happily around the kitchen, but he had to know. He couldn't hear Mattie's voice and raced from the kitchen and headed for the stairs, terror filling his heart and mind.

He was almost to the second floor when the birthing room door opened, and his mother stepped out. He was almost afraid to see her face again but forced himself to look. He owed it to Mattie.

John looked at his mother's eyes and broke down in tears when he did, putting his left hand against the hallway wall for support.

Winnie quickly walked to her son and put her hand on his shoulder.

"What's wrong, John?" she asked.

John looked at his mother, wiped the tears from his eyes, and said, "I'm okay, Mama."

Winnie smiled and said, "You should be. You have a beautiful little girl and Mattie is doing fine."

He nodded and whispered, "I know, Mama. I could see it in your eyes. I was just so afraid that it would be like the last time."

Winnie took his arm and said, "Well, it's not. Now you go and sit down in the main room and I'll come and get you when you can see Mattie and your new daughter."

John nodded, then kissed his mother, slowly walked down the stairs and took a seat in one of the chairs. Once he was seated, he buried his face in his hands and the tears began to flow again, only these were from relief and happiness for his beloved Mattie.

After a few minutes, he raised his eyes, used his sleeves to dry his face and sat back in the cushions. He didn't think about debts or guilt anymore. He only thought of Mattie and the love that they shared.

Twenty minutes later, his mother startled him when she tapped his shoulder and said, "John, Mattie wants to see you now."

John smiled at his mother as he stood and walked with her up the stairs. She opened the birthing room door and he followed her inside and quickly turned to see Mattie.

THE DEBT

The moment his eyes beheld his wife, he understood what it was that had bothered him all those years.

He quietly walked to Mattie and took the chair by her bed.

Mattie's hair was matted down, but her face was almost angelic as she smiled softly at him while their new little girl suckled at her breast.

"We have a little girl," she said quietly as she beamed.

John reached out and gently touched her still damp cheek, then his daughter's tiny back before he leaned over and barely touched Mattie's lips with his.

"She's as beautiful as her mother," John said as he smiled at Mattie.

"John, for all the wonderful things you've done to make me so happy, nothing will ever match this. Thank you for loving me so much."

"How could I not?" he asked as he let his eyes absorb the love that she passed into his own eyes.

Mrs. Rider told him he had to leave now, so he stood, kissed his wife once more then kissed his daughter's head before he turned and backed out of the room, still smiling at Mattie.

Once outside, he just walked to the big bedroom next door, and without lighting a lamp, laid down in the large bed where he and Mattie had spent so much enjoyable time together and closed his eyes.

For nine years, he'd wondered why he'd been so tortured trying to understand why he couldn't get over the loss of Nellie. He first believed it was a horrible guilt for being the cause of her death, then he began to believe he had an obligation to fulfill, much like the debt that Mattie had felt.

But the moment his eyes fell on Mattie he understood what had bothered him so terribly all these years. When he'd been waiting in the kitchen while Nellie had undergone her labor to deliver Jamey, he'd spent hours imagining a happy, radiant Nellie with their newborn son at her breast, only to have it turned into the nightmare of her death. He'd gone from the pinnacle of an imagined joy to the very pit of despair in seconds and it had left a massive cavern in his heart and soul.

Tonight, he'd spent those same hours terrified of losing his beloved Mattie for the same reason. He couldn't picture her as the joyful mother of a newborn baby, no matter how hard he tried. He was waiting for the horrible news that he'd lost her. For hours, he'd wallowed in the mire of doom and anticipated pain that would arrive when he found Mattie cold and lifeless.

When he saw his mother's smiling face as she prepared to give him the joyous news, he knew that he hadn't lost Mattie, and it had overwhelmed him. But the moment he'd seen Mattie's radiance, he was struck with the revelation that the nagging feeling of guilt or obligation to Nellie would no longer bother him because he had misunderstood its origin from the start. Nellie would never have burdened him with any kind of debt. It wasn't in her nature.

The debt he had owed was to himself, yet he could never be the one to satisfy it. The only person who could was lying in a bed just fifteen feet away with their new baby girl.

That giant canyon in his heart and soul he'd created when he lost his beloved Nellie could only be filled had been filled with the love he'd received from his beloved Mattie.

THE DEBT

A love they would share with the little girl they had just created.

EPILOGUE

July 11, 1892

"You got one, Millie!" Jamey shouted as his six-year-old sister landed the flashing cutthroat trout by just backing away from the stream until the fish began flopping on the side of the stream.

Jamey trotted over to the fish and handled getting it off the hook while Millie beamed at her parents watching from a nearby blanket.

"I didn't think she'd catch one so quickly," Mattie said as she leaned against John's chest.

He laughed and said, "I'm just glad the fish didn't pull her into the water."

"Jamey would have dived in to save her anyway. He's a bit protective of his little sister."

"He's protective of all of them, it's just that Millie is the only one old enough to come out here and fish. He'll have his hands full when they're all out here."

She looked as Jamey displayed Millie's catch to his sister and asked, "Are you disappointed that I haven't given Jamey a brother?"

John smiled and kissed the top of Mattie's head and replied, "Of course, not. Jamey's the king of the castle and his sisters all adore him. He has a brother of sorts in Ruth and Pete's Johnny anyway."

"Did you know that Ruth is pregnant again?"

"So soon? I thought that would be impossible."

Mattie laughed and said, "We've had four girls in six years and you still think it's impossible to get pregnant after six months."

John rested his hands softly on Mattie's shoulders as he leaned back on the saddle and felt her warmth against his legs. Six years and four babies, but only Millie, now proudly showing her first fish to her parents, had created that enormous shift from despair to the pinnacle of joy. It made his oldest daughter special to him in ways that he couldn't describe.

He loved all of his children, but since that day she was born, John felt he owed a debt to her for letting Mattie live. Unlike the earlier sense of debt, he had no intention of ever satisfying this one because each day, he made a payment with his love.

1	Rock Creek	12/26/2016
2	North of Denton	01/02/2017
3	Fort Selden	01/07/2017
4	Scotts Bluff	01/14/2017
5	South of Denver	01/22/2017
6	Miles City	01/28/2017
7	Hopewell	02/04/2017
8	Nueva Luz	02/12/2017
9	The Witch of Dakota	02/19/2017
10	Baker City	03/13/2017
11	The Gun Smith	03/21/2017
12	Gus	03/24/2017
13	Wilmore	04/06/2017
14	Mister Thor	04/20/2017
15	Nora	04/26/2017
16	Max	05/09/2017
17	Hunting Pearl	05/14/2017
18	Bessie	05/25/2017
19	The Last Four	05/29/2017
20	Zack	06/12/2017
21	Finding Bucky	06/21/2017
22	The Debt	06/30/2017
23	The Scalawags	07/11/2017
24	The Stampede	07/20/2017
25	The Wake of the Bertrand	07/31/2017
26	Cole	08/09/2017
27	Luke	09/05/2017
28	The Eclipse	09/21/2017
29	A.J. Smith	10/03/2017
30	Slow John	11/05/2017
31	The Second Star	11/15/2017
32	Tate	12/03/2017
33	Virgil's Herd	12/14/2017
34	Marsh's Valley	01/01/2018
35	Alex Paine	01/18/2018
36	Ben Gray	02/05/2018

THE DEBT

37	War Adams	03/05/2018
38	Mac's Cabin	03/21/2018
39	Will Scott	04/13/2018
40	Sheriff Joe	04/22/2018
41	Chance	05/17/2018
42	Doc Holt	06/17/2018
43	Ted Shepard	07/13/2018
44	Haven	07/30/2018
45	Sam's County	08/15/2018
46	Matt Dunne	09/10/2018
47	Conn Jackson	10/05/2018
48	Gabe Owens	10/27/2018
49	Abandoned	11/19/2018
50	Retribution	12/21/2018
51	Inevitable	02/04/2019
52	Scandal in Topeka	03/18/2019
53	Return to Hardeman County	04/10/2019
54	Deception	06/02/2019
55	The Silver Widows	06/27/2019
56	Hitch	08/21/2019
57	Dylan's Journey	09/10/2019
58	Bryn's War	11/06/2019
59	Huw's Legacy	11/30/2019
60	Lynn's Search	12/22/2019
61	Bethan's Choice	02/10/2020
62	Rhody Jones	03/11/2020

Made in the USA
San Bernardino, CA
04 May 2020